Life on the Alaska Frontier

G.E. Sherman

ISBN-13: 978-0989421799
ISBN-10: 0989421791

FLEETING EDGE PRESS, 2015

To Vicki

I wanted the gold, and I sought it;
I scrabbled and mucked like a slave.
Was it famine or scurvy—I fought it;
I hurled my youth into a grave.

I wanted the gold, and I got it—
Came out with a fortune last fall,
Yet somehow life's not what I thought it,
And somehow the gold isn't all.

The Spell of the Yukon-Robert Service

The Trail to the Fortymile
0 10 20 30 40 50 60 70 80 miles
Chicken
Kechumstuk
Tanacross
Mentasta Pass
Indian Pass
Slana
Chistochina
Gulkana
Tazlina
Copper Center
Tonsina
Kimball Pass
Ernestine
Tiekel
Ptarmigan Drop
Valdez
Wortmanns

Books in the
***Life on the Alaska Frontier* series**

I. Forging North

II. Fortymile

Contents

Part I

A Plan

August 5, 1903

At the sound of approaching hoof beats, the telegraph clerk ceased sorting through the reams of incoming messages and looked up.

"Here he comes again," said the clerk to the telegraph operator.

"Who?" said the operator without looking up.

"That John Palmer fella. He's been in here every day for a week. I keep telling him we got nothing for him."

The clerk quickly looked down as the door swung open, pretending not to notice as he randomly shuffled the yellow message sheets.

"Good morning," said John Palmer.

"Oh, good morning, sir, didn't notice you come in."

"Anything for me today?"

"Let me check," said the clerk. He flipped through the stack, knowing full well there was nothing. "No, sorry Mr. Palmer. There's nothing here."

"Are you sure? I'm expecting a very important message from Preston Van Sant. Please look again."

The clerk flipped through the stack again, slower this time as he feebly worked to appease the customer.

"No, definitely nothing yet."

John placed both hands on the counter and leaned in. "It is imperative that I receive the wire from Van Sant."

"I understand, sir, but nothing has come in. Perhaps tomorrow?"

"Perhaps," said John as he wheeled around to leave, slamming the door behind him.

"Not my fault," called the clerk in a voice inaudible beyond the office walls. Satisfied, he returned to sorting.

Palmer untied the horse and mounted up, staring ahead for a long moment. He took off his hat and wiped his forehead. The dusty streets of Valdez had coated him well during his ride in from the boarding house. He and the horse were both tired of the daily trip to fetch a wire that wasn't there. *Where in the hell is Van Sant?* he thought, as he turned the horse toward home.

* * *

The long ride back to Stella's boarding house gave Palmer too much time to reflect. Ever since the house in Seattle burned, killing his wife and destroying everything they had, Van Sant faithfully wired them money. *Emily and I are nearly out of money*, the thought echoing repeatedly through his mind.

The towering mountains and hanging glaciers did little to distract him from his quandary. Being stuck in Alaska with no means of support didn't appeal to him, and certainly didn't bode well for his daughter. *Preston must have met with some calamity*.

The horse suddenly quickened its pace, jolting Palmer from his daze. She always did it when close to home. Within two minutes she was standing at the barn door, pawing the ground and shaking her head up and down as she nickered.

"Hello, Father," called Emily from the front porch. "Did it come?"

As his daughter waited for an answer, John dismounted and tied up the horse. He took off his hat and slapped it three times against his leg, the dust flying up into a cloud that nearly enveloped him. Stepping up on the porch, he slumped into the rocking chair.

"Well?" said Emily.

"No. Not a word. Something must have happened to Preston."

The smile faded from her face. "Whatever will we do?"

"I'm not sure," he said, pulling his pipe from his vest pocket and tamping tobacco in the bowl. "We'll be out of money soon, and we don't have enough for passage on a steamer to Seattle."

"You aren't making me feel any better, Father."

John lit the pipe, and stared out across the Alaska landscape as if waiting for the answer to come to him. "Perhaps you and Thomas should get married now," he said, his gaze never wavering.

"But Father, I—"

"No, bad idea. He's no better off than we are at present."

Before she could respond, the front door opened and Stella came bustling through, carrying a tray with steaming coffee and fresh rhubarb pie.

"I heard you come back and figured you needed some refreshment." Stella sat the tray down and began passing out coffee and pie. "How did it go?"

"It didn't. Still no word from Van Sant. I think some tragedy may have befallen him."

"Odd. Perhaps you can contact one of his colleagues and ask about him."

"Well, I have to do something. We're almost out of

money."

"You know you are welcome to stay here as long as you want. I've got plenty of room."

"I know, Stella. I just hate to impose. You've been so good to us all summer."

"No imposition at all. I enjoy the company, and your daughter has been a great help around here," said Stella, passing a wink in Emily's direction.

Emily sat silently, her head in her hands, staring at the holes in the rough cut boards of the porch. "I wish Thomas was here. When are you supposed to meet him?"

John pulled his pocket watch from his vest and flipped it open. "Soon Emily—in fact I must get the wagon hitched and get moving."

* * *

It was an unusual summer—hot and dry, with only a little rain. The glacier-fed streams raged in late afternoon, pushed by the massive snow melt in the ice fields. One had to be careful crossing streams in weather like this—a trickle in early morning might be a raging torrent come evening.

Today's prospecting trip was a bust. Thomas now stood on the far side of the unnamed creek, his walking stick grasped firmly, but feeling inadequate for the task at hand. He crossed early morning with little trouble, but now the creek was running fast and hard, a full two feet higher than before. *Going to get wet, no doubt about it.*

After watching for an hour, he decided the water level wasn't dropping—the choice was to cross or spend the night on this side. He thought about it for a moment, but the idea of spending another night sleeping in the open in the backcountry didn't much appeal to him. No, he would cross, yet the sound of what seemed to be bushel-sized boulders bouncing under the current was worrying.

Three steps in, he was in trouble. The frigid gray water piled up against his legs, threatening to sweep his feet from under him. With the walking stick on the downstream side, he leaned into it and tried to shuffle slowly forward to avoid rolling an ankle on a boulder. The cold water had an instant numbing effect—already his muscles were tightening and resisting efforts to move forward. The current washed the gravel from beneath his feet, making him unsteady and forcing him to move faster than he wanted.

In an instant he was underwater, the walking stick failing him and the current sweeping him under before he could react. The heavy pack pulled him to the bottom as he struggled to free his arms. The .45-70 was slung over his shoulder and across his chest, preventing him from dropping the load. His lungs burned, screaming for oxygen.

So this is how it ends, he thought. In an instant, the last four months flashed before him—his unfortunate landing in Alaska, Stella rescuing him, Emily and her father traveling from Seattle in search of him, and the joyous reunion. Now all that was for naught—his dreams shattered in a moment of impatience.

The pack caught the bottom and the current rolled him, crashing him into a submerged boulder. The breath escaped his lungs—everything within him resisting the urge to inhale until that final moment that would bring the end.

The sunlight hit him square in the face as he suddenly broke the surface. He sucked in large gulps of air as the water whirled around his waist. The current tortured him against one last boulder before bouncing him into a gentle back eddy no deeper than knee level. He sat still in the water for a moment, pulling in large breaths of air as the current swirled slowly around. *That was too close*, he thought as he stumbled to stand, his pack still hanging from one shoulder. As he clawed his way up the short bank to dry land, he paused to reach back over his shoulder for the .45-70—it was gone.

* * *

Thomas stood on the bank, shivering in the long shadows of the late afternoon sun. He stared at the raging gray water that nearly took his life—somewhere in there was the rifle, the rifle that Stella had so ceremoniously given to him as if giving up a part of her departed husband. *I have to find it*, he thought, unable to picture telling Stella about the loss.

The idea quickly passed, the water too swift and clouded with glacial silt. Thomas could only see a few inches below the surface and by now the current likely carried it far downstream. Now he faced the reality of the situation—unarmed, soaking wet, and the sun beginning its slow descent towards the horizon. Opening the wet pack, he found the hatchet and began cutting low branches of dead, dried spruce and stacking them on the bank. Satisfied he had enough, he pulled the tin of matches from the pack, unwrapping it from the oil cloth. *I hope these are dry*, he thought as he opened the tin.

The first two matches failed to strike. Thomas took another and held it up, looking at it intently before trying again. The match lit and he bent down to light the kindling, starting with a small dried up twig still attached to the branches. Upon contact with the flame, the twig glowed a bright red, becoming an ember that curled up and dropped from the branch, then died.

He began to shiver as the sun slid below the mountain peak behind him. Going to the nearest spruce tree, he pulled big clumps of green moss hanging from the lower branches, then broke off a handful of small, dry twigs. With the moss tucked under the spruce kindling, Thomas took another match and tried again. The moss lit and flickered, quickly waning as he carefully placed the small twigs in a pyramid fashion around the flame. Blowing gently he nursed the flame until the spruce ignited. The resin took off with a vengeance and within a few seconds the flames were leaping two feet into the air. Quickly, he piled on more branches to keep the fire going.

Standing as close as safety allowed, he rubbed his hands over the flame and began to warm. His front side hot and clothes steaming, he turned around to do the same to his cold, soggy backside. It took several cycles of front to back before the shivering subsided and his core temperature approached normal.

He looked again at the creek and swore under his breath. *I wonder where the .45-70 ended up?* With the hatchet, Thomas blazed several of the trees along the bank to mark the spot where he emerged, planning to return when the water subsided.

It was still daylight, but only an hour or two remained before the temperature would begin to drop rapidly. He now faced the prospect of spending the night without shelter or pushing forward, trying to reach the trail two thousand feet below where Palmer would hopefully be waiting with the wagon.

Stowing the hatchet, he pulled the gold pan from the pack and, with several trips to the creek, doused the fire. *At least I'm on the right side of the creek*, he thought as he stashed the gold pan, slung the pack over his right shoulder, and started walking.

* * *

Palmer lit his pipe for the third time, staring up the mountainside for any sign of Thomas. "Come on son, it's getting late," he said, scanning the treeline for movement. Palmer didn't relish being out after dark. From his seat on the wagon he listened intently for any sound in the brush, more concerned about grizzly bears than the approach of Thomas.

He tapped his pipe on the edge of the seat, the ash falling to the ground, embers dying as they floated downward. The horse perked her ears up for a moment, then resumed her blank stare. Palmer's thoughts began to drift back to the issue at hand. *I've got to get in touch with someone about Preston. I can't fathom—*

The crashing sound in the brush snapped him back to attention, whirling his head to the right in an attempt to locate the source. Immediately his hand went to the Colt .45 Peacemaker strapped to his hip. The horse was staring in the direction of the noise, ears perked and nostrils flaring.

"Easy horse," he said, patting her neck. He continued to stare into the wall of trees, gripping the reins tightly in one hand and the Peacemaker in the other.

Suddenly, and with utter silence, a cow moose slipped out of the trees and onto the trail, two calves following close behind. The moose was a mere thirty feet away, staring at the horse with no apparent fear. Stella's one and only horse had spent its entire life in the Alaska wilderness. A moose or even three were of no concern to her—she nonchalantly began to munch on a few sprigs of grass.

Palmer loosened his grip on the .45 a bit, unsure if the cow felt threatened. His fears were allayed in short order as she sauntered across the trail and down the small hill along the river, her calves in tow. Palmer breathed a sigh of relief and holstered the pistol.

The loud crack behind him startled him to his feet as the wagon shook. Palmer lost his balance as he tried to whirl around and fell to the ground, nearly knocking the wind out of him.

A roar of laughter erupted from the back of the wagon, then quickly ceased.

"Oh John, Sorry. Didn't know you were going to take a nose dive."

Palmer stood up and turned to see Thomas, grinning from ear to ear and holding a broken tree limb in his left hand.

"I'm not sure that's the way to treat your future father-in-law," said John as he brushed the dirt from his pants and attempted to regain some semblance of dignity.

"I couldn't resist. I came out behind the wagon and saw you staring down the cow moose so I waited and—well, you know the rest."

"Very funny," said John as he climbed up into the wagon. "Can we get out of here now before it gets dark?"

"Yes—and take care of that pistol. It's the only firearm we have left."

John stared at Thomas as he swung up into the wagon, waiting.

"I lost it in the creek, and Stella is going to kill me."

* * *

The sun was below the horizon, but enough light remained to allow John and Thomas to get the horse in her stall and stow things for the night. Thomas was sure the occupants of the boarding house heard them arrive, but as yet no one bothered to look out the back door. He was both relieved and nervous, unsure how to tell Stella about the loss of her late husband's rifle.

John closed the barn door. "Let's go Thomas. Might as well face the music sooner rather than later."

Thomas sighed and trudged up the back steps, hesitated, then swung the door open. The smell of Stella's moose stew and the sound of hearty conversation filled the air. *Stella must have boarders.* This was good—he could delay telling her about the .45-70.

As they entered the dining room, Thomas counted two extras at the table—a couple of rough looking characters that were long overdue for a bath and definitely needed a shave.

Stella was the first to see them. "John, Thomas, come on in and eat. About time you fellows got here. We have boarders."

"I can see that," said Thomas, crossing the room and extending his hand.

"Name's Olson," said the scruffiest of the two, returning the handshake. "And this here is my partner Clyde."

Clyde nodded, but didn't get up.

John nodded to both and took a chair at the head of the table, with Emily on his left. "Partners? What business you fellows in?"

"We're miners," said Olson. "Just come off the Fortymile."

Thomas interest was immediately piqued. He pulled up a chair across the table from the two. "Kinda early to be quitting for the season isn't it?"

Clyde and Olson exchanged glances, neither looking as though they were ready to speak.

Clyde shuffled in his chair, leaned back, and put his hands behind his head. "Well, it's a long story. We're getting out of the business and heading back to Seattle."

"Hard luck on the gold fields eh?" said John.

Clyde shot Olson another glance, then smiled. "On the contrary, we've made our fortune and now we're off to enjoy it. Got a claim for sale if you're interested."

Thomas stood. "Really? Where? How much you want for it?"

"Well, it's a rich claim and we could make a lot more money if we continued to mine it," said Clyde. "It would probably take at least—"

"You look like a good fellow," said Olson. "I think we can make you a special deal."

"Yeah," said Clyde, "a special deal."

"Well how much?" said Thomas.

Olson stroked his scruffy beard, then looked at Thomas. "We figure there's a million left in gold there, but we're tired of the country and just to settle all our affairs here, we can let you have it for five thousand dollars."

"Here you go," said Stella as she scurried in from the kitchen and placed huge bowls of stew in front of Thomas and John. "Eat up before it gets cold."

"Five thousand dollars?" said John. "Would you consider less?"

Emily had been pushing the remnants of her stew around with her spoon, but now looked up with renewed interest. "Are you thinking of buying it, Father?"

"Well, I might be interested in partnering with Thomas, if the price is right."

"How much less?" said Clyde.

"Excuse us for a moment, would you?" said John, motioning for Thomas to follow him to the kitchen.

"Certainly, gents. Talk it over."

* * *

"I don't have two thousand, let alone five," said Thomas, his voice lowered, "and I'm not taking charity, John."

"I'm not talking about charity, Thomas. I'm talking about forming a partnership. Fifty-fifty after the initial investment is paid off."

"There's a little over a thousand dollars from my hunting efforts, but that includes Stella's share—and it's all I'm going to have since the game laws went into effect."

"Well, it was inevitable that Congress would put some laws in place here—too bad it put an end to your hunting."

"I can take two more moose and that's it for the year, and the way prices are going, that won't bring much profit—especially after I split it with Stella."

"I say we offer them three thousand. You throw your hunting money into the pot and I'll make up the difference."

"I can live with that."

Stella walked into the kitchen. Thomas looked back toward the dining room and noticed Clyde and Olson where having a conference of their own, turned towards the corner to prevent Emily from listening in.

"You boys thinking about buying a claim?" said Stella.

"We are," said John.

"Well, plopping down money is the easy part. Have you thought about what happens after that?"

"What do you mean?" said Thomas.

"Oh, little things like, where do you get money for supplies, how do you get to the Fortymile, and what happens to Emily."

John and Thomas looked at each other, brows furrowed. They hadn't thought about the implications, especially when it came to Emily.

"You guys figure it out yet?" yelled Clyde from the dining room.

John didn't answer. "Stella, we are going to offer them three thousand. We'll sort out the details later."

"I wouldn't rush into anything. Have they shown you any gold?"

"Good point. Let's see."

* * *

"We're interested," said John, "but we'd like to see some gold from the claim first."

Clyde grinned and reached into his vest pocket, pulling out a small leather bag with a drawstring. He opened the bag and dumped the contents on the table cloth. "How's this?"

Thomas stared, eyes wide. The gold nuggets glowed in the flickering lamplight. They were large, as big as a pinto bean, yet rough and craggy—what miners referred to as having "character."

"Oh my," said Emily, gazing at the field of gold before her.

"That's impressive," said John. "This is from your Fortymile claim?"

"Yes sir," said Olson. "Every bit of it."

"Looks fantastic," said Thomas.

"So, what do you think gents? You buying?" said Clyde.

"We're willing to offer you three thousand cash for it," said John.

"That's nearly half what we're asking," said Olson. "What do you think Clyde?"

"I don't think we can let it go for that. We got too much invested."

"Invested?" said John. "Is there equipment on the claim?"

"Oh yeah," said Clyde. "Everything you need to show up and start moving gravel."

Olson laughed. "Yeah, everything."

"Well I'm afraid we can't offer you any more than—"

"How about thirty-five hundred and you boys can stay here for free until you catch your ship south?" said Stella.

Thomas and John both stared at her.

"Stella, I can't ask you to do that after all you've done for me," said Thomas.

Stella smiled. "It's not a problem—we're partners right? First hunting, and soon to be mining."

"We'll take it," said Clyde. "When can we have our money?"

"We can get it together in a day or two. I need to get money wired from my bank in Seattle," said John.

"That'll be fine," said Clyde, "but we leave in three days so if you don't have the money in two, deal's off."

"You'll have it," said John.

"Now if you'll excuse us gents, I think we'll retire to our rooms," said Clyde.

"One last thing," said Thomas. "I assume you can provide claim maps and directions for us."

"Of course," said Olson. "You'll have everything you need."

"Goodnight then," said John, the two miners already halfway up the stairs.

Thomas was smiling ear to ear, his dream of striking it rich seemingly within reach.

"You look like a little boy who just got his first puppy," said Emily. She waited until the sound of doors shutting echoed down the stairs, then turned to her father. "How will you get the money? Preston seems to have gone missing."

"Not to worry my dear, I'm wiring the bank directly first thing in the morning."

* * *

August 6, 1903

Thomas rolled over in bed, awake again for what seemed like the fifth time. The excitement of becoming a claim owner, coupled with the dread of telling Stella about the loss of the .45-70 kept sleep from him. He looked at his watch, just readable in the early morning light. *Only four o'clock. Going to be a long day.*

He lay staring at the shadows on the ceiling, waiting for the sound of Stella in the kitchen. He knew it would be soon—she was always up early, especially when boarders were in the house.

He nearly drifted off when the sounds reached him—a door opening, the squeaky pump handle being worked, and the unmistakable slam of the cast iron stove door after it was stoked. It was time—he dressed slowly and quietly began the descent to the task before him.

"You're up very early, Thomas."

"Couldn't sleep."

"Ah, the excitement of last evening kept you awake I suppose."

"That, and something else."

"Oh? Did you have any luck on your prospecting trip? With the events of last night I didn't even ask."

"No, Stella. In fact, I had terrible luck."

Stella could hear the serious tone in his voice. She

sat the coffee pot on the stove to perk and turned to face him. "What happened?"

Thomas shifted his weight from one foot to the other, the whole time looking at the floor.

"Must be serious. It's not gonna get any easier—now out with it."

"I lost the gun, Stella. I lost the .45-70."

Her expression remained firm. "How?"

"I fell into the creek trying to cross while it was too high. I nearly drowned, and when I finally crawled out, it had been ripped from my shoulder. I'm so, so sorry. I know what that gun meant to you."

Stella looked at the young man, remorse written all over his face. She smiled.

"Thomas, you mean more to me than a gun. You are like the son Wesley and I never had. He was lost to me a long time ago—that rifle is nothing compared to you making it back alive."

"I'll get it back for you, Stella. I promise."

She stepped forward and hugged him, not saying anything for a brief moment. "If you can do it without risking your life, fine. If not, let the mountains keep it."

"I'll get it back. Besides, I'm going to need it on the Fortymile."

Stella smiled at his enthusiasm. "I suggest you wait until the water goes down."

"Definitely. I won't make that mistake again."

Thomas grabbed a coffee cup and headed to the table. "I'm ready when it is," he called quietly over his shoulder.

* * *

It was over an hour before anyone else woke. The

smell of coffee and bacon frying finally wafted upstairs and brought the remainder of the group out, one by one.

John was first, making his way to the kitchen and pouring a steaming cup of black coffee from the oversized pot warming on the wood-fired stove.

"Good Morning, Stella," he said as he made his way to the table and took a seat across from Thomas.

"Mornin', John. Ready for some breakfast?"

"I'm always ready to eat your cooking."

Thomas thought he saw Stella blush a bit, but wasn't sure.

She shoved another stick of wood into the kitchen stove. "I'll have some fried potatoes, bacon, and eggs for you in a jiffy."

Thomas looked up from his coffee cup. "I want you to be honest with me John. Are you comfortable with this mining deal?"

"I know the risks, Thomas. There are no guarantees in a venture like this, but from the gold we saw, I think it's going to work out."

"We're going to need a bunch of supplies. We need to find out what is already on the claim."

"True, we need to get those boys to give us a full accounting, but the first order of business is to get to the telegraph office and wire the bank."

"We haven't budgeted for supplies. I should go with you and talk to Neal at the store. He'll have a good idea what we need and what it's going to cost."

"Let's do that first. That way I'll know how much money we're going to need. Do you know how much you have to contribute?"

"I haven't counted it in a while, but I'll do that right now, assuming those mangy fellas don't come downstairs.

If they do, distract them."

"Will do."

Thomas went to the kitchen and looked at the wood box next to the stove. It was nearly clear full. Stella must have gone out before he got up and filled it.

"Sorry I let the wood get low."

"Don't worry about it. I filled it this morning."

"Now it's heavy and I have to move it."

"I heard."

Thomas quietly slid the box along the wall to the right, exposing the small hatch near the floor. He pulled his knife from the sheath and getting down on hands and knees, slid it into the crack and popped the hatch open. There on the small shelf was the mason jar holding all the earnings from the sale of moose and sheep meat to the store in town.

"Think you have enough?" said Stella.

"Don't know. Supplies are something we hadn't considered and half of this is yours."

"Count it and see what we have."

Thomas dumped the money on the counter next to the stove and began counting. Selling game meat to the local store had paid fairly well, but as Thomas continued counting his doubts began to grow.

"Nine hundred and seventy dollars, so my share is—"

"Four hundred eighty-five."

"You're fast at that," said Thomas, stuffing cash back in the jar.

A creak at the top of the stairs caught their attention.

"That might be Clyde or Olson," said Stella. "Better get that jar put away."

Thomas quickly shoved the rest of the cash into the

jar, then put it on the shelf and closed the hatch. Just as he finished sliding the wood box into place, Clyde walked into the kitchen.

"Good morning, what you folks up to?"

"Just stocking up on wood," said Thomas, the tips of his ears turning red.

"Coffee?" said Clyde.

"Have a seat and I'll bring you some," said Stella. "I'm working on breakfast for everyone."

Clyde headed to the table, moved Thomas' coffee cup to the side and took his chair.

Annoyed, Thomas moved across the table and sat next to John. He glared at Clyde and wondered what kind of man they were dealing with.

Clyde stared straight at him, a twisted smile on his face. "Oh, did I take your seat?"

Thomas broke it off. "No problem Clyde, sit anywhere you like."

"I can't wait to get out of this God-forsaken country," said Clyde as he pulled out the chair next to him and propped up his feet. "I'm sick of the cold, bugs, and the people."

"Looked to me like Alaska treated you pretty well, judging by that bag of gold," said John.

Clyde turned and looked out the window at the early morning sunrise. "We worked ourselves to the bone for that."

Thomas shot a knowing glance at John. *Were they making a mistake here?*

"So this claim we're buying doesn't give up her gold easily?" said John.

"No, you misunderstand. Mining is hard work, no matter how rich the ground is. Them nuggets don't just pop out of the ground for the picking. That ground is plenty rich, and we done all the hard work getting things set up for you."

This eased Thomas' doubts some, but he realized they were stepping into the unknown. Between him and John, their mining knowledge was limited.

Stella brought Clyde a cup of coffee, then began serving breakfast. Olson finally came down, his hair a mess and eyes puffy like he had been hitting the bottle. Emily was the last to arrive at the table, perfectly groomed and looking radiant as usual.

The conversation around breakfast centered on the claim, mining, the equipment, and everything else about the Fortymile. John and Thomas had no end of questions—Clyde and Olson firing off answers as quick as they asked.

"Is there a cabin on the claim?" said John.

"Yeah," said Olson. "She's a real nice cabin. Got a wood stove, bunks—pretty much everything you need to set up shop."

"So I'm wondering," said Thomas, "what do we need to take for supplies?"

Clyde looked at Olson for a moment. "We left most of the mining equipment there. You're gonna need food and such, of course."

"And you probably oughta take a couple of new picks and shovels. We pretty much wore them out."

"What about axes, saws, and rope?"

"Better take that too. You oughta go prepared. If you take more than you need you can always sell it to your neighbors—probably at a profit."

Thomas realized he should be taking notes. "What about—"

"When can we get our money?" said Olson.

"We're headed off to town right after breakfast. If everything goes right, we may be able to get it for you later today," said John.

"Good," said Clyde, proceeding to stuff an oversize bite of fried potatoes into his mouth.

* * *

At the sound of the door opening, the proprietor of the store looked up from behind the counter, glasses perched on the end of his nose.

"Thomas—good to see you. Got another moose for me?" asked Noel Parker.

"Not this time Noel. I'm pretty much done hunting, what with all the new regulations."

"Oh well. It was good while it lasted. Game's getting scarce around here anyway. What can I do for you?"

"John and I are buying a mining claim and we need an idea of what provisions are going to cost."

"Mornin', John," said Noel as he shuffled some papers from under the counter. "Here's my recommended list of provisions for a year," he said, handing a copy to Thomas. "Mining, eh? Whereabouts?"

"The Fortymile," said John.

"Well that's a far piece from here. When you heading up?"

Thomas was too absorbed in scanning the list of provisions and didn't look up, his finger running down the page from item to item.

"We haven't really talked about it," said John, "but we would like get up there yet this season and take a look."

"Better go prepared in case you have to spend the winter."

Thomas looked up from the paper. "Do we really need three hundred pounds of flour and a hundred-fifty of bacon? Seems like a lot."

"That list of provisions is to keep you in grub for a year. If you try to buy anything up north it's going to cost you three or four times what you'd pay here."

"I see," said John. "Let me take a look, Thomas."

Thomas handed the paper to John. It was an extensive list. In addition to food items, there was clothing, as well as hardware and tools.

John rubbed the back of his neck and sighed. "Whew."

"We have a lot of it already," said Thomas. "We probably need some warmer clothes in case the weather turns foul."

"I think you're better outfitted than I am," said John. "We're going to have to rely on your judgment Noel. Can you give us an estimate of what it all might cost?"

"You bet. Cross off anything you already have and I can work up a price for you in an hour or so."

"I need to wire my bank for some money. Can you give me a rough idea of how much we're talking about?"

"Well, if you were to buy everything on this list, I'd typically charge you about five hundred dollars, give or take a hundred."

John raised his eyebrows and rubbed his chin. "That's a lot of money."

"This ain't Seattle, I got big shipping costs getting this stuff up here."

"Okay, do what you can. We'll be back after I send a telegram and you can give us a final number then."

"Sounds fine. Anything else?"

Thomas spoke up. "I'm going to need a rifle."

* * *

The clerk winced as Palmer and Thomas came up the steps. "Here he comes again," he said to the telegraph operator who was busy keying a message.

"Morning, Mr. Palmer. Sorry there's still nothing for you."

"No problem. I need to send a wire to my bank today."

The clerk looked somewhat relieved as he handed John a form. "Here, write out your message and we'll get it out for you today."

"This is very important. Is there any way you can expedite my message."

"Well, there's a bunch ahead of you, but we can do it—just cost you extra."

"That's fine."

John paused, then scribbled out the message.

```
MANAGER
DEXTER HORTON AND COMPANY
SEATTLE, WASHINGTON

DEAR SIR,

I NEED WIRED TO ME IMMEDIATELY THE SUM
OF FOUR THOUSAND DOLLARS. MY BANK
IDENTIFICATION NUMBER IS 6836. PLEASE
EXPEDITE AS I AM IN NEED OF FUNDS
BEFORE END OF DAY TOMORROW.

JOHN W. PALMER
VALDEZ, ALASKA
```

John handed the message and pencil to the clerk, who counted up the words as he read.

"You know, it's unlikely the bank can wire the funds the same day. It takes time to get your message delivered to the bank."

John sighed heavily, but realized he was probably unreasonable in his expectations.

"I need the funds by midday tomorrow. Do you think that is possible?"

"Well, in my experience, it's usually possible to get it the next day."

"Fine. How much for the message and expedited service?"

"That'll be two bucks, and we'll get it out next."

John paid the fee and waited for the message to be sent. The clerk stood looking at him, pencil in both hands. It snapped in two. He took a deep breath and turned, looking at the operator tapping on the telegraph key.

"How soon can I expect a response?"

"Like I said, I doubt you'll get anything back today, but you're welcome to check back later. The office is open until six."

"I hope we get an answer sooner rather than later—we don't have a lot of time to close this deal," John said to Thomas as they left the office. "Let's go see what Noel's come up with."

* * *

"That's the best price you can quote?" said John as he looked through the estimate. It included a lot of things he doubted were necessary, but his lack of experience left him unsure.

"That's what I would take if I was headed north. I think four hundred dollars is a fair price."

"I could buy all this for less than a third of that in Seattle."

"That's fine, but when you pay to ship it here, the price goes up. I'd think you'd know that after spending the summer here."

"I think it's fair John," said Thomas. "Noel's always been square with me."

John handed the list to Noel. "Can you put the stuff together for us and have it ready next week?"

"Sure can. I can have it ready for you tomorrow if you want."

"No, we won't be ready to leave for several days."

"I didn't see a rifle on the list," said Thomas.

Noel held up his index finger, turned, and went into the back room, a place Thomas had never seen. He returned with something wrapped in oil cloth and set it on the counter.

"This is brand new," said Noel as he worked at unwrapping the package. As he unwound the last of it, Thomas was greeted by the sight—a shiny blue repeating rifle.

"What is it?" asked Thomas.

Noel picked it up and worked at wiping it down with his handkerchief. "It's a Model 1873 Winchester carbine, .44-40 caliber."

"It's short."

"That's right—twenty inch barrel. Just right for toting through the brush."

Noel wiped the barrel down one last time, then handed it to him. Thomas was instantly in love. The .45-70 was special, but this gun was new, shiny, and felt right as he hefted it, then snapped it to his shoulder. He had to have it.

"How does she shoot?"

Noel laughed. "That's the gun that won the west. Pretty much says it all."

"How much?"

Noel thought for a moment. "Well, I can let you have it for twenty-five dollars, and I'll throw in a box of cartridges for you."

Thomas didn't have to think twice about it. "I'll take it, can you—"

"Wait a minute," said John. "Do you have another?"

"Matter of fact I do."

"How about you give us two of them and three boxes of cartridges for forty dollars?"

Noel crossed his arms, brow furrowed, then smiled. "You drive a hard bargain Mr. Palmer. You got a deal."

"I was going to come back for it," said Thomas. "I'm not carrying enough cash."

"No problem. I'll pay for them now and you can repay me later."

Thomas rubbed the back of his neck and sighed.

John counted out the cash and laid it on the counter. "Don't worry about it Thomas. You're not taking any charity, just a very short term loan."

"Let me grab the other one and I'll get your cartridges," said Noel as he headed for the back room.

"I feel like I'm not pulling my own weight here, John. You're paying for everything up front and bearing the majority of the costs."

"It's okay Thomas. You can square up with me once we're rolling in gold."

Noel returned with the other rifle, carefully wrapped them in brown paper, then tied it all together with a string. He took four boxes of .44-40 cartridges from the shelf behind him and placed them on the counter. "An extra box because you've been good customers," he said, then grinned from ear to ear.

"Thanks, Noel. We really appreciate it," said Thomas as he scooped up the package.

John took the cartridges and turned towards the door. "We'll be in touch regarding the rest of the supplies."

"I look forward to it."

As they headed for the door, Noel said, "Thomas, what happened to the .45-70?"

"It's a long story. I'll tell you sometime."

"Fair enough," said Noel as the door closed behind them.

* * *

John thought about returning to the telegraph office, but knew there would be no word this soon. On the return trip to Stella's, Thomas drove the wagon and the two discussed how to proceed with their venture.

"I'm not sure I'm comfortable leaving Emily for a couple of months," said John, "even though I'm sure Stella would keep a close eye on her."

"I know," said Thomas. "I'm a bit torn—but anxious to get going.

"Me too, but I keep wondering if it's even worth heading up there this late in the season."

"I think we need to get up there and get a look at it, if nothing else to be prepared for a full season of mining next year."

"Sound reasonable."

"Let's plan to go and be back before the hard freeze in September."

"I'm thinking now that perhaps we shouldn't purchase everything on Noel's list. On the other hand, we would be set for next season."

Thomas laughed. "I say we go for it since we're spending your money instead of mine."

John smiled. "Works for me. Now all we need is for the bank to come through."

* * *

"How did it go?" called Emily from the porch as they pulled up in the wagon.

"We got the telegram off," said John. "I think I'll go back to town later this afternoon and see if there's an answer."

"Go on in," said Thomas. "I'll take care of the horse."

John headed up the steps to the porch as Thomas pulled the wagon around back to the barn. He unhitched the horse and gave her a quick brush down, then took the new rifles and cartridges into the shed. He unwrapped one of the Winchesters and wiped the rest of the factory oil from it, then did the same to the other. They were identical, yet Thomas hefted each one, raising it to his shoulder as if ready to fire. He placed them side by side on the bench and continued to contemplate which he would choose to be his own.

"You still putting the horse away?" called John from the back steps of the house.

"No, got that done. Come on out here for a minute."

Emily overheard the conversation and tagged along, close behind her father. They entered the shed to find Thomas still staring at the rifles.

"Which one do you want?" said Thomas.

"You bought guns?" said Emily.

"Yes, dear. We are going to need them up north," said John.

John turned to Thomas. "Makes no difference to me, Thomas. You pick."

Thomas stared at the nearly identical firearms. The only difference was the wood grain of the stock. One had more character to it, with pronounced grain in a pattern that caught his eye. "I'll take this one if you don't mind."

"That's fine by me. Shall we put a few rounds through them before lunch?"

"I'd like to. Where are our miner friends?"

"They went into town—mentioned looking for something to drink," said Emily.

"I hope they don't get drunk and head back here," said John.

"If they do, I'll put them in their place," said Stella, who was listening from the back porch.

"I bet you would," said John.

"Come on in and have a piece of pie before you start shooting up the countryside."

* * *

"Recoil's not bad," said Thomas as he ejected the cartridge and jacked in another round. "Let me set up a target and you can give it a go, John."

Thomas walked the fifty yards to the stake he had driven in the ground, removed the shot up target, and replaced it with a gallon coffee can, turning it upside down and dropping it over the stake. He jogged back to the makeshift firing line.

"I'm surprised the rifle was nearly right on. I barely had to adjust the sights at all."

John shoved some cartridges into the magazine and worked the lever. "Let's see how mine does."

"How much shooting have you done?"

"Some, but mostly with scatter guns."

"Well give it a go and we'll see how you do."

John raised the carbine to his shoulder and took aim. At fifty yards through open sights, the coffee can was a decent sized target. John watched as the sights swayed back and forth across the target. He tightened his grip to steady it, but that only seemed to make it worse. Jerking the trigger, the rifle sounded off. Dirt behind the target flew up in a small dust cloud—the can remained intact.

"I think the sights are off."

Thomas laughed. "Are you sure about that?"

"Here you give it a try and see."

Thomas took the Winchester and lined up the can in the sights. He let out his breath slowly, held it, and squeezed the trigger. The bullet struck the bottom left edge of the can and set it spinning on the stake. Thomas racked another cartridge into the chamber and fired again, this time hitting a little higher but still to the left.

"It's off by a bit. I'll adjust the sights for you—unless you want to do it."

"Be my guest."

Thomas adjusted the sights and after several more shots, had the rifle dialed in. "Try it now," he said, handing it to John.

After studying Thomas' shooting technique while he was sighting it in, John attempted to copy him. He took his time, controlled his breathing, and squeezed the trigger.

"Good shot." said Thomas. "Run a couple more rounds through it and I'll do the same with mine."

Twenty minutes later, the coffee can had surrendered to the barrage of .44 caliber bullets from the Winchesters and Thomas declared the rifles ready for action.

"I've sighted them in so they shoot a couple inches high at fifty yards, that way they should be right on at a hundred. Most of our shooting will be inside that range I expect."

"Makes sense," said John. "Let's see if Stella has wrangled some lunch for us, then we'll head back to town to see if the bank has wired the money—if you want to come along."

"Sounds good," said Thomas. "And I'm hungry."

* * *

After lunch Thomas cleaned both rifles, double checking every part of the mechanisms to make sure they were in perfect order.

John asked Emily if she wanted to go along into town, but she declined, saying her and Stella were planning something special for dinner to celebrate the purchase of the mining claim.

It was late afternoon when the wagon approached the telegraph office. As they drew closer, John's anticipation grew.

"I sure hope the bank wired the money. Clyde and Olson are moving on tomorrow and if we don't get the money I'm afraid we'll lose out."

"I'm sure it will work out," said Thomas, hiding his doubt.

They pulled up to the telegraph office and John was off the wagon before it rolled to a stop.

"I'll wait with the horse," said Thomas, as John took the three steps to the office in one bound and swung the door open.

"Good afternoon, sir," said the clerk.

John, totally out of character, dispensed with the amenities and said, "Anything for me? Anything at all."

The clerk reached over and pulled the top message off a stack. "This just came in for you," he said as he handed the folded sheet to John.

John took it and wasted no time in reading.

AUGUST 6, 1903

JOHN PALMER
VALDEZ, ALASKA

REGARDING YOUR REQUEST FOR FUNDS, WE REGRET TO INFORM YOU THAT THE ACCOUNT WITH IDENTIFICATION NUMBER 6836 WAS CLOSED AT YOUR REQUEST ON MAY 5.

YOUR AGENT, MR. VAN SANT PRESENTED REQUIRED DOCUMENTATION TO WITHDRAW ALL FUNDS. WE SUGGEST YOU CONTACT HIM REGARDING DISPOSITION OF YOUR ASSETS.

MARTIN SLONGER, MANAGER
DEXTER HORTON AND COMPANY
SEATTLE

His hands dropped to his side, his eyes staring straight ahead. He read it again, hands now shaking, every muscle in his neck tightening.

"Are you okay, sir?" asked the clerk.

John crumpled the paper into a wad and stuffed it into his pocket. "No, I am not okay," he said as he left the office.

* * *

"Surely it's a mistake," said Thomas. "It doesn't make any sense."

"I'm afraid it makes a lot of sense. This is why I haven't been able to contact Preston. He closed my account, stole all the money, and has been doling it out to me as I asked to hide the fact. Now he's gone who knows where," said John, hanging his head.

Thomas didn't know what to say as he turned the wagon and headed out of town. It was clear John needed some time to absorb his current situation, so Thomas kept silent as the horse plodded on. After a mile or so, John finally looked up.

"I guess we are out of the mining business before we started. I'm nearly broke and have no idea what to tell Emily. I need to get to Seattle and hunt down Van Sant."

"How do you know he is even there? If it were me, I wouldn't stick around the same town where I just stole a man's entire fortune."

"You're right Thomas, there is no point in blindly trying to search for him."

"Is there anyone else you can contact that might know where he went?"

John thought for a moment, realizing he actually knew little about Van Sant's associates. "There is one fellow I could try to contact—a partner in his failed law firm. He might know where he is, but even so, I'm afraid it sinks our deal for the gold claim. We don't have the money."

Thomas knew from the moment John read him the telegram that the dream was over. The loss of the gold claim hurt, but not as much as losing one's life savings. This would have lasting implications for John and Emily, especially in light of the death of Lydia.

"First my wife dies in a fire that destroys my home and all our belongings, and now a trusted friend has stabbed me in the back. I guess I know now a little of what you went through."

"I did feel pretty lost after being shot and robbed the first day I got here, but Stella was there for me. I don't know what I would have done without her."

"Emily and I are in an awkward position now. It appears we must rely on Stella's kindness even more—a position I detest."

* * *

August 7, 1903

She quickly gathered her bag and made way to the gang plank, taking her place beside the smartly dressed gentleman. He smiled at her, reached out his hand and took hers, squeezing it for a brief moment before letting go.

"I'm scared," she said, looking up at him warily.

"Don't worry yourself, it will be fine."

The noise on the ship grew as passengers disembarked, some fighting for position among the throng.

A barrel-chested miner shoved his way in front of them, dislodging the bag from her hand and nearly knocking her to the deck.

Retribution was swift. Her companion grabbed the bearded man by his hair, and in one swift move, yanked him backwards to the deck, nearly winding him. Before he could try to get up, a boot was placed firmly across his throat, the pressure firm enough to hold him.

"I think you owe the lady an apology."

Hate in his eyes, the miner struggled. The pressure increased, and he relented. Struggling for a breath, he managed, "Sorry, ma'am."

"I think you can do better than that."

"I...I'm terribly sorry for jostling you, ma'am. I hope you will forgive me."

She nodded, saying nothing. Removing his boot from

the miner's throat, her companion reached down and offered a hand. He took it, and her companion helped him to his feet. Their eyes met—the miner's hand clenched into a fist. Reason prevailed and, relaxing his hand, he turned to step away.

"Pick up her bag and hand it to her."

"What?"

"I said pick up her bag and hand it to her."

The miner obliged, righting the bag and handing it to her. He took a step to walk away.

"One more thing, cockroach. If I see you even looking at this lady again, I will shoot you in your tracks."

"I'm sorry, sir," said the miner as he backed away and turned, crossing to the port side of the ship. With both hands tightly gripping the rail, he stared out across the bay, his back to the man and woman. *That man is as savage as a meat axe*, he thought as his pulse slowly returned to normal.

"He didn't hurt me," she said.

"These Johnny-come-lately miners are scum—ignorant, uneducated, rude, and the underbelly of society. I will deal with them as I would a rabid dog."

"How long must we be here?" she said, staring at the sea of undesirables streaming from the ship.

"Long enough," he said.

"What do you intend to do?"

"I intend to find him, and when I do, put a bullet between his eyes."

She looked down, unable to look him in the eye. "Must you?"

He didn't answer.

Other passengers witnessed the altercation with the miner, and for some reason, a path seemed to clear ahead of the man and woman as they moved forward. As the sun cleared the mountains and began to warm the August air, they reached the end of the dock. Two steps later they were standing on the dry, dusty streets of Valdez, Alaska.

* * *

"I won't take no for an answer," said Stella.

"I can't let you do this, Stella," said John. "It's too much."

Thomas joined in, "Yes, Stella, we can't accept it."

"Look you two, I've been saving this money for five years, ever since Wesley disappeared. It's not doing me any good sitting here."

Stella handed a bundle wrapped in brown paper to John. "That's four thousand dollars. With what Thomas has, it's enough to buy the claim and outfit yourself."

Thomas shook his head, his forehead wrinkled and brows knit together.

John pushed the bundle back towards Stella, but she put her hands top and bottom over his and held them there. "No, you take it," she said softly.

Emily entered the kitchen and stopped, realizing she walked into the middle of something. Stella's hands dropped away.

"What is going on?" said Emily, the tips of her ears visibly turning red.

"Stella is funding our mining venture, dear. Four thousand dollars."

"Oh my, that's a lot of money."

"That's what we told her," said Thomas, "but she insists."

"I swear, Stella, I will find Preston and get my money back. And when I do, I will pay you back every cent, plus interest."

Stella smiled. "I'm not worried, John."

"I don't know how to thank you, Stella," said Thomas. "You've done everything for me and now for Emily and John. I feel like I can never repay your kindness."

"Enough talk, now scoot. Those boys will be coming downstairs for breakfast soon and I need to get busy. Take some coffee and make plans while I get to cooking."

"I'll help you," said Emily.

Thomas and John grabbed a cup of coffee and headed for the dining room. Sitting across from each other, they began to make plans for their trip north.

"I'm worried that we're getting started too late in the year," said John.

"I know, but I've talked to a lot of miners passing through and some stay all winter."

"That doesn't sound good to me."

"They mine frozen gravel in the winter using shafts, then sluice it in the summer."

"How do they mine it in the winter?"

"Well, from what I've been told, they thaw the gravel by building a fire on it, then dig it out and pile it up. That's about all I know about it, but it doesn't matter—our claim is a placer."

"Placer?"

"Yeah. We'll be mining thawed gravel on the surface and moving it through a sluice box to get the gold."

"Sounds easier than the other."

"Still hard work, but definitely easier than mining frozen ground."

"I think we should plan to get up there and get out before the hard freeze," said John. "We can get the lay of the land, do a little mining, and get things ready for a full season starting in the spring."

"Makes sense to me."

"Me too," said Emily from the kitchen. "I don't want either of you gone that long."

Thomas and John looked at each other and smiled. "Yes, dear," they both said at once.

* * *

"Morning," said Clyde as he shuffled into the dining room, Olson following close behind. "Got our money?"

"Mornin' to you, too," said Thomas, his voice sharp as he stared at them.

"Well, let's see it."

John started to stand from the table. Thomas turned toward him and raised his hand, stopping him.

"I've been thinking," said Thomas. "You boys are leaving soon and the way I see it, you've got no other prospects. We're willing to pay you two thousand for the claim sight unseen."

John's eyes widened as both Stella and Emily turned towards Thomas.

"You're crazy," said Clyde. "We had a deal—you saw the gold that claim produced."

Thomas stood firm, arms crossed. "We've got no guarantees. Maybe we'll just walk away."

"You calling me a liar?" said Clyde, his face tightening.

John couldn't read the miners to tell what was going through their heads. *Thomas is going to mess this up. What is he doing?*

The miners pulled out a chair and sat down, Clyde still staring at Thomas. Emily thought it was a glare.

"The price stands," said Clyde.

Olson shuffled in his chair, looking down at the table. Thomas immediately knew he was making ground.

"Well then, we're out," said Thomas.

"Clyde I think we—"

"Quiet, Olson," said Clyde, his fist slamming the table. "We'll come down to three thousand and that's it."

John opened his mouth, but Thomas beat him to it. "No, two thousand or we walk away."

Clyde tensed, then let out a sigh. "Damn you, Thornton. You drive a hard bargain, but you got us between a rock and a hard place."

Thomas thrust out his hand. "Shake on it and you've got your money."

Clyde stood and reluctantly raised his hand, surprised at the strength of the grip that met his.

"Deal," said Clyde.

"Relax and have some breakfast, then we'll complete our business," said Thomas, winking at John.

* * *

Breakfast was a tense affair with little conversation. Clyde and Olson ate quickly, stuffing food in their mouths as though they had been lost in the wilderness for months. Finishing, they returned to their room and packed quickly, eager to move on.

Clyde stepped off the stairs and into the sitting room. "We're ready to leave—where's the money?"

"You're an impatient sort, aren't you?" said John.

"Just don't want to spend any more time here than I have to since you dressed us down."

"I wouldn't call it that. More like shrewd negotiation."

"Whatever you want to call it. Pay up and we're on our way."

John pulled a bulging envelope from his vest pocket and handed it to Clyde. "Count it."

"I plan to," said Clyde, opening the envelope and thumbing through the bills.

Olson waited impatiently. Thomas thought he was beginning to sweat a bit around the brim of his hat. *I wonder...*

"Looks like it's all here." Clyde stuffed it into his bag and headed for the door.

"Wait a minute," said Thomas. "What about the papers and documents?"

Clyde paused and reached into the pocket of his coat, producing a single crumpled piece of paper. He handed it to Thomas.

Thomas looked at the crudely drawn claim map that reminded him of something a child would create. "That's it?"

"Yup," said Clyde, turning for the door.

Thomas grabbed him firmly by the arm. "What about all the records, equipment lists, and deed?"

Clyde yanked his arm away sharply, tearing it from Thomas' grip. "That's all you get."

Thomas stepped forward, his fist clenching. "I want the rest of it now."

"Back off, plow boy. You don't want no trouble now," said Clyde, pulling back his coat to reveal the butt of a revolver protruding from his waist band.

"Let them go, Thomas," said Emily. "It's not worth it."

"Listen to the girl, plow boy."

"I swear, if you cheated us I will hunt you down and

I'll have every penny back."

Clyde glared, let his coat fall back to hide the revolver, then smiled. "Nice doing business with you," he said as he followed Olson out the door.

Thomas started to follow, but Emily gently hooked her arm through his. "Let it go, Thomas."

"I hope we didn't just make a huge mistake."

"Me too, Thomas—me too," said John.

* * *

August 8, 1903

"You and the lady checking out, sir?" said the clerk as he pushed his glasses up on his nose.

"No, but I am looking for some information."

"Sure, what can I help you with?"

"I'm looking for John Palmer. He came here earlier in the summer with his daughter."

"Oh, you a friend of his?"

The man folded his gloved hands and placed them on the counter, leaned in, and stared at the clerk.

"Uh, yes," the clerk said stammering. "I know him. They stayed at the hotel here when they first arrived."

"Where can I find them?" said the man, his voice low and raspy, gaze never wavering.

"They're living out at Stella's boarding house."

"How do I get there?"

"Well, you can get one of the fellas with a wagon to take you and the lady out there, but it may be a while. Most of them are busy with the new load of miners that came in on the steamer this morning."

"Just give me directions then."

"Head to the east end of this street. You'll pick up the trail there."

"How far?"

"To the boarding house? It's several miles. I don't think you want to walk it."

"Never mind, I have other business to attend to beforehand. Where can I send a telegram?"

"Telegraph office is just down the street, near the general store. You can't miss it."

"One more thing. I need a horse."

"Check with the blacksmith, he might be able to help you out."

Without thanks, he pulled his hat down low, turned, and left the hotel.

"Odd man he is," said the clerk to himself.

* * *

"You realize how far it is to the Fortymile, don't you?" said Noel as he dropped the last of the supplies on the counter. "Seems you're going to spend all yer time gettin' there and back."

John began stacking the supplies in Thomas' arms. "Yes, we know. I'm hoping we can make good time."

"Well, the trail can be a bit sloppy this time of year, but since it's been a dry year you might luck out. Don't know what it's like north of here though."

"We've heard it's in pretty good shape," said Thomas, peering over the stack of goods in his arms. "That's enough, John."

Thomas took the load to the wagon and piled it on. It was a lot of supplies, more than he wanted to haul north, but Noel assured him they needed it. As he entered the store, he found John counting out bills one by one, placing them on the counter.

"That should cover it."

"Thanks, John. I wish you and Thomas the best of luck. When you heading out?"

"Tomorrow morning. Time is short and we want to get up there and back before the snow flies."

"I think you're forgetting something," said Noel.

John and Thomas looked at each other, then back at him.

"I think you need another horse."

Thomas slapped his forehead and ran his hand back through his hair. "Tarnation, how could we not think about that?"

"You're greenhorns," said Noel. "That's why."

Thomas frowned. John didn't know how to take it, but then Noel let a grin slip and they realized he was having fun with them.

"You're right, we are," said Thomas. "I just assumed we'd take the horse and wagon, but that leaves Stella and Emily with no transportation. Where are we going to find a horse or two in this town?"

"What about those two fellas you bought the claim from? If they're catching a steamer south they're gonna want to get rid of their horses."

"I'm not going anywhere near those two snakes. Just about had a gun drawn on me when we last dealt with them."

Noel frowned and shook his head. "Well, the blacksmith Fenton keeps a few nags around—buys them off fellas coming and going. You might check with him."

"I guess that's our next stop," said John. "Thanks, Noel, hopefully we'll see you in October."

"Good luck, fellas. I'll check in with the ladies when I can."

"Thanks," said Thomas. "We better get going—have

a lot to do yet today."

* * *

"Two hundred a piece," said Fenton. "That's my price and a deal at that."

John and Thomas stood staring at the horses. They looked to be a bit rougher than Stella's horse. The Appaloosa looked to be in the best shape. The other was a breed Thomas couldn't identify—she was just a nondescript horse. *More like a nag*, thought Thomas.

Thomas checked their mouths, then went about examining each hoof to make sure they were in good shape. He patted their ribs.

"They're a bit scrawny," he said.

"They just come off the trail a week ago," said Fenton. "They look a lot better now than they did then."

"You got anything else?"

"Nope, that's it. I had one other, but a fella bought her a couple hours ago. With the new batch of cheechakos that just landed, I expect these will be gone by today."

"Good enough, Thomas?" said John.

Thomas nodded, knowing they had no other options.

"We'll take 'em," said John, reaching for his wallet. "Good thing we saved a few dollars on the claim," he said, winking at Thomas.

"You need a wagon? Got a few behind the stable there."

"I guess we better," said John. "Can't rob everything from Stella. Let's take a look."

There were three wagons to choose from. Two looked far too heavy to drag across a land rife with swamps and deep mud holes. The remaining wagon looked serviceable and in good repair.

"What do you want for that one?" said Thomas, pointing at it.

A crooked smile wrapped across Fenton's dirty, wrinkled face. "I'll make you a real good deal on that one."

"I'm sure you will," said John.

* * *

Thomas finished hitching the Appaloosa to the wagon, then tied the nag on behind.

"Ready?" said John.

"Yes, let's get back and start packing up. You got anything else you need to do before we head out?"

"Yes, come to think of it, I do. I need to send a telegram."

John drove Stella's wagon with the supplies, while Thomas handled the new wagon, the nag in tow. It was a short trip to the telegraph office.

"I'll wait here with the gear," said Thomas.

"Sounds good," said John. "This won't take long."

As John entered the telegraph office, he thought the clerk seemed a bit wary, perhaps nervous.

"Very sorry—nothing for you today, Mr. Palmer."

John smiled. "I'm not expecting anything. I just want to send one."

"Oh, very good, sir," he said, handing Palmer a blank form.

John quickly scribbled out a message and handed it back to the clerk.

POLICE CHIEF
SEATTLE, WASHINGTON

DEAR SIR,

MY BANK ACCOUNT AT DEXTER HORTON AND COMPANY HAS BEEN ROBBED OF ALL FUNDS. MY LAWYER, PRESTON VAN SANT WAS THE ONLY ONE AUTHORIZED TO ACCESS FUNDS ON MY BEHALF. I BELIEVE HE HAS ABSCONDED WITH MY MONEY AS I HAVE BEEN UNABLE TO CONTACT HIM. PLEASE INVESTIGATE AND NOTIFY ME OF ANY PROGRESS.

YOUR HELP IS GREATLY APPRECIATED.

JOHN W. PALMER
VALDEZ, ALASKA

The clerk counted up the words. "Two-bits for this one, sir."

John put the coins on the counter. "That'll go out today?"

"Yes, sir, we'll have it out of here in an hour or two."

"Thanks," said John as he left the office.

Thomas was standing beside the new wagon, smoking a cigarette. "Everything okay?"

"Yes, just took care of something I should have done days ago, but hoped I wouldn't have to. With any luck, by the time we return from the Fortymile, the police in Seattle will have found my money."

* * *

"Did you find him," asked the woman as he closed the door to their hotel room.

"Yes, I know where Palmer is staying."

"When will you do it?"

"Tomorrow. You'll stay here and out of sight while I ride out to the boarding house where he's living."

"I wish there was another way."

"There isn't. Besides, he's only getting what he deserves."

"You won't hurt the girl, will you?"

"No," he said, comfortable with the lie. *Not unless I have to.*

She sighed and slumped into the overstuffed chair beside the bed, crying softly. "This is wrong in so many ways."

He stood firm, not moving to comfort her and offering no words to ease her pain.

"Can't we forget about this and just leave?"

"No. We've been over all this many times. I suggest you compose yourself. I'll hear no more about this from you until it's done."

She ceased crying and looked out the window. *So far from home—how have I come to this point?*

* * *

Part II

Journey

August 9, 1903

Thomas dragged himself downstairs and shuffled to the kitchen, hoping to find coffee. He could hear Stella working away at the stove, a good sign that his search would be successful.

"Morning, Thomas," said Stella. "I'm surprised you're up this early after that late night."

"Yes, I'm surprised too. All that sorting and packing kept John and me up well past midnight."

"Anxious to get going I suppose."

"Yes. We've got a long way to go and I'm ready to get moving."

"I can't say I'm thrilled at having you and John head up there this time of year. The trail can be bad and winter's coming."

"I know, but this is a good way for us to know what we need for next year. We'll be back in time to help you get ready for winter."

"Don't worry about that. You two just take care of yourselves."

"We will do our best. I wonder if I need to go wake up John."

"No need," came the voice from the living room. "I'm up and ready for coffee."

"I'll get some breakfast started," said Stella.

John and Thomas each grabbed a cup of coffee from the big pot on the stove and took a seat in the dining room.

"Are we ready?" said John?

"I think so," said Thomas. "We've gone over the list twice."

"Good thing Stella had all that extra tack in the shed. I'd hate to walk all the way."

"Now all we have to do is decide who gets to ride and who drives the wagon."

"I'll let you drive the wagon," said John. "I don't want to be responsible for all our gear ending up upside down in a river."

Thomas wrinkled his brow and feigned annoyance. "Thanks—that's not going to happen."

"It better not," said Stella from the kitchen.

John and Thomas often forgot that Stella's hearing was something of legend. "Boy that Stella is a good cook," said Thomas softly.

"I heard that," said the voice from the kitchen.

"Good thing we only have nice things to say about her," said John as he took another gulp of coffee, sat it down, and smiled.

Emily came down from her room, looking prim and proper as usual as she took a seat in the dining room. "What time are you leaving?"

"Right after breakfast," said Thomas.

"I'm glad you are going and yet I wish you weren't," she said, looking first at her father and then to Thomas.

"I know, dear," said her father. "We will only be gone a couple of months. The time will pass quickly."

"I will worry the whole time you are gone, just as I did when Thomas was up here all alone."

"I wasn't alone. Stella was taking good care of me after I was shot and robbed."

"I know, but yet I had no idea what was happening to you."

John finished his coffee and stood to fetch another. "There are telegraph stations all along the trail. We will keep in touch with you as we can. Just don't go running to the telegraph office every day."

"Yes, Father. I will try, but it will be hard."

"Breakfast's on," said Stella as she carried a bowl of fried potatoes and a huge platter of scrambled eggs to the table.

"I'll get the bacon and coffee," said Emily as she jumped up and scampered to the kitchen.

* * *

It didn't take long after breakfast for Thomas and John to load the last of their gear and hitch up the wagon. With the extra tack of Stella's, they would be able to ride one horse while the other pulled the load.

Thomas cinched the canvas down tight over the wagonload of supplies and double checked the hitch. Satisfied, he pulled the wagon around front, then returned to bring the nag up.

Emily and Stella were standing on the front porch, talking to John as Thomas walked up.

"Well, I guess this is it," said Thomas.

Emily ran to him and hugged him tightly, surprising him with her strength. He kissed her gently on the forehead and she stepped back, tears visible in her eyes.

"I'll be okay."

"I know."

Thomas turned to Stella and gave her a hug. "Thanks for everything. We couldn't do it without you."

Stella smiled. "You be careful. I don't want to have to come to the Fortymile to rescue you."

"We'll be careful," said Thomas, patting her back as the hug faded.

Emily hugged her father and reiterated the plea for caution and safety.

"I want you to be careful as well," said John.

"I'll take good care of her," said Stella.

"I am sure you will," said John, stretching his hand out to shake hers.

She took his hand, then pulled him to her and gave him an open hug.

"I want you to come back safely," she said softly.

John remained silent, looking at the woman that had given of herself for him and Emily.

"Thank you," he said at last. "For everything."

"Well, let's be off," said Thomas. "Daylight's burning."

With one last wave, Thomas jumped up into the wagon and waited for John to untie the nag and mount up. He noticed the horse was a bit uneasy, attempting to turn as John tried to get his foot in the stirrup. They went around for nearly a full circle before John finally got the best of her and pulled himself up into the saddle.

"I hope she settles down some," said John.

"I'm sure she will, once she gets used to us."

As they pulled away from the house and headed toward Keystone Canyon, Emily and Stella waved and watched. Each time Thomas looked back, they waved again. He couldn't tell, but from a distance it looked like Emily was crying openly now. The last time he looked back, they were gone—the boarding house no longer visible from the curve in the trail.

"I guess we're off," said Thomas.

"I'd say so," said John. "May God be with us."

* * *

He left mid-afternoon, headed east along the trail. In no hurry, he took in the scenery as the horse plodded slowly along. Several times he checked inside his coat, patting the .45 caliber revolver that was loaded and ready. Malice turned to tranquil resolution, the goal fixed firmly in his mind. There was no panic or fear, only a detached calm flowing through him.

The scene played repeatedly in his mind over the last year. That final moment when justice would be meted out—all wrongs would be righted in one swift moment of retribution.

Unsure of how far it was to the boarding house, he traveled slowly. His plan required a certain level of stealth—a cautious approach. As he drew near, the realization that he had no plan of escape came crashing upon him. Justice must be served, but not at the expense of freedom.

He passed a couple of old, dilapidated cabins, rounded a corner, and caught his first glimpse of what he believed to be the boarding house. He backed the horse and turned her off the trail, then dismounted, tying her off to the nearest spruce. Pulling his hat low, he packed his pipe with tobacco and lit up, hoping to appear as a traveler taking a respite from a long ride. His true motive was to watch the house, waiting for an opportunity—waiting for the object of his obsession to appear.

An hour passed with no sign of activity from the boarding house. He noticed smoke rising from the chimney, which meant someone was likely at home. Walking up and knocking on the door was not in his best interest—the fewer people that saw him, the better. He tapped the ashes out of his pipe and packed in fresh tobacco. *One more smoke and then I must do something*, he thought.

The sound of a horse and wagon coming from beyond the boarding house caught his attention. He shuffled a bit, pulled his collar up, and tried to put on a casual air. The horse and wagon passed the boarding house and the driver noticed him standing alongside the trail.

"Afternoon," said the driver. "Got troubles?"

He had nothing but disdain for these people, and yet, he had to play the part to avoid raising suspicion. "No troubles here, friend—just having a smoke and enjoying the scenery," he said, feigning cordiality.

"If yer hungry, Stella makes a mean moose stew—probably has some simmering right now."

"Ah," he said. "I was wondering if that was Stella's place."

"Yep, sure is. She don't mind drop-ins for a meal."

"Thank you for the information. I may do just that."

"You headed for the gold fields?"

He was tired of the conversation, yet continued the act. "No, I'm looking into business opportunities along the trail."

"Plenty of competition there. Already a bunch of roadhouses along the route, but I wish you luck."

Time to move him along. "Thanks. Don't let me hold you up, I'm getting ready to saddle up in a moment."

The driver nodded. "Good day, then," he said as he slapped the reins against the horse and the wagon lurched forward.

He watched him roll out of sight, around the corner,

and down the trail toward Valdez.

I'm wasting time, he thought. *Might as well try the direct approach.*

* * *

"May I help you," said the woman that answered the door in short order after his first knock. He sized her up—she was probably in her early fifties, with graying hair and a pleasant look about her.

"I'm looking for John Palmer. I was told he was staying here."

Stella looked at the man, dressed more smartly than the typical sort that got off the boat. He wore his hat pulled low, which she thought was odd for a clear day in early August. "You a friend of his?"

"No, ma'am, not at all. He loaned me a few dollars a while back and I wanted to repay his kindness."

"Well you just missed him. He headed for the Fortymile this morning."

This wasn't expected, yet he quickly realized it could work to his advantage. "When will he be back?"

"I'm not sure. Might be a while. I can give him the money if you like."

"Thank you, but I prefer to settle my debts in person. I suppose his daughter went with him as well."

Stella stood silent for an instant. By nature she had learned to be suspicious of the characters that crossed her doorstep—at least until she could size them up. Most turned out to be okay, some were to be avoided. She decided not to give him any more information.

"I'm afraid I have to get back to my kitchen. Would you like to leave a message for Mr. Palmer?"

Though irritated at her dodge, he had what he needed. "No message, I'll catch up with him at a later date."

"I'm sorry you rode out here for nothing."

He turned and started down the stairs of the porch. "I'm not."

* * *

"Who was that?" said Emily as she came down the stairs from her room.

"Some gentlemanly looking fellow calling for your father."

"What did he want?"

"He said he owes him some money."

"Did he leave his name?"

"No, and I didn't think to ask. I said I would take the money or he could leave a message. He declined."

"Must be someone Father met in town."

"I told him your father could be gone for a while so I don't expect he will be back anytime soon. Odd, though. He asked about you."

"Really?"

"Yes, he wanted to know if you went with your father. I dodged his question—none of his business really and we don't know him from Adam."

"I hope he doesn't come back until Father is home."

* * *

"He's gone north on the trail," the man said as he took off his coat and holster, placing them on the bed.

"Now what?" said the woman. "I don't look forward to sitting around this hotel waiting."

He stared at her—the stare that always struck fear in her heart. She turned away, wishing she'd kept the complaint to herself.

"This will work to my advantage, but I must travel quickly. With him on the trail I can catch him alone—no witnesses that way."

She sighed. "What of me?"

"I'm heading to the general store for supplies and gear. If I leave early morning he will only have a day lead. I can catch him if I travel light."

He reached into his vest pocket and pulled out his wallet, opening it to reveal a healthy wad of cash. "Here is enough money to get you by. Wait here at the hotel for a week. If I'm not back by then, take the first steamer to San Francisco—you can't be seen in Seattle."

He pulled several more hundred dollar bills from the wallet. "This should cover first-class passage."

"I'm worried about traveling alone."

"It's first class. Stay in your cabin if you like—you'll be fine."

She sighed again and started to speak, but thought better of it. Angering him was never a good idea.

"Do you understand?"

"Yes, Preston. I understand."

* * *

August 10, 1903

"We're going to have to do better than yesterday," said Thomas as he hitched up the wagon. "Wortmans Roadhouse was good for an overnighter, but less than twenty miles in a day is not."

"You're right," said John, "and yesterday was some of the better part of the trail. Not sure what we can do to cover more ground."

"I think we're just going to have to push harder, travel longer, and camp out rather than stay at the roadhouses."

John weighed the options and decided he preferred a roadhouse and a real bed to a tent and the cold ground. "I would prefer to stay indoors if possible."

"We may have to swap out the horses. That wagon is quite a load for one horse, especially on some of the rougher parts of the trail," said Thomas.

"I thought coming through the canyon was rough enough. What's our next stop?"

Thomas had studied the map of the trail he got from Noel for days and nearly had it memorized. He pulled it out of his vest pocket and smoothed it out on the wagon seat.

"Getting over the pass is our goal for today. I'd like to make it past Tiekel but that's probably pushing it given the uphill climb we've got in front of us."

John looked over Thomas' shoulder at the map. "How far is Tiekel?"

"About thirty miles from here and we've got several river crossings."

"Let's hope the bridges are in one piece. Noel did mention the army has been working on trail improvements this summer."

Thomas folded the map and put it away. He looked up at the mountains that surrounded him on all sides and felt both excitement and anxiety—he was finally on the way to fulfilling his dream.

"You want to drive or ride?" said Thomas.

"I'll ride for now."

Thomas checked the load one last time, making sure everything was secure. In spite of Noel's advice, and after much debate, they decided to leave half of the supplies at Stella's rather than drag a year's worth of goods for a two month stay. This cut down the load on the wagon and Thomas was sure it was a good plan, since they had no idea if they would be able to safely store so much food on the claim. With tools, gold pans, rope, and other mining essentials, the wagon was plenty heavy.

Thomas jumped up in the wagon and with a ceremonial wave of his arm, they started toward Thompson Pass and the slow crawl up the mountain. The route would take them to the summit of the pass, then down along the banks of Ptarmigan Creek to the Tsina River. The trail followed the river for many miles to the confluence with the Tiekel River, their goal for the day. The hardest part of the day's journey would be the steep climb up the pass.

At first the going was easy. The route from Wortman's to the start of the ascent was a fairly gentle climb, following the contour of the mountain just above the Lowe River. After four miles they reached the ascent into the pass, a climb of one thousand feet. The Appaloosa started strong, but began to slow when they neared the summit.

"We're going to have to rest the horse for a bit," said Thomas as he pulled the wagon to a stop near a small lake that lay just off the trail. "She's lathered up pretty good."

John pulled up beside him. "The old nag seems to be doing fine."

"That's because she only has you to haul around."

John laughed. "Shall we swap them out?"

Thomas pulled out his tobacco pouch and rolled a cigarette. "No, let's take a rest and water them."

John dismounted and tied the nag off to the wagon. "A smoke sounds like a good idea," he said, loading his pipe.

Thomas took a long drag on his cigarette and blew it out slowly. "Only about six miles into it and here we are resting."

"I expect it will be easier going once we reach the top."

"Yes, at least it's mostly downhill."

Thomas unhitched the Appaloosa and led her to the water for a drink. John did the same with the nag. They rested the horses until the Appaloosa had cooled down, then hitched up to continue the ascent to the summit.

Within the hour, they had mastered the climb and were looking down the long valley towards the Tsina river.

"Another twenty-three miles or so and we're done for the day," said Thomas.

John shook his head. "We'd better get to it."

* * *

He had been on the trail since early morning, driving the horse hard to catch up with Palmer. He figured he could travel nearly twice as fast, since he was traveling light. *Besides, this couldn't take more than a day—two at most.*

It took nearly an hour to get past Stella's. He slowed as he passed, looking to make sure there was no sign of Palmer. *After all, she may have lied.* Seeing nothing but smoke rising from the chimney, he pressed on.

The trail from the boarding house to the canyon was fairly flat and Van Sant made good time, pushing the horse hard. He passed Camp Comfort without slowing down, resolving to press on until dark. Two miles later he was traversing Keystone Canyon—the trail more difficult, and the progress slower. He continually kicked his heels into the ribs of the horse, and each time she snorted and raised her head up and down, but kept the same pace over the rutted, uneven trail that skirted the high wall of the canyon.

I'll never catch him at this pace.

By noon he was at the base of the pass. Though he acquired a trail map, in his hurry to leave, he failed to study the route well enough to know what was ahead. He stopped at the lake next to the trail and looked up the mountain. Despite his impatience, he decided to have a quick bite to eat and allow the horse to drink and feed for a few moments. Dismounting, he tied her off to a nearby alder and pulled the map out of his pack.

I'm guessing he made it at least this far the first day. He studied the map, wondering where Palmer was, and more importantly, where he would spend the night. Looking up from the map, a string of several horses caught his attention. They were negotiating their way down the last steep section of the pass before they hit the river bottom.

Van Sant could see three horses and two men—he waited until they reached the small lake.

"Good afternoon," he said, trying to be personable. "How are things up the trail?"

The men stopped their caravan and allowed the horses to water. "Not too bad," said the short fellow in the lead. "Some rough spots here and there, but the bridges are in good shape, as long as the water doesn't come up too much."

"Good news. I'm trying to catch up with my partner. Perhaps you've seen him."

"We seen lots of folks in the last several days. What's his outfit look like?"

This was a problem. Van Sant had no idea how Palmer was traveling, but he had to think quickly. "His name is Palmer. A tall fellow and a solid build."

The miner laughed. "You just described about half the folks between here and the Fortymile, except the women. Well, some of the women."

Van Sant cursed himself for not interrogating the woman at the boarding house. "He's around my age and may have been traveling with his daughter."

"He's your partner and you don't know if his daughter is with him?"

"He left before me," said Van Sant, a hint of a glare forming on his face.

"Ain't seen nobody traveling with a young lady in the last several days," said the second miner.

This is getting me nowhere, thought Van Sant. In a last attempt he said, "He can't be more than a day ahead of me if that helps."

The lead miner scratched his head for a minute. "We seen two old coots headed north today, plus an outfit of four with two wagons—oh, and two fellows traveling with two horses and a wagon."

Doesn't make sense—unless the woman lied to me, thought Van Sant. "What about the last two you mentioned?"

"Well that could'a been your partner I guess, but he ain't travelling alone—and there weren't no girl with 'em."

Thornton, thought Van Sant. *I forgot about Thornton.*

"Where were they at? I'm pretty sure that's him. I forget he said he was hiring some help."

"You sure don't seem to know much about your business, mister."

"Never mind that. Just tell me where you saw them."

"They was just past Ptarmigan Drop, I think."

"How far is that from here?"

The miner shook his head and gave Van Sant a funny look. He started to say something but thought better of it, deciding instead to answer his question. "About seven miles from here, near the Tsina River."

Though Van Sant felt nothing but contempt for the two, he managed to remain civil. "Thank you for the information."

"Sure. You're traveling pretty light there—hope you don't get yourself in trouble."

Van Sant didn't answer. He untied the horse and mounted up, then whipped the reins across the horse's neck and pointed her up the trail.

The miners looked at each other and shrugged, then continued on their way.

* * *

Van Sant pushed the horse hard up the pass, all the while trying to formulate a new plan. Dealing with Palmer was one thing—having Thornton in the way was another. He had nothing against the young man, but there could be no witnesses. It was unfortunate, but he knew what he had to do.

I need to catch them at night, while they are camped, he thought. The only kink in that plan was if they were staying at one of the roadhouses. He reached back and pulled the map from the pack strapped behind him. The nearest roadhouse was Summit, but they were beyond that. Tracing the trail on the map, he tried to determine where they might end up for the night. The most likely spots were either the Beaver Dam or Tiekell Roadhouse. Either one could be a problem—he was still sixteen miles from Beaver Dam and twenty-six miles from Tiekell.

I can't just walk into a roadhouse and create a scene. I need to catch them along the trail.

This time of year it was light enough to travel until after ten at night, something that surprised Van Sant after arriving in Valdez. *The only solution is to get in front of them, then wait.*

It was a good plan, the weak link being he couldn't be sure when he was past them. He resigned himself to traveling until dark, something he hoped Palmer wouldn't do. Yes, he would find a place to camp with a good vantage point and wait. He sighed, then whipped the horse once again. *Going to be a long day.*

* * *

Thomas looked back to make sure John was keeping up. They made good time after reaching the summit of Thompson Pass. He wanted to keep pushing, to put as much trail behind them as possible. It was a long way yet to the Fortymile and they didn't have a lot of time before winter.

"Doing fine back there?" he yelled.

"No worries here," said John, riding up next to the wagon. "How much farther to Tiekell?"

"Not sure. Maybe a couple of miles or so."

"What do you think? Should we see if we can bunk at the roadhouse?"

"We've got a fair amount of daylight left. I say we press on and camp when we can't see to travel any further."

John sighed, but not loud enough to be heard. He wasn't too thrilled about spending the night along the trail, but knew why Thomas was pushing so hard. The trip was easy so far, but he wasn't foolish enough to believe there wasn't adversity ahead. "Okay, but only if you promise I can sleep in a real bed at least once before we hit the Fortymile."

Thomas laughed. "You don't like camping?"

"I'll let you know when I decide."

Thomas was prepared to rough it the whole way. He mentally prepared for this life long before he set foot on the *North Wind* and sailed from Seattle. John on the other hand, was another matter entirely. He was a victim of circumstance—drawn here by the pleas of his daughter and now stuck because of Van Sant. Thomas hoped Palmer had the intestinal fortitude to make the trip.

"We can stay at Tiekell if you like," said Thomas, giving Palmer an out.

"No, let's press on. No worries here. I'll let you know when I'm ready to give up."

"Good. We should be able to make at least twenty more miles before we lose the light."

John slapped Thomas on the back and took the lead. "Alright, let's pick up the pace."

* * *

The mountains cast long shadows, the twilight enveloping the trail and turning the world into shades of gray.

"Whoa," said John as he pulled the nag to a stop. Thomas pulled up alongside and brought the wagon to a halt.

"Had enough?"

"I think it's time to make camp, Thomas."

"Sounds fine by me. We've made good progress today."

"I'll unpack the tent."

"Hold up a minute. I don't want to camp right next to the trail if we can help it."

"Oh?"

While they had passed few travelers, there were enough to make Thomas wary. The last thing he wanted was to get waylaid by trail bandits. Though not common, there were plenty of stories about men being beaten and robbed along the trail. Awake he wasn't worried—being hijacked in your sleep was another thing.

"Maybe I'm being overly cautious, but I'd feel better if our outfit wasn't sitting in plain sight for everyone to see."

"Might be hard to get the wagon off the trail and out of sight."

"Here, let me take the nag and run up the trail a bit and see if I can find a spot."

"Okay, but don't be gone long. It's going to get pretty dark here soon."

Thomas swung up into the saddle and pointed the nag up the trail. He was looking for a spot to pull the wagon off without getting stuck in a swamp or shook apart in a boulder pile. The trail followed the contour of the hillside through mostly rocky ground. He rode nearly a quarter of a mile and was about to give up the search when he spotted his goal—an old creek bed intersecting the trail, snaking gently upwards and around a bend, hidden by a small draw. Thomas pushed the nag ahead and up the draw, finding the ground solid, lacking large rocks, with plenty of grass growing on the banks. Just beyond, he could see a small pond rimmed by willow. *Perfect, water for the horses as well.*

After a hundred yards, the trail was hidden from view. *This will do nicely,* he thought as he turned the nag around and headed slowly towards the trail, not pushing the horse too hard in the fading light. As he reached the trail, the nag balked. He nudged her in the ribs, then heard it—a gunshot.

* * *

Thomas kicked the nag into high gear, headed back to where he left John and their gear. *A gunshot—bear, bandits?* He hoped neither, but whatever it was, he feared John wasn't prepared to deal with it alone.

He rounded the last bend of the trail and the wagon came into sight. The horse was tied off to a scrub willow, but in the fading light, John was nowhere to be seen. Thomas dismounted, pulled the carbine from its sheath, and strained to locate John. Behind him came a noise from downslope. He whirled around, gun raised as the shadow moved forward.

"Camp meat!" called John as he paused and held up a brace of ptarmigan. "Two in one shot." He smiled as he reached the trail and handed the scattergun to Thomas.

"You had me worried. I'm off looking for an inconspicuous place and next thing I hear is a gunshot. I thought maybe a bear or bandits got you."

"I couldn't resist. They came winging down the slope and landed just below me, so I pulled out the shotgun and gave it a go."

"Well, fresh meat is good, but we need to get moving before we can't see our hand in front of our face."

John jumped up on the wagon, tossing the birds into the back. "Right—lead the way."

Thomas mounted up and headed up the trail to the old creek bed. By the time they got the wagon up the draw and around the bend, it was nearly dark.

"Break out the tent and I'll get a small fire going," said Thomas as he headed up the draw towards the only stand of spruce he could see in the dark.

In the dark, John dug around under the canvas, then pulled out several candles from a box near the back. "We should have put the lanterns and kerosene where it was easy to get to—candles will have to do for tonight."

"Let's remember that next time we pack up."

Candles did little to push the darkness aside, but provided enough light for John to pull the tent from the wagon and find the stakes and poles. Sweeping his foot back and forth across the ground, he searched for a reasonably flat spot devoid of rocks and major lumps. It would have been easier if he could see.

Thomas was out of sight—John could hear the axe striking a tree and the sound of branches snapping. Setting up camp in the dark was not something John cared to repeat. *Ten p.m. is a little too late to call it a day.*

Thomas returned carrying an armful of dry spruce branches, dropping them unceremoniously on the ground.

"Seen any rocks?"

"Rocks?"

"Big ones for a fire ring—don't want to burn up the tent and our wagon."

"I kicked a couple out of the ground, but I'm sure there's plenty to be found."

One by one, Thomas gathered up large rocks, rolling most out of the moss covered ground. It didn't take long for him to have a small ring assembled and a nice little fire snapping and popping in the dark.

"Don't want to make it too big, since we're trying to lay low here," said Thomas. "Let me help you with the tent."

In short order, they had the tent up, horses staked out where they could feed, and the ptarmigan dressed out and ready to fry up. After a quick meal, Thomas fetched another batch of wood and stoked the fire for the night. He grabbed the carbine and placed it in the tent next to his bedroll. Checking the horses one last time, they crawled into the tent and closed it up. Sleep came quickly under the clear mountain sky.

August 11, 1903

It was still early when Van Sant finished saddling the horse and securing his meager supplies. His plan to press on up the trail had come to an early end. By the time he reached Beaver Dam Roadhouse, it was dark and he was tired, cold, and hungry. He chose to stay at the roadhouse, and his inquiries regarding his quarry were unfruitful. No one had seen Palmer.

Strengthened by the tar-like coffee of the roadhouse and a stack of griddle cakes, he resolved to push even harder. He wasn't outfitted for a lengthy trip, yet he would not stop—his future and freedom depended on it. There were ways to supply one's self on the trail, and he was not above resorting to them.

Palmer could be a half-day or more ahead of him, yet he was confident he could catch up. Traveling light with a horse, he would make much better time than a heavily loaded wagon. As he turned the horse up the trail, a light drizzle began to fall. He pulled his collar up around his neck, tipped his brimmed hat down low and whipped the horse into a gallop.

* * *

"Rain. That's going to make the trail messy if it keeps up," said Thomas as he rolled out of the tent, hoping the fire still lived in the embers.

"More fun for today, then," said John. "Nothing like packing up wet gear."

Thomas grabbed the axe and turned toward the stand of spruce. "Maybe it will clear once we get down the valley aways. Get the coffee pot ready and I'll have a fire for you in a few minutes."

John rummaged through the wagon, looking for the coffee pot, the sound of axe hitting wood drifting through the early morning drizzle. At last he found it, dumped a healthy portion of grounds in and waited.

Thomas returned with an armload of damp wood and set about trying to get the fire going. The coals were still warm under the ash, but the rain worked hard to snuff the life out of them. With much fiddling and a bit of cussing, he finally got the fire going and, before long, the coffee was boiling away.

"Nothing like beaver pond coffee," said Thomas, spitting out the last gulp of brown water and grounds.

John smiled. "No beavers, just swamp water."

It didn't take long for them to finish their meal of bacon, along with biscuits Stella packed for them. They worked quickly to break camp, stowing their bedding separate from the wet tent and securing everything under a large oil cloth on the wagon.

"Better get your fish on," said Thomas.

"Fish?"

Thomas laughed. "Your rain slicker. What, you aren't up on the frontier lingo?"

"Not yet—not sure I want to be."

"I'm sure we'll get into better weather once we get out of the mountains."

"Hope you're right, otherwise it's going to be a long miserable day."

Two hours later they were descending the muddy trail that became more slippery with every step. The drizzle turned to a steady, cold rain, chilling them to the bone as they slipped along. Thomas let John lead with the nag, while he drove the wagon. At times the slope worried him, the mud making the wagon sideslip toward the edge of the trail, threatening to send the whole rig tumbling down the mountain. Fortunately the Appaloosa was strong and sure footed, but progress was slow.

Steadily they descended, the rain increasing its pounding, sending muddy rivulets down the trail ahead of them. Thomas began to think they should stop—wait it out rather than risk an accident. *I'll give it another hour, then we'll see.*

Within thirty minutes the rain began to let up, the sky becoming lighter as if the sun was working to push through. Two miles down the trail the sun broke through, chasing the last of the rain clouds from view. They stopped and pulled the wet tent from the wagon, draping it across the top of the gear so it could dry in the sun.

"Told ya," said Thomas.

"You should have been a fortune teller. I'm glad the rain is done with—I was close to heading back to Stella's."

For a brief moment, Thomas thought he was serious, but then caught the twinkle in his eye. "Better buck up. Before the trip is over, we're likely to see worse than that."

"Oh, good news," said John, now wondering if maybe he underestimated the nature of this adventure.

Thomas laughed. "Life's tough in the far north."

"How far are we aiming for today?"

"Terrain is getting easier for the most part, so I'm

hoping for thirty miles today. Of course that depends on the trail condition—and we do have a pretty good climb to get through Kimball Pass. If we can make it to at least Donaldson Roadhouse we'll be doing well. That's about twenty miles from here I think."

"That puts us how far from the Fortymile?"

"Let's see," said Thomas, adding up the mileage in his head. "I don't remember exactly, but I think we'll still be about three hundred miles away."

"At this rate it's going to take us ten more days to get there."

"I know it's not ideal. Ten or twelve days each way, that leaves us only about forty days on the claim before we have to head back—if we want to get home before the temperatures drop."

"Well I'm not keen on wintering out there, especially since we didn't plan for it and neither did the women folk."

"The only way we can speed things up is to cache half our supplies to lighten the wagon. We might be able to cut three or four days travel time that way."

"And if we get stuck up there?"

"It certainly puts us at risk. I'm pretty sure we won't be able to readily buy supplies out there, but we may be able to procure something in Chicken."

"Should we do it?"

Thomas hesitated. It was a risk, offloading supplies when heading to the interior with winter less than two months away. *Poor timing all the way around*, he thought. "How much money do we have with us?"

John, thought for a moment. "Several hundred, I think."

"Not sure that's enough."

"I have an idea." What if we sell what we don't need at the next roadhouse?"

"That might work. We certainly don't need a hundred and fifty pounds of flour and seventy-five in bacon over the next two months."

"Well, if we do, they'll have to roll us back to Valdez."

Thomas laughed at the image of them being rolled along the trail and down the mountain. "My only concern is that we get a fair price."

"If not, we'll cache it then, okay?"

"Sounds like a plan," said Thomas. "Let's see if we can't pick up the pace a bit."

* * *

"Damn," Van Sant cursed aloud as he dismounted. In his efforts to push the horse, she had slipped on the muddy trail, nearly throwing him off. Now she stood, one leg held up in the air and looking like she wasn't going anywhere.

He wasn't much of a horseman. She was either sprained or had a fracture, but he had no way of knowing. He pulled her by the reins in an effort to get her to walk. She resisted—he pulled harder, cursing at her the entire time. Finally she took a step, faltered and went down, rolling on her side and bathing the pack and his gear in the wet mud—her travel was over.

Without hesitation, he pulled his revolver and shot her in the head. She convulsed, legs flailing the air, nearly striking him as he jumped back. Slowly her nervous system shutdown and the movements stopped. Now he was in a spot, faced with first retrieving his gear, and then figuring out how to continue his journey. *Ten miles to the next roadhouse I bet.*

He struggled to free the pack and gear from the dead horse. She of course, had fallen on the hitch side, making it impossible for him to reach. His only hope was to either cut it off or try to roll her over, without sending her off the edge of the trail and down the steep mountainside.

Grasping her by the hind leg, he pulled it up, then backed towards the edge of the trail. Slipping in the mud, he lost his footing and fell backwards, further soaking him. More cursing ensued, followed by another attempt. This time the horse started to roll, but without grabbing the other hind leg she wasn't going to come over. *This isn't working.*

He opened the pack and dug around, finally finding the fifty feet of rope he brought just in case. Tying it off to the upper leg, he pulled the leg up as far as he could, then slowly backed off the trail and down the slope, keeping the rope taught. Reaching a stand of scrub willow about thirty feet away, he tied the rope off. The willow bent and the leg dropped halfway down. After another bout of cursing, he was able to pull the rope tight again and secure it to the base of the three inch willow trunk, then head up the hill.

He was now able to lift the lower leg, and with much straining and choice words, get the horse rolled halfway over. He grabbed the rope, held it tight and descended to the willow patch where he snugged it up. Another trip up and he was able to straighten out her head, grab a front leg, and in one nearly monumental effort, flip her over on her other side.

Without warning, the momentum slid the horse off the trail, and she began rolling down the mountain. Van Sant leapt forward, trying to keep out of the way as the horse headed to the valley bottom. She crashed through the willow patch, then reached the end of the rope and stopped, head downhill and laying on her side.

Van Sant reached the horse, expecting the worst. To his surprise, she landed on the proper side for him to loose the pack. Then he saw it—in his anger and impatience, he failed to even think about removing his rifle from the scabbard. It now lay broken, the stock splintered in half. He picked it up and heaved it as hard as he could down the mountain. "I should shoot you again," he said to the horse.

* * *

The Ernestine Roadhouse was only a year old and Thomas could immediately tell the difference between it and the older establishments they passed on the trail. He tied off the horse and waited for John to ride up and do the same. He wasn't sure if selling half their supplies was a good idea. After all, Ernestine's was only sixty-two miles from Valdez—it wasn't likely they were desperate for resupply.

"Ready?" said John as he tied off the nag.

"As ready as I'll ever be. I just hope we don't take a bath on this deal."

John opened the door and held it for Thomas to enter. "Me too."

The roadhouse was well built, with sawn lumber siding and real windows. There were a few travelers inside, seated at tables and enjoying a freshly cooked, noon meal.

"Greetings," said the man as he approached, wiping his hands on a dirty towel and slinging it over his shoulder. "Looking for something to eat?"

"Yes," said Thomas, "and we'd like to talk a little business with you as well."

The proprietor cocked his head and looked at them, as though sizing up their intentions. He was justifiably wary, having witnessed many grifters pass through, offering get-rich schemes or other useless wares.

"Have a seat and I'll fetch you some stew and fresh biscuits, then we'll talk."

Thomas and John nodded and found a small table in the corner with a view of the front—perfect for keeping an eye on their horses and wagon. Within a few minutes, their meal arrived.

"Here you go. Now what do you have in mind?", said the proprietor, standing with arms crossed.

Nodding in John's direction, Thomas decided to let the businessman do the negotiations.

"Well, sir, we find ourselves in a bit of a predicament."

"Oh?" said the proprietor, maintaining his stance.

"We are attempting to make a quick trip to the Fortymile, and return before freeze up, but we are over-supplied and it's slowing us down. We'd like to see if you are interested in purchasing some of our food stuffs."

"I'm pretty well stocked. What do you have?"

"We've got the basic staples—flour, bacon, beans, sugar, and dried fruit."

The man rubbed his stubbled chin and looked out the window in the direction of the wagon, then back to the table. "Finish up your stew and we'll have a look."

"Thank you, sir."

"Name's Miller," he said as he turned and walked toward the kitchen.

John and Thomas ate quickly, a sense of urgency driving them, even though they had more than a week's travel ahead of them.

"How much should we ask?" said Thomas.

"If we are lucky enough to sell half, it would be good to get two hundred for it."

"That's sounds good. I would think that's a deal for him, since we're not charging him transportation."

"Yes. Should be cheaper than what he pays to get it from Valdez."

It didn't take long for them to finish the meal. "Not bad," said Thomas, "but nowhere near as good as Stella's food".

John shook his head in agreement.

Thomas shuffled back and forth in his seat, looking back toward the kitchen in an effort to get Miller to notice. Finally, as he finished clearing the table in the far corner of the room, Miller looked their way. John raised a finger and caught his attention.

"Done?" he said.

"Yes, sir, and I must say it was the best hot meal we have had on the trail," said John. It wasn't a lie—apart from their camp food this was the only place they had eaten.

"Thanks. Let me clear this away and we'll have a look at your goods. Meet you at your wagon."

John and Thomas nodded, then headed out the door to unpack the wagon enough so Miller could examine the supplies.

"Do we need to pull all of this out?" said John.

"No, let's just get it opened up enough so he can see what we have, plus we can show him the bill of sale from Noel if you have it."

"I think I brought it. Let me look."

John pulled out the satchel containing the crude claim map and a few other papers he thought would be useful.

"Ah, here it is."

Miller came out the door and shuffled over to the wagon. "All right, gents, what's the deal?"

"We'd like to sell roughly half of our food stuffs. Here's a bill of sale from our supplier in Valdez," said John, handing the paper over.

Miller slowly looked through the list, running his finger over each item and looking at the price.

They immediately realized showing him the bill was a mistake—with the prices known, Miller had the advantage.

"I don't really need all this," said Miller, handing the bill back to John.

"We'll make you a good deal," said Thomas.

"How good?"

Thomas looked at John—they should have talked about this better beforehand. John shrugged his shoulders and turned back to Miller.

"How about two hundred for exactly half of all the food stuffs?" said John.

Miller rubbed his chin, staring at the goods in the wagon. "No, don't think so. I'll give you one-fifty and throw in your meal."

"That's way less than what you would pay to have the same delivered here," said John, hoping to bolster their position.

Miller paused, then turned toward the roadhouse door. "Pay me for the meal and be on your way then."

They were in a spot. Getting rid of nearly five hundred pounds of weight on the wagon would allow them to travel faster and longer, giving them more time on the Fortymile.

"Wait," said Thomas, looking at John.

Miller turned, staring at them.

"You have a deal," said John, moving forward with extended hand.

"Good," said Miller, returning the handshake. "Leave your man here and I'll send my boy out to bag stuff up and unload. Let's go inside and settle up."

Your man? thought Thomas, nearly laughing out loud. *I guess I know my place now.*

John returned with Miller to the roadhouse. Within minutes a scruffy young fellow who looked like he was overdue for his yearly bath and shave returned with some sacks and a wooden crate. He and Thomas worked at dividing the supplies, a job that turned out to be, in large part, guesswork. Thomas helped the fellow unload and carry the goods around the back of the roadhouse to a small storage building.

After six trips they were done and Thomas stood waiting at the wagon, not wanting to interfere with the transaction going on inside—especially now that his station in life was clear.

Shortly, John returned, a huge grin on his face.

"What did you do, talk him back up to our price?" said Thomas.

"No, but look."

He pulled a bottle from his coat pocket, removed the cork and into his hand, poured a pile of gold dust and small nuggets.

Thomas eyes widened as he looked at the bottle, then John's hand, then back to the bottle.

John was smiling as though he'd just struck the motherlode. "He paid us in gold,"

Thomas held out his hand. "Let me have some."

John poured a bit into Thomas' hand, then carefully

put the gold in his own back in the bottle.

"Amazing," said Thomas, the gold fever rising inside him. He had seen gold before, but there was a difference—this was *their* gold. "How much?"

"Right around eight ounces. Come on, let's get it back in the bottle and get out of here before someone sees us looking all moonstruck."

"All right—our first Alaska gold!"

With the gold safely stowed, they hit the trail, happy to be traveling lighter, despite the fact it cost them a fair bit. Thomas could feel the difference in the way the wagon rode over the ruts and rocks in the trail. Just in time too, for before them lay Kimball Pass, another climb of nearly fifteen hundred feet.

* * *

Van Sant wiped the sweat from his brow and sat down on a large rock next to the trail. Lugging his gear up the hill from the dead horse was agonizing, taking much longer than expected. He now faced a dilemma—what should he leave behind. The pack and gear the horse carried was far too heavy for him to pack on his back. Unless his luck changed, he would be walking until dark to reach some semblance of civilization.

At least the weather had improved, rain giving way to broken clouds and sunshine. Van Sant began unpacking the gear, spreading wet items across a large granite boulder to dry. He sorted things into essential and non-essential piles. He needed a tent and sleeping gear, some food, ammunition, and other hardware. In reality he could afford to leave little behind—he was already traveling too light.

As he contemplated how to repack, his attention was drawn to the sound of voices coming up the trail from

Beaver Dam. He quickly stood, closed his coat and turned, waiting to see who was coming. Within a minute, two horses rounded the bend, each carrying what Van Sant judged to be tenderfoots—newcomers fresh off the boat.

"Aye there," said the man in the lead. "Having a bit of trouble are we?"

Van Sant hid the disdain from his face, and put on his best smile. "Yes, lost my horse."

"Name's Wilson," said the man in the lead. "Where's your horse gone to?"

Van Sant pointed down the hill to the willow patch. "Dead."

"Well you are in a peck of trouble, sir."

"Yes I am. You fellows traveling alone?" asked Van Sant, looking beyond them.

"Just me and my partner Bill," said Wilson, motioning to the man on the horse behind him.

"I wonder if you can give me a hand."

"Sure mister, what can we do for you?"

"Well, I have more gear down there below the horse, but I've turned my ankle bringing up the first load. Could you fetch the rest of it for me?"

Wilson looked back at Bill, who nodded his approval. "Sure, mister. A man's gotta help each other out up here."

He dismounted and tied his horse off to a root protruding from the cut-bank along the trail. Bill swung off his horse, nearly falling, then tied her off to the root.

"Where's your gear, I don't see it from here."

"Just downhill from the horse a bit. It went flying off when she finally stopped."

"We'll fetch it for you in short order," said Wilson as he and Bill stepped off the trail and headed down the hill.

Van Sant waited until they nearly reached the horse,

stretched out his hand, and fired.

Wilson dropped immediately, rolling head over heels twice before stopping, blood spewing from his chest cavity as he gasped for breath, eyes wide open in shock.

Bill turned, "What the..."

He never finished the sentence. Van Sant fired a single shot, hitting the man mid-chest and knocking him to the ground. The horses were spooked, pulling tight against the reins, but were unable to flee.

Van Sant moved quickly down to the men, separated by only a few feet. Wilson was dead, his partner still struggling for breath, yet conscious. "Why?" he managed to whisper between gasps.

Van Sant looked at him coldly. "Because I can," he said, cocking the revolver and putting a single slug into the man's forehead. "Neither of you would have made it anyway," he said to the dead men. "I did you a favor."

Working quickly, he relieved the men of what little cash they carried, then dragged each down past the horse, deeper into the willow patch where they couldn't be seen from above.

The final problem was the horse. If one looked carefully it could be seen from the trail. It wouldn't be long before the eagles and ravens descended, making travelers curious about the kill. Van Sant decided discovering a dead horse was one thing—the men an entirely different matter. One at a time, he struggled to drag each body further downhill and into thicker cover.

It took nearly an hour to move the bodies another fifty yards downslope and cover them with alpine moss, all the while hoping no one else would venture along the trail and discover him. He returned to the dead horse and removed the rope, then pondered whether it was better to conceal it, or leave it as a natural death. Anyone finding it would assume it the source of that horrible, unmistakable smell, and hopefully look no further. He left the horse as it was, and trudged uphill to the trail to inspect his newly gained supplies.

The men where fairly well outfitted. Van Sant was happy to find he was now the proud owner of a lever-action .45-70, an old Henry Model 1860 repeating rifle, food, a new tent, and mining gear. His survey was brief. *I've got to get out of here.*

He didn't unpack, but quickly stuffed his muddy gear back into the pack and lashed it to one of the horses, put a long lead on Bill's horse, then mounted up. With the other horse in tow, he made his way up the trail a good half mile or so. Judging he was now a comfortable distance from the murder scene, Van Sant stopped to sort through the gear.

Don't need mining gear, he thought as he systematically removed the short handled shovels, a pick and gold pans from the pack frames, tossing them as far as he could into the high brush that lined the trail. It took less than half an hour to repack the mixture of his and the dead men's gear. Though the gear and a second horse would slow him down a bit, he wasn't about to be caught stranded a second time.

Van Sant mounted up and, without so much as a thought for the two lifeless bodies in the brush behind him, continued his quest.

* * *

Thomas brought the wagon to a stop at the summit of Kimball Pass. A lake to the east would provide water for the horses, a break they deserved after the climb out of the valley. John brought up the rear, dismounted, and tied off his horse.

"That was quite a climb," said Thomas.

"Yes," said John. "The horses are ready for a rest."

"It's all downhill from here, at least until we hit the Tonsina."

The lake was almost a half mile long, perched at the summit of the pass and a common rest stop for travelers. Remnants of camps dotted the area next to the lake, but all were unoccupied.

"Let's rest here for a bit and let the horses graze," said Thomas.

John agreed and after watering them, set about staking out the horses so they could feed.

Thomas spread the map out on the wagon seat and studied the route.

"How much further to Tonsina?" said John.

"Well, we've made a little over five miles since the Ernestine Roadhouse. We'd have done better if most of it wasn't uphill." Thomas ran his finger along the route on the map to Tonsina. "Looks like another ten or twelve miles to the river crossing."

"We should be able to make that by dark, don't you think?"

"Should be able to. If we can make it that far, we'll only be two hundred and seventy miles from Chicken."

"Only—seems like a big only to me."

"Once we hit Tonsina we should be able to pick up the pace. There aren't any mountain passes for nearly a hundred miles."

"Suits me fine. Let's rest for a bit longer and then get moving."

Within a matter of minutes, the mosquitos and red flies discovered them. With no wind, they gathered in larger and larger numbers until both man and horse could bear it no longer. The mosquitos were one thing, but the red flies were voracious. They swarmed about your head, flew into your ears and nose, and when they connected, took a good-sized chunk of flesh.

"Let's get out of here," shouted Thomas, pulling on his head net and dashing to untie the horses.

John followed, and in short order they were underway, pressing hard and hoping for a breath of wind to push the bugs away.

"Glad we're not camping here for the night," yelled Thomas as he pushed the horse and wagon harder down the trail.

"Me too," said John. "Me too."

* * *

Three hours from Kimball Pass, John and Thomas stood looking at the one-lane bridge across the Tonsina River, waiting for their turn to cross. The bridge was constructed of rough-cut logs and timber, but looked to be sturdy.

Crossing the river without a bridge was something Thomas didn't want to think about. The recent rains brought the water level up and it was a muddy torrent, churning to the point where they could hear boulders being rolled downstream.

The narrow bridge allowed two horses to pass, but with a wagon it was a one-way affair. Three near-empty wagons were making their way towards them in single file.

"Wonder why they're empty," said John.

"Must be coming back after hauling goods north," said Thomas.

The first of the wagons cleared the bridge. Thomas held the reins solid as they passed, tipping his hat to the driver who barely acknowledged him. *Not very friendly*, thought Thomas.

Despite the snub, Thomas and John nodded at each driver as they passed. The last cleared the bridge and as he passed, offered his opinion, "More tenderfoots headed for destruction."

"Mind your own business," shouted Thomas impulsively.

The driver pulled up the reins and stopped, put his hand on his sidearm, and stared directly at them, saying nothing for what seemed like forever.

After an increasingly uncomfortable silence, he spoke.

"Wanna make something of it?"

With his temper flaring, all the potential responses flew through Thomas' mind.

It was John who broke the silence. "We don't want any trouble, mister."

"Thought so," said the driver smugly as he whipped the reins and the wagon lurched forward, heading up the trail toward his compatriots.

When he was out of earshot, Thomas finally spoke. "He's an idiot."

"We have to be careful out here," said John. "There's a lot of people with short fuses and short on brains."

"You're right. I just hate to be pushed around."

"Forget it. Let's get across the bridge and figure out where we're going to camp. The day is getting long and I'm getting hungry."

As they crossed the bridge, the confrontation replayed in his mind, the anger and humiliation burning inside him. *One day,* thought Thomas, *One day.*

* * *

Thomas drove the last tent stake into the ground. "There, we're set for the night, except of course for getting some dinner."

John tossed another chunk of wood on the fire and proceeded to stir the pot of beans. "Almost ready."

Thomas snickered. "I hope it's as good as Miller's food at the roadhouse."

John ignored the sarcasm, dished up a heaping plate of beans, tossed the last of Stella's biscuits on top, and thrust it in Thomas' direction.

"Thanks," said Thomas as he sat down and looked out across the valley, beyond the Tonsina bridge to the never ending mixture of water and mountains. "Quite a view."

"It certainly is. I'm glad we decided to camp on the bluff."

"Me too. There's just enough of a breeze to keep some of the bugs away."

Finishing up his meal, Thomas said, "We should be able to get an early start tomorrow."

"How far are we aiming for?"

"I'll have to get the map to be sure, but I'm pretty sure we can make Copper Center."

"That sounds good. I'll pay for the meal and a real bed for the night."

"I'll hold you to that. It's probably only a little over twenty miles—we could push farther but I think a bit of civilization sounds good—at least for one night."

"Good, let's get some rest and move out early to make sure I get that warm bed tomorrow night."

* * *

It was nearly dark when Van Sant reached the summit of Kimball Pass. Had this whole saga started a few days earlier, there would have been a full moon to guide him, but now the darkness swirled around him as it settled upon the peaks of the mountains.

He stopped by the large lake in the pass at one of the abandoned campsites, finding a fire ring and a small bit of wood. Staking the horses out where they could feed, he unloaded and worked to set up camp. The more he moved through the grass and short brush, the more the mosquitos and red flies swarmed about him. Cursing, he stopped unpacking and worked to start a fire, hoping the smoke would stave off the incessant onslaught.

By the time the tent was set up, he was sporting a multitude of welts. He forgot about eating and climbed into the tent, leaving the horses to fend off the bugs.

Curse this God forsaken place. Pulling the tent closed, his thoughts raced, forming and rejecting plans for his obsession. At last he could fight it no longer. As his eyes finally closed, a final thought lingered, then slowly faded. *Where is Palmer....*

* * *

August 12, 1903

Crossing the Klutina River, the first glimpse of Copper Center came into view.

"I can taste that hot meal now," said John, yelling from behind the wagon.

Thomas cleared the bridge and pulled back on the reins. "Whoa."

Setting the brake, he hopped down from the wagon and walked back to John's horse. "You know, it's still pretty early in the day. We could make a few more miles before the horses are ready for a rest."

John looked down from the horse, saying nothing.

"I know you wanted to stop in Copper Center, but Tazlina has a new roadhouse we can stay at—only a year old."

"I guess one's as good as the other. I'm all for getting to the Fortymile sooner."

"You know, if we had done this not too long ago, we would've come floating down the Klutina right here, after climbing over the Valdez Glacier."

"Seems like that might have been faster."

"Not really. First you had to travel up and over the glacier, scaling several vertical ice walls. Once you get to the top, you slip and slide down the mountain with all your gear to Klutina Lake, then chop down trees, saw lumber, make a boat, traverse ten or more miles of lake, then shoot the rapids to get here—all without losing your outfit or your life."

"Sounds like fun. I guess our way is better."

"No doubt. A lot of men gave up at Copper Center, sold their outfit, and headed home, risking a boat ride down the Copper River and its rapids."

"I'll stick to this old nag and the trail. How's it look from here to Tazlina?"

Thomas pulled out the map and traced his finger along the route. "Looks pretty flat all the way. No mountains—maybe a couple of bluffs to climb out of the Copper River bottom. Should make for a pretty quick trip."

"Good. I wonder if I can get a steak at Tazlina."

"I'm sure you can," said Thomas. "Might be porcupine though."

* * *

Van Sant carelessly threw the last of his camp on the pack horse and saddled up, anxious to leave the bug-ridden pass behind. It was early, the wind calm with a bite in the air, a sign that fall in the high country wasn't far away. He was thankful for the temperatures—the mosquitoes that plagued him the night before hadn't roused yet.

Only about twelve miles to Tonsina, he thought as he pushed the horses hard down Kimball Pass.

By noon he neared the bank of the Tonsina River, hoping to cross quickly and perhaps get something to eat, as well as some information. As he started across the bridge, he realized there was a problem.

"What's going on here?" he said as he approached a team of horses stopped halfway across the river.

Two men were bent over, looking under the wagon that had taken on a severe list to the left.

"Broke axle," said one of the men as he stood and looked at Van Sant.

"Yep, it's a bad one," said the second man.

"I have to get across now. Move your wagon."

The two looked at each other and grinned. "Mister, this wagon ain't going nowhere for a good while and there ain't room for you to get a horse around it."

Van Sant took a deep breath, all the while glaring at the two. "Unload the blasted thing and drag it off the bridge."

"Mister, we got over five hundred pounds of freight on this wagon and we aren't about to haul it off this bridge by hand. We already stacked half off the wagon so we can get it lifted."

"Yep," said the other. "You might as well back up and relax, mister. We might have to walk into Tonsina for help before it's over. Unless you want to lend us your horse."

Van Sant glared, then reached for his sidearm. The taller of the two caught the move and beat him to it, pulling a lever action rifle from the wagon scabbard and getting the drop on him. "Not a good idea, mister."

Van Sant slowly raised his hand away from his belt, barely able to contain his rage, but realizing he had no option.

"Best back them horses off this bridge and go back the way you came."

I could take them, he thought, but this would be a public execution, not a hidden crime like the last.

"You'll pay," said Van Sant as he backed his horse and turned, leading the pack horse behind him.

"Doubt it, mister", said the tall one as they both broke into laughter, further infuriating Van Sant as he cleared the bridge and headed down river along the gravel bed.

"Idiot," said the short one, not realizing how close he and his partner had come.

* * *

Thornton and Palmer pulled up to the Tazlina Roadhouse, situated on a high bluff above the Copper River.

"I expected something a bit fancier," said John.

It was a somewhat crude log structure with few windows, but was new. Judging by the number of horses and wagons outside, the roadhouse was doing well.

"Wonder if there is any room in the inn," said John.

"Don't know. One way to find out I guess."

"Sure, we got room for you, if you don't mind sharing a bed," said the large round woman that met them as they entered.

They looked at each other for a moment, sizing up the situation.

"Works for me," said Thomas, "if the bed isn't too small."

"I'm happy to pay for two rooms," said John.

"Well, we got one. Take it or leave it."

"We'll take it," said Thomas. "I'll sleep on the floor."

She cocked her head and smiled at them, revealing the lack of two front teeth. "There's a chair in there too."

"That's fine. I'm John Palmer and this is my partner Thomas Thornton."

"I'm Ethel. Pleased to meet you."

Pleasantries exchanged, Thomas said, "Can we get something to eat?"

"You bet. Have a chair and I'll bring it out."

"I was wondering if we could have steak," said John.

She laughed out loud. "You'll get stew and biscuits like everyone else, love."

"Works for me," said Thomas, rolling his eyes as she walked away. "Guess you'll have to wait until we shoot a moose to get that steak."

"Guess so," said John.

The woman quickly returned with two large steaming bowls of stew and a plate of biscuits with butter, plopping them down in the middle of the table.

"Smells good," said Thomas. "What's the meat in it?"

"Not sure," she said.

"You're not sure?"

"Nope. We just keep that big pot of stew going, throwing in more meat as it comes in the door. Might be bear, moose, or maybe porcupine."

Thomas laughed out loud and looked straight at John. "Told ya."

* * *

The Tonsina was running high and fast as Van Sant picked his way downstream, looking for a place to cross. *They must have crossed this before there was a bridge.*

The water was a blue gray, typical of all glacier fed streams in Alaska. As he continued downstream, Van Sant scanned for a narrow section that would be the quickest to cross. The channel just above a small island seemed the most likely, and he judged it to be about one hundred feet across. Though he had some experience with horses, he knew this was something different—he'd never crossed deep water and never on a horse that might have to swim for it.

Now or never, he thought as he pointed the horse into the river and kicked hard into her ribs. The horse balked at first, angering him and earning it yet a swifter kick. The horse lunged forward into the water, splashing the freezing spray all over him. The pack horse was behind, resisting and making progress slow. The horse was unsteady, slipping over melon sized boulders which caused her to lurch and struggle for balance.

Halfway across, the water was up to the stirrups. *This isn't going to be too bad.* The thought had no more formed when the horse plunged underwater, taking Van Sant up to his neck. The deepening of the channel was unexpected and the horse stepped headlong into water deep enough to submerge it. The current now took over, sweeping them downstream as the horse surfaced and snorted, its nostrils now barely above the freezing torrent. He lost his grip on the pack horse lead, cursed for not tying it off, and watched the horse swirl downstream, struggling in panic to swim for shore as he continued to spur his horse forward.

As the horse neared shore, she frantically scrambled to get her hooves in touch with the river bottom, so much so that she stumbled and rolled to the downstream side, throwing Van Sant into the river. As he surfaced, he struggled to keep his head above water, the extreme cold squeezing at his chest, making it difficult to breathe.

After what seemed like forever, he felt the boulders of river bottom bashing against his backside. Twisting to look downstream he saw why—he was in the shallows just above the island, his horses nowhere in sight and forty feet of glacial water between him and the far shore. He hauled himself out and sat on the bank, shivering to the bone, unable to stop shaking.

Though the mid-August temperatures were nearing seventy, Van Sant bordered on hypothermia. He moved to position himself in the sun, stripped off his soaked outer layers, and tried to warm himself. With all his provisions on the pack horse, he had no means to start a fire. Laying back, his face to the sun, he closed his eyes.

* * *

"How was your stew and biscuits, fellas?" said Ethel as she cleared away their plates.

"Best I've had on the trail," said Thomas, stretching the truth a bit.

"Glad you liked it. Where you fellas headed?"

"We're on our way to our gold claim in the Fortymile."

"Ah. What creek you on?"

"Angel Creek."

"Never heard of it," she said as she walked away.

Thomas smiled. "Wonder why she asked?"

"Making conversation I guess. Anyway, we ought to be able to get an early start tomorrow, what with a big meal and a good night's sleep instead of huddled in that miserable tent," said John.

Thomas looked at him and grinned. "So you are getting tired of camping,"

"Nope. Just looking forward to a change. Be nice to get to the claim and settle into our own cabin."

"Sure will. I'm going to check the wagon and then let's call it a day."

"Sounds good to me."

* * *

At first the sound was distant, growing louder and more distinct, until Van Sant opened his eyes to find his horse snorting and staring at him a few feet away.

The late afternoon sun finally had warmed him enough to where he could function. Cautiously he stood and moved toward the horse, talking calmly until he was close enough to reach the reins. Tying her to a small spruce tree, he surveyed the damage.

The saddle was still intact, loosely secured to the horse, as was the empty scabbard. The rifle was gone, along with his pack. His only hope was to find the other horse and hope that the rest of his gear wasn't lost. *Perhaps she made it to the island,* he thought.

The shoreline of the island was difficult to traverse—trees grew almost to the waterline with a steep drop off the bank into the water. Van Sant left the horse tied at the upstream end of the island and made his way slowly through the trees, negotiating a mixture of spruce and alder. Had he not stolen the pack horse, he might have been able to call her by name. Of course, he wasn't even sure the horse *was* on the island.

He made his way through the woods, paralleling the southern shore of the island until he reached the downstream tip. Here the channel to the far shore was even wider. *Looks like almost sixty feet.*

Seeing no sign of the horse, he made his way back upstream along the north shoreline. He hadn't gone far when something on the opposite shore caught his attention—it was the pack horse, standing in tall grass, the lead hanging to the ground. The horse looked his way, seemed uninterested, and turned its head forward.

Van Sant realized what happened. With the wider channel at the downstream end of the island, the water must be shallower. The pack horse, probably in a panic, had continued across and was now safely on the other shore. Not wanting to spook the horse, he immediately retreated into the woods and moved quickly back upstream where the other horse was tethered.

Reaching the horse, he untied and led her back through the woods, moving downstream to where he spotted the pack horse. She was still there, but had moved a hundred feet or so. He continued to the downstream tip of the island, intent on crossing where it looked shallower.

Mounting up, he pointed the horse toward the opposite shore and nudged her forward. She wanted none of it, balking before ever reaching the water. Van Sant took a different tact, talking quietly to her and patting her neck to reassure her. The pack horse was now looking at them from some two hundred feet away. He worried that the commotion would spook her and his supplies would be on a dead run through the timber.

Again he tried to coax her to cross and again she refused to enter the water. Still wet from the dunking, his patience was exhausted. He kicked her hard in the ribs, causing her to lurch forward. Once she hit the water, panic ensued and Van Sant held on for the ride. She surged forward, headed toward the pack horse, water coming up over her knees. Halfway across, Van Sant prepared for the worst, clutching the saddle horn tightly and pressing his legs hard against her ribs.

To his surprise, the water wasn't as deep now, a fact that seemed to calm the horse as she reached the shallows of the shoreline. It was over in less than a minute—he was safe on the other shore, though somewhat wetter from the crossing. The pack horse meandered their way and Van Sant had no problem grabbing her lead. It looked like his remaining gear was intact, but completely soaked—tent, bedroll, clothes, and the other rifle—all wet.

Van Sant rode back upstream along the shoreline and within a few minutes, the bridge came into view. It was empty.

* * *

August 13, 1903

After a decent night's rest and a five o'clock breakfast of griddle cakes and coffee, Thornton and Palmer said goodbye to Ethel, thanked her for the accommodations, and headed north on the trail.

As they traveled, John couldn't help noticing Thomas seemed to be deep in thought, scratching his head now and then, and looking bewildered.

"What's the matter?" said John.

"Oh nothing, I just keep thinking I'm forgetting something."

John grinned. "Someone's birthday?"

"Maybe, but that's not it. Just something nagging me in the back of my mind."

"I'm sure you'll think of it eventually. What's the goal for today?"

"I'm hoping we can make thirty or more miles. That would put us past the Gakona Roadhouse."

"Works for me. Looks like a night in the tent coming up."

"Blast it," said Thomas suddenly.

"What is it?"

"I remember what's nagging me."

"Well?"

"We should have sent a telegram to Stella and Emily while we were at Copper Center."

"You're right. We've been so focused on our trip I'm afraid we've neglected that rather important task. Where's the next telegraph station?"

"Not sure. Let's stop and take a look at the map before we go any further."

Thomas stopped the wagon and pulled out the map, spreading it across the seat. "Looks like the next possibility is Gulkana Station."

"How far?"

"Well, I'm guessing we're about five miles out of Tazlina, so that would make it about another twenty miles."

"Let's make sure we stop there long enough to get a message out."

"Yep," said Thomas, "we sure better."

* * *

Van Sant downed the last of his coffee and motioned to the middle-aged woman for a refill. After the ordeal of the previous day, he decided a night in the tent wasn't at all welcomed. Backtracking, he spent the night at the Donaldson Roadhouse, even though it meant falling further behind his quarry.

"I'm looking for some friends of mine," he said to the woman. "I wonder if you might have seen them."

"We get a lot of folks coming through here."

"The name's John Palmer, and he's traveling with a younger man named Thornton."

"Those names don't sound familiar. Which way were they headed?"

"North," said Van Sant as he proceeded to give a vague description of both the men and their outfit.

"That description could fit a lot of people. Sorry, can't help you."

Van Sant took one last gulp of coffee, dropped a dollar on the table, and walked out the door, slamming it as he left.

He pulled out the map, hoping the bath it took the day before hadn't rendered it useless. Looking at it, he realized his progress yesterday only amounted to twelve miles. *Palmer's probably making at least twice that a day*, he thought. *I'll never catch him at this rate.*

Doing the math in his head, he guessed they could be as far as Gulkana by now. He was forty miles behind and his hopes of catching them before they reached the Fortymile were fading. Stuffing the map into the pack, he mounted up and sat there, mulling over his options. He could push on, spending another ten days on the trail and deal with Palmer once he reached their mining claim, always holding out hope of overtaking them before that. The other option was to turn back, stick around Valdez and wait for their return. The thought of being stuck in that town for what could be months didn't appeal to him.

Then it came to him—he would make them come to him. He leapt from the horse and burst back into the roadhouse. The woman gave him a look, but before she could say anything, Van Sant said, "Where's the nearest telegraph station?"

She looked at him, seeing nothing but arrogance.

"Well?" Van Sant demanded.

"Look mister, you'd catch a lot more flies with honey than vinegar."

Van Sant glared. "I don't need a morality lesson from a second rate bush tramp."

The woman stepped aside and Van Sant was staring at

the business end of a shotgun, held by a man he assumed was her husband.

"I suggest you back out slowly and get on your horse."

"Or?" said Van Sant, his hand moving slowly for his holster.

"Or you'll feel the sting of this shotgun. I've shot men for less," he said, bluffing.

Two men seated in the far corner now stood up and pulled back their coats, revealing they were armed as well.

Van Sant relaxed, dropping his hand and smiling. "Just looking for a little information."

"Tonsina Station is just across the bridge a ways. Now get out and don't come back."

Van Sant tipped his hat to the woman in a mocking gesture and turned, quietly shutting the door as he left.

* * *

Palmer handed the message to the telegraph operator at Gulkana Station.

"You sure you want to send all that? Gonna be expensive."

"How much?"

"Fifty cents a word, not including the address. We throw that in for free."

"Generous of you."

"So that's...let me see..."

"Twelve fifty."

"That's right."

"A lot steeper than in Valdez."

"Well, this ain't Valdez."

John took the message and cut out bits here and there, trimming it down to twenty words, all the while thinking he was being gouged. He handed it to the operator who proceeded to read it out loud.

```
STELLA BAIRD
VALDEZ, ALASKA

ALL FINE HERE.
WILL LOOK FOR REPLY AT
CHISTOCHINA AND
INDIAN RIVER.
LOVE TO YOU AND EMILY.

JOHN AND THOMAS
```

"Send it," said John, handing the operator ten dollars.

"Will do, have it there before dark. You're in luck—not much traffic today."

"That's good to hear," said John as he donned his hat and headed for the door, Thomas in tow.

"Come back again," said the operator, stashing the bill in his shirt pocket and turning back to the key.

Thomas jumped up on the wagon and took the reins. "That was steep, John."

"Yes, but necessary."

"Do you think we'll get a quick reply?"

"I think so, I slipped Jack a few bucks before we left, asking him to check for telegrams once a day and drive them out to Stella's."

"Do you think he's dependable?"

Smiling, John mounted up. "Solid as a rock."

* * *

"You sure you want to send this to every station up the line?" said the telegraph operator at Tonsina.

"You have a hearing problem?" said Van Sant, his brow furrowed and eyes as sharp as steel.

"Okay, mister, but it's gotta be one of the strangest messages I've sent."

"That's none of your business, just send it, and do it quickly."

```
JOHN PALMER

RETURN VALDEZ IMMEDIATELY.
EMILY IN DIRE TROUBLE.

STELLA
```

The operator counted up the words. "Four bucks, mister."

Van Sant slapped the money down on the rough wood counter and stood there, arms crossed.

"Anything else?"

Van Sant stood glaring, arms crossed. "I'm going to stand here until you send that message."

"Look, I got several ahead of you here."

Van Sant pulled back his long coat with his right hand, and paused.

"Okay, mister, no need for pulling out your iron," said the operator as he sat down and began pounding the telegraph key.

Van Sant stood, staring for the short time it took for the operator to finish.

"Done."

"To all stations?"

"Yep."

Van Sant whirled around and exited, slamming the door so hard it bounced open.

"Idiot," said the operator. *Guess he doesn't know Morse code—his message goes last.*

He turned back to his work, smiling and humming

di-dah-di-di-dit, di-dah-di-di-dit.

* * *

August 14, 1903

Thomas stepped out of the Gakona Roadhouse, an early morning cup of coffee steaming in his hand. The sun was just rising above the mountains, casting a glow across the winding Copper River. He marveled at the size of this country, how easily one could be swallowed up in it, never to be heard from again.

After sending the telegram, they traveled a mere mile or two before reaching the roadhouse and, with no argument from either side, decided to call it a day. A good evening meal, a good night's rest, and a hearty breakfast left Thomas ready to charge forward up the trail.

"I may have some bad news," said John as he joined Thomas outside.

"Oh?"

"I just heard from the proprietor that the trail gets rougher from here on—not as wide and maybe difficult for the wagon."

The enthusiasm Thomas felt moments before waned by the smallest amount. With each day, their time on the Fortymile slipped away, consumed on the trail.

"Well, we'll just have to push harder."

"Somehow I knew you'd say that."

Thomas smiled. His future father-in-law was beginning to know him well. "We better get packed up and started. Sounds like a long day."

"What's our goal today, assuming the trail cooperates?"

Thomas studied the map the night before, running figures in his head, calculating how far they could go, how long it would take, and when they would reach the claim. It was a never ending and always changing chore, governed by each day's progress.

"I'm hoping we can make twenty-five to thirty miles today. That would put us near Chistochina, if all goes well."

"And how far from the claim will that leave us?"

Thomas already knew the answer. "Just over a hundred and eighty miles."

John frowned. Five days on the trail and they weren't even halfway there.

Thomas couldn't help but notice. "What's the matter?"

"Well," said John, pausing as if he wasn't sure how to say what he was thinking, then finally expressing his concern without prettying it up. "Five days out and we're not halfway, trail's getting worse, and time's slipping by."

Thomas shared his concern, but wouldn't let it sway his resolve, "You don't want to turn back, do you?"

"No, but I sure wish we could move faster."

"Only way to do that is to ditch the wagon and go light with supplies—not sure that's a good idea."

John sipped his coffee and stared out across the valley, the sound of the Gakona River whispering in his ear as it rushed towards the Copper. Thomas waited.

"No, I don't think that's wise, at least not yet," said John.

"Let's push hard as we dare and see how it goes."

John nodded in agreement, but also resolved to leave the claim in plenty of time to make it back to Valdez before winter, even if he had to twist Thomas' arm to do so.

Thomas gulped the last of his coffee. "Let's pack up and get going."

* * *

It was a good plan, but not without complications. Van Sant had no idea when and if Palmer would get the telegram. He assumed Palmer or Thornton would visit a telegraph office to report their progress back to Valdez. It was just a matter of when.

His second problem was logistical. Not knowing when to expect them to come rushing back down the trail meant he had a choice—keep traveling or stay put. Traveling forward had one advantage—he could accomplish his task sooner. Of course it also meant he couldn't control *where* the meeting took place. In the end, he decided ambush was the best course of action.

After sending the telegrams, he continued on, but at a more leisurely pace, all the while keeping an eye out for the perfect location. Finding nothing suitable and not desiring a night in the tent, he lodged at Copper Center. Mid-morning found him traveling along the bluffs of the Copper River, headed for Tazlina, still searching.

I need somewhere remote, he thought, instantly realizing this was easier said than done, what with the number of travelers on the trail. He needed to be able to see up and down the trail, but most of all, he needed no witnesses. He refined his search, looking for a comfortable vantage point where he could see them coming, and if necessary, fall in behind them unnoticed, patiently following until the opportune moment.

He thought about taking the high ground, shooting them down at first sight and moving on. This was the safest. Reason and ego battled in his mind, but in the end his arrogance won—he would have his say, face to face.

With each oncoming traveler, he went on high alert just in case, but each time it proved unnecessary. He crossed the Tazlina River, thought about stopping in for a meal at the roadhouse, but dismissed the idea—it might mean missing them.

Beyond the Tazlina, the trail climbed the bluff above the river. Extending to the southwest back toward the river was a crescent-shaped, narrow ridge, providing a view of over a mile of the trail. This was his spot—it meant camping in a tent, but was an acceptable inconvenience. He left the trail and worked his way south along the ridge, looking for a vantage point that both gave him some measure of cover, but also allowed an unobstructed view of the trail.

Satisfied, Van Sant tied off the horses, unloaded a portion of the supplies and set about making camp. Within an hour he had the tent up, a small fire going, and the branches that blocked his view trimmed. He smiled as he scanned the valley and the trail below. *It shouldn't be more than a day or so before I have him*, he thought.

There was but one doubt that gnawed at him—what if Palmer traveled at night?

* * *

Thornton bounced the wagon to a stop and hopped off. The trail out of Gakona had been rough, but nothing worse than what they'd seen thus far.

"Trouble?" said John.

"Nope—just thought I'd give my backside a break and let the horses graze for a few minutes."

"Good idea. I think I might be getting saddle sores."

Thomas laughed. "You ain't seen nothing yet."

"Might as well have lunch since it's about that time."

"Agreed."

With the pressure of the trail upon them, no fire was built—they ate hardtack and jerky, washing it down with the warm water in their canteens.

"Sure miss Stella's cooking," said John.

"Me too," said Thomas. "What I wouldn't give for a big pot of her moose stew and homemade biscuits."

"Stop—you're torturing me."

Thomas just laughed, wiped his mouth with his hand, and set about retrieving the map. "Looks like we're over halfway to Chistochina. We might be able to press on and make a good day of it."

"Sounds fine, but I do want to check for a telegram at Chistochina."

"Of course. I'm getting antsy wondering about Emily and Stella."

"From what I've seen, Stella can take care of herself—been doing it alone for quite a while."

"No doubt there," said Thomas. "No doubt."

Lunch finished, they loaded up and pressed on, pausing briefly at a small stream to water the horses. The trail did have its ups and downs—some places were deeply rutted, not so much from traffic, but from erosion during spring thaw. As snow melted, the runoff took the path of least resistance, running down the trail and eroding the ruts deeper. It slowed their travel and Thomas constantly worried that dropping into a rut would break an axle or wheel.

It was drawing late in the day when they reached Chistochina, but still early enough to hope the telegraph station was open. Thomas wasn't worried—since the telegraph operators generally lived in the back of the office, he would just beat on the door if necessary.

As it turned out, the operator was still busy tidying up the office and sorting the messages of the day.

"Hello," said John as they entered.

"Greetings," said the operator. "Need to send a telegram?"

"Actually we're looking to see if we received anything."

"I'll look. What's yer name?"

"John Palmer or Thomas Thornton."

"Hmm, Palmer, that sounds familiar." He rubbed his chin, laughed, then started flipping through the day's messages. "I should be able to remember them all. We don't get that much traffic through here on any given day. Ah, here we go," he said, handing the message to John.

JOHN PALMER/THOMAS THORNTON
CHISTOCHINA/INDIAN RIVER

ALL WELL IN VALDEZ SINCE YOU LEFT.
WE MISS YOU BOTH.
PLEASE SEND WORD MORE OFTEN.

STELLA AND EMILY

"Well, that's good news," said John as he handed the telegram to Thomas.

"Yes, one less thing to worry about."

"Thank you, sir, we'll be on our way," said John as he nodded to the operator, then headed for the door.

"Hold up a minute. I got another one for you."

John and Thomas looked at each other for an instant,

then John returned and took the telegram from the operator. As he read, the color drained from his face.

"We have to go back."

* * *

Thomas took the telegram and quickly read it. "This doesn't make any sense. Give me the first one."

John reached into his pocket and gave it to Thomas. He tried to decipher the date and time at the top, but it was scrawled in the operators handwriting.

"When were these sent?" said Thomas, thrusting them back at the operator.

"Can't read my writing? I'm not as careful scribbling out the top part as I am with the actual message. Uh...well...this one about your daughter's trouble came in late last night. I think it was nearly the last I received before shutting down."

"And the other?" said Thomas.

"I got it this morning, shortly before lunch time. Odd though..."

"What's odd," said John.

"The one signed by the two women was sent from Valdez Station. The other came from Tonsina."

Thomas and John looked at each other, unsure what to make of it.

"What does that mean?" said Thomas.

"Well, it means it originated in Tonsina and was telegraphed from there by the operator, old Bob."

"There's no way Stella is in Tonsina," said Thomas.

"Agreed," said John. "Is there anything else you can tell us from the messages?"

"Well, the one about the trouble was sent to all stations north, so somebody really wanted to make sure you got it."

"I'm still worried about Stella and Emily," said John. "We need to sort this out."

"Why don't I just get on the line and ask old Bob if he remembers who sent it?"

"You can do that?" said John.

The operator smiled and pushed his glasses back up on his nose. "Sure, happy to. Won't even charge you. Bob should still be up and operating since it's not too late."

The operator sat down at the key and started sending code at a rate which made John and Thomas think there was no way anyone could understand it. He paused, sent a couple more strings of code, then started writing furiously as the response came in. It took a minute or two and in the end, the operator would laugh out loud, tap on the key some more, then laugh again.

"It's like they're conversing in person," said Thomas.

"A bit odd," said John, "but I guess it's normal for them."

The operator put down his pencil and stood up, carrying the furiously scribbled note.

"Well", said John, "was Bob able to help us?"

He smiled and handed the note to John. "Bob's always helpful. That message was sent by a tall man with an angry disposition. Bob said he almost drew a gun on him to make him send the message right away."

"I have no idea who that could be, but it obviously wasn't Stella. Did you get a name?"

"Weren't no lady, that's for sure, but he never told Bob his name either."

"What were you laughing about there at the end?"

"Well, since the fella was such a mean cuss, Bob pretended to send his message right away, but instead sent the code us operators use for *wait a second.* Tricked him and got him to leave. Bob sent the message later."

"Who is this guy?" Thomas said to John. "And why does he want us to head back?"

"I have no idea Thomas, I really don't. But whoever he is, he's up to something."

"What shall we do?"

"I say we press on, but only after confirming that Stella and Emily are really safe."

John turned to the operator. "Is there any way we can get an urgent message to Valdez and request an immediate response?"

"Kind of late in the day for that, but I can send it no problem. Might be till morning until we can get a response."

"We've made better than thirty miles today," said Thomas. "Let's send the message, camp here for the night, and wait till we hear something."

"Agreed," said John, motioning for the operator to hand him paper and pencil. "I'll keep it brief, just asking to confirm they are fine."

"I'll send it for you gratis," said the operator. "You fellas had enough for one day I think."

John and Thomas thanked him repeatedly, then watched as he sent the message to Valdez.

"It'll be morning before you hear. Come back first thing and we'll see if we get something."

Thanking him one last time, they left the telegraph station, looking around for a camp site. A nice level spot toward the river caught their eye. They spent little time setting up camp, ate the same as they had for lunch, then turned in to get some rest.

"Going to be a long night," said John.

"True, but I'm sure they're okay."

"I hope so, or we're dropping gear and heading back tomorrow."

* * *

August 15, 1903

Thomas was up early, thinking of hot coffee after forcing himself to crawl out of the tent into the chill of the morning. Though only mid-August, the temperature at night dipped into the mid-thirties. His options were limited—go cut wood, build a fire, and make coffee, or try to scrounge a cup.

John rolled over inside the tent, still half awake. "What's going on?"

"Nothing. Just trying to figure out how to get some coffee."

"How about the telegraph office?"

"Not sure he's up and about. Don't want to go making him mad."

"Too early anyway," said John, not moving.

Thomas pulled his coat tight about his neck and surveyed the town. It wasn't much, just a stop on the way for miners headed to and from the Fortymile. Thomas heard that miners destined for the Nabesna and Chisana-White River districts tended to overnight at Slana rather than Chistochina. The few cabins that made up the town housed trappers and others that scratched out a living catering to travelers in one way or another. *Surely someone must have a cup of coffee.*

Thomas heard a door open and, in the distance, saw

the telegraph operator exit the cabin that served as both office and home. Carrying a bucket, he scurried around back, flung the contents into the brush, then turned back towards the door. Thomas walked briskly towards him, hoping to inquire about his immediate need.

"Mornin'," said the man, pausing for Thomas to reach him. "No word yet from Valdez," he said.

"I didn't expect so," said Thomas. "I was wondering if there's some place around here to get a cup of coffee, and maybe a hot meal."

"See that cabin over there, just beyond your tent and towards the river?"

"Yes."

"That's Mrs. White's place—widow woman. She don't board people, but she serves up food—I'm sure she's up already."

"Thanks. We'll wander over there and get some breakfast, then check back with you to see if anything has come in."

The man nodded and returned to the office. Thomas shuffled back to camp, hands in his pockets to shield them from the nip in the air. Reaching the tent, he slapped the side hard and made a growling noise. From inside, John bolted upright and scrambled around, causing sudden alarm from Thomas.

"Don't shoot!" said Thomas, knowing full well the scatter gun was laying between their bedrolls. "It's just me," he said, trying to hold back the laughter.

"Darn poor way to roust a guy," said John.

"Yeah, but it got the blood moving, didn't it?"

"I'll remember to return the favor when you least expect it. Just remember, if you want to marry my daughter, you better watch your step."

Thomas laughed, "Yes, sir!"

"Any word yet?"

"Nope, but I found us a place to eat. Come on, get up and let's grab some coffee. I can't wait much longer."

* * *

Mrs. White set heaping plates of fried potatoes and bacon before them, then scooted off to fetch more coffee.

Thomas and John ate hungrily, both commenting that Mrs. White was a lot like Stella in the cooking department.

"Simple but good," said Thomas. "Just what I like."

"Nice to have a hot meal, especially after the last two," said John, recalling the sumptuous fare of hardtack and jerky that graced their previous dining.

With a cup of hot, strong coffee cradled in his hands, Thomas' thoughts turned to their current situation. "I'm not real worried about the women, but I'm sure anxious to hear from them."

"Same here. Mighty odd circumstance we have going on, what with the message and all. When we get the good word from Stella and Emily it still won't solve the mystery."

"Got a mystery, do you?" said Mrs. White as she picked up the empty plates.

"Yes, ma'am, we do," said John.

John and Thomas told her of their travels and odd message. Before long they were listening to her life story and how she landed in Chistochina.

"My husband came to prospect the Fortymile in 1894 and eventually staked some claims up on Fortyfive Pup, then set about to mine it."

"Where's Fortyfive Pup?," said Thomas.

Mrs. White went on to relate the complete story of Fortyfive Pup, a small stream north of Chicken. Her husband built a cabin there and sent for her the following year. The journey was long and arduous, especially for a woman traveling alone. She eventually made it to Chicken after a long trip down the Yukon and overland by pack train from Eagle. Life on the claim was hard, with short summers and long cold winters. Though the color was good when panning the creek, the pay was covered by tens of feet of frozen muck—permafrost that never thawed unless disturbed. They spent two years trying to work it, but the small creek was at times a mere trickle, with not enough water to even run the sluice boxes. The thawing muck along the high creek bank would slough into the boxes, sometimes stopping work for days. They finally gave it up, selling out to someone with more money who could mine it properly.

"What became of it?" said Thomas.

"Don't know. We packed up and left that fall to head south. Unfortunately my husband fell ill and we didn't get any further than Chicken. He died and I stayed there for a while until I caught a ride with a pack train and ended up here."

"Sorry to hear that," said Thomas. "Why did you stay in Alaska?"

"Not sure. I have no family now and I'm content here. Besides, I get to meet a lot of interesting people since the trail has opened up."

She smiled and headed to her small kitchen, leaving John and Thomas lost in thought.

Finally Thomas spoke, "Sounds like their claim was in the same general area as ours."

"It does. I'm wondering what conditions we'll find. I certainly hope we can mine the darn thing."

"Well, those fellows we bought the claim from swore by it. And he did have a pocket full of nuggets."

"I hope you're right."

Thomas gulped his coffee and moved the cup to the edge of the table, hoping for more. "We should know in another week or two when we get there."

"Better not take another week, or I'm going to turn around right now."

"It might." Thomas pulled out his pocket watch and looked at the time—eight-thirty. "If we can make thirty miles or better a day, we'll be there in six, but we probably won't make that today. We've been sitting here for over two hours already."

John started to say something, but was interrupted by the door swinging hard open and banging against the wall. Sheepishly closing the door, the telegraph operator entered. "Morning, Matilda—I mean Mrs. White."

She just smiled and turned to get him his usual cup of coffee. He sat down at the table and said, "You're in luck—got a response from Valdez already."

"Where is it?" said John, thrusting his hand forward.

"Uh, I didn't write it down—got it right here," said the operator, tapping his balding head.

"Don't keep us in suspense."

"I was in too much of a hurry to write it down, but the short of it is, your friends in Valdez are fine. Someone named Jack rode out and checked on them and they assured him everything was fine, but they're curious about why you inquired."

"You're sure that's all of it?" said Thomas.

"Yep, got it direct from my operator friend in Valdez—no relays."

"Well, that's a relief," said John. "I suppose we should

send something else to try and put them at ease."

"Probably a good idea," said Thomas.

"I'll be back over at the office as soon as I finish my coffee and get the morning gossip from Matilda—I mean Mrs. White."

"Thanks for delivering the news. We'll pack up and be over to send a message in a bit then," said John.

"See you in a bit."

As they left Mrs. White's cabin, Thomas looked at John and whispered, "Is there really that much gossip to catch up on in Chistochina?"

* * *

John finished packing the wagon while Thomas studied the map. Each kept glancing towards Mrs. White's, waiting for the telegraph man to exit.

"What's it look like?" said John.

The topographic map was fairly detailed, the army having done considerable surveying for both the trail and the telegraph line. From it, Thomas could get a general idea of the terrain that lay before them, as well as the distance yet to travel.

"Looks fairly gentle from here all the way to Indian River. We have to cross the Chistochina River not far from here. After Indian River the trail leaves the banks of the Copper and heads up into some higher country."

"Steep?"

"Not really, looks like we have to climb only five hundred feet or so before the trail levels out."

"Going to be tough to make thirty miles then. Where do you think we'll end up for the night?"

"If it's good going on the level, we might be able to make Slana. That's twenty-seven miles from here."

"All we can do is try, if we ever get going this morning."

Loaded up, they moved their outfit the short distance to the telegraph station, hoping in some way it would spur the operator to return, despite the fact that he couldn't see them from inside Mrs. White's place. Thomas sat up on the wagon, rolled a cigarette, and blew smoke rings while John fiddled with the gear lashings and his pack frame. Two cigarettes later, as Thomas was busy drumming his fingers on the wagon seat, the door to Mrs. White's place burst open and the operator came on a dead run, covering the hundred or so yards in a time that would practically make a race horse proud.

"I'm late! Supposed to be back on the line by nine and it's ten after," he said between gasps. "They're going to fire me if I keep it up—third time this month," he said, flinging the door to the office open and nearly falling inside.

Thomas and John smothered their laughs, not wanting to risk upsetting him, given they needed him for one more task.

"I'll go send the message," said John. "Anything specific you want me to add?"

"No, just don't let on about the mysterious telegram."

"Of course. I'll come up with something."

John found the operator taking down a message when he entered.

"Whew," said the man. "Looks like not much traffic yet so I dodged another one."

John reached across the counter, took a pencil and the message pad, and scratched out a brief telegram:

STELLA BAIRD
VALDEZ, ALASKA

```
SORRY ABOUT THE CONFUSION.
WIRES GOT CROSSED SOMEHOW.
GLAD YOU ARE WELL, WILL
CONTACT AGAIN WITHIN A FEW DAYS.

JOHN
```

"Can you send this right away?"

The operator stood, took the message, and counted up the words. "I guess I'll have to make you pay for this one."

"No problem. How much?"

"I'll still throw in the Chistochina discount though—how's five dollars sound?"

John dug into his pocket and counted out the payment. "Sounds less than the going rate we paid in Gulkana."

"Thanks. You fellas heading out then?"

"Yes, but do me a favor. If someone happens in to send a telegram to me about my daughter, please try to get a name, then send it forward to me."

"I can do that. I'll share the word with my fellows back south as well. Where do we forward it to?"

"We'll definitely check at Tanana Crossing when we get there. To be safe, can you forward it on to the station at Chicken?"

"Sure, can do. I wish you fellas the best."

"Thanks for all your help, we better get going—got a long day ahead to keep on schedule."

The man nodded in John's direction and turned back to his telegraph key. Though Stella and Emily were safe, John worried about the mysterious stranger. *It's someone who knows we're on the trail and where.*

"Message sent," said John as he mounted up. "Let's see if we can put some miles behind us."

"I'm ready," said Thomas, releasing the brake on the wagon and pointing the horses east.

* * *

The first six miles out of Chistochina went quickly, as they crossed the river and traveled along the gravel of the outwash plain, eventually reaching the bluffs that bordered the Copper River. Here the ground was level and the remaining five miles to Indian River seemed to float by.

Thomas wished all the trail was like this, but he knew it wasn't so—there were some pretty good climbs ahead of them, and the first was coming up fast. At Indian River, they stopped briefly to water the horses and let them graze for a bit. Once across the river, the trail swung northwest and climbed out of the valley, gaining about five hundred feet of elevation before turning east along the base of the Alaska Range.

To the south, the expanse of the Copper River valley lay before them, bathed in sunlight. Beyond that, the Wrangell Mountains rose a staggering seven thousand feet above, hiding treasures unknown. Thomas stopped the wagon and stared out across the vastness of the country, wondering how those first explorers managed to find their way through the maze of lakes, mountains, ice cold rivers, and swamps. The hardship of the trail seemed to evaporate as he thought of how grueling it could be.

"Can't imagine striking out cross country like the early fellows did," said Thomas, still taking in the view.

"We have it easier, that's for sure," said John. "A trail and bridges—what more could you ask for?"

"It'd be a tough go if we had to cross some of those rivers without a bridge. Guess we better get moving.

I figure another ten miles or so to Slana, then we head north."

"What's our stop for the night?"

"Well, we could stay at Slana, but if you're game and the horses are holding up, I think we should push on and camp somewhere in Indian Pass."

"Works for me. I'm all for making up for lost time."

* * *

The stop in Slana was short, just long enough to stretch their legs and tend to the horses. At just past seven in the evening, they had two hours of daylight left, enough time to put a few more miles behind them. The trail turned north and wound it's way around mountain peaks, then headed into the long, narrow valley that made up the pass.

The shadows grew long by the time Thomas pulled the wagon to a stop, set the brake, and slowly climbed down.

"Man, am I stiff from bouncing on this seat all day."

John dismounted and tied the nag off to the wagon. "I know what you mean."

"Don't have much time to set up camp. We didn't make it as far as I hoped."

"What creek is this?"

"I think it's Porcupine Creek, but I'll know for sure when I look at the map. Better set up camp first though—we're losing daylight."

John nodded and began to unpack the gear needed for another night on the trail. They found a spot off the trail suitable for camp and moved the wagon and horses nearby. Thomas unhitched the horse from the wagon and staked her out, then removed the saddle and pack from the nag and did the same with her. He patted her side soundly, feeling a bit of regret at how hard they were pushing the pair. Their success depended wholly on the two animals—taking good care of them was essential.

Thomas helped set up the tent and get the gear needed for the night arranged inside. Though their camp was in a small patch of meadow, the brush was thick along the creek, making navigation off the trail a challenge.

With camp set up, John set about cutting some wood to build a fire.

"While you're doing that, I'm going to take the horses to the creek for some water."

"Better take the carbine with you—bears."

Through over nearly two hundred miles of trail, the bears had been scarce. Thomas thought it unusual, but realized the berry crop was probably ripe in the high country. *Maybe we'll catch one when we get up higher.*

Thomas led the horses the hundred yards or so to the creek, threading his way through the alders to find the path of least resistance. The horses drank for what seemed like forever, while Thomas thought about alders, a horse, and a charging grizzly—a scene he was happy not to repeat.

The horses finished drinking and Thomas turned from the creek. As he did, he caught a flash of brown in the brush to his right. He dropped the leads and swung the carbine up, adrenaline already on overload.

The beast emerged from the hole in the alders—it was a porcupine. *You scared me half to death*, thought Thomas. For an instant he considered shooting it out of spite, but dismissed the idea. *Best save the ammo for a real need.*

He returned to camp without incident and staked the

horses out for the night. Returning to the camp fire, he found John with a big grin on his face.

"What's so funny?"

"See a bear down there, did you?"

"No."

"I saw the porcupine come out of the brush, cross the trail and head in your direction. I figured with all the bear talk it might spook you."

"Didn't bother me a bit."

"Oh, so you always jump two feet off the ground with a carbine to your shoulder?"

"Oh, you saw that."

"Sure did—most fun I had all day."

"Glad I could entertain you, but I've had enough fun for one day. Let's cook a can of beans. I'm tired and hungry."

They ate a quick meal, made sure the gear was stowed for the night and turned in. Thomas put the shotgun between them as they crawled into their beds. Thomas was nearly asleep when he heard John snickering.

"What now?"

"Oh nothing," said John, barely containing himself. "Hope that porcupine doesn't get your scent and track you down in your sleep. They're killers you know."

"You better hope not, because at the first sound of a critter, I'm going to start spraying lead in all directions."

"Maybe I better keep the gun over here," said John as he rolled over, laughed once more, and fell asleep.

* * *

August 16, 1903

The raven circled, set its wings, and sailed smoothly to an effortless landing atop the leaning spruce. Bobbing his head twice, he proceeded to announce his presence, cawing loudly and repeatedly.

The explosion was sudden, black feathers swirling down from the top of the tree as the lifeless body hit the ground with a resounding thud.

Van Sant holstered his revolver and grunted with satisfaction as he spit tobacco on the ground. *Damn birds.*

Two days of sitting on the ridge, watching each and every wagon go by wore what little patience he had razor thin.

They should have turned around by now, he thought as he pulled a fresh wad of tobacco from the pouch and stuffed it in his lip. *Something must be wrong.*

He kicked the dead bird over the edge of the ridge, watching it tumble down to join the others, then stared out across the valley. It was possible that somehow he had missed Palmer, especially if they passed in darkness. The flaw in his plan now became evident—he had no idea if Palmer was ahead or behind him—headed to the Fortymile or on his way back to Valdez.

Idiot, he thought in a rare moment of introspection. It was time to move, but which direction. *Might as well flip a coin*, he thought as he began to break camp.

* * *

Thomas finished securing the canvas tarp over the wagon, then looked around camp to make sure nothing was left behind. The morning sun was still hidden below the steep peaks of Porcupine Creek, leaving a biting chill in the mid-August air.

"Feels like fall," said John.

"Certainly has that feel to the air, at least here in the valley."

"I hope we don't freeze on the mining claim."

"Might have to spend the winter," said Thomas, knowing that his joke might go either way.

John cinched the saddle one last time on the nag, then mounted up, smiling in Thomas' direction. "I'm turning around now."

"No going back now, the gold's waiting for us."

"I hope so."

Thomas hopped up on the wagon and slapped the reins. The horse turned and looked back at him. For a moment he thought perhaps the horse was giving him the evil eye. He raised the reins for a second slap, but she lurched forward, nearly tumbling him backward off the seat—they were off.

The trail through the long Porcupine Creek valley was fairly flat and built on the gravel previously deposited by the stream. This made for easy going, with no mud or ruts to slow progress. In fact, the trail was wide enough that the wagon and John's nag could ride side by side.

"How far you figure today?" asked John.

Thomas studied the map the previous evening. He was worried—their trek was taking a long time, but he saw no way to speed thing up.

"I'm hoping for twenty-five to thirty miles today. The route is pretty flat all the way to Tanana Crossing. If the trail is in good shape, we should be able to get through Mentasta Pass and maybe all the way to Mineral Lake."

"I'll take your word for it," said John, having decided early on to leave the navigation to Thomas.

"That will put us a mere one hundred and thirty miles from the claim," said Thomas jokingly.

"Mere, humph."

"Well, if the horses are up to it and we can keep pushing twenty to thirty miles a day, we'll be there in another five days or so. Only problem is, once we cross the Tanana, things get a lot more hilly."

"Maybe we should have floated down the Yukon," said John, laughing at the possibility.

"We'll make it. My only concern is timing our return. If we get stuck in the Fortymile country over the winter neither you or the women will be very happy."

"But you will?"

"Truth told, I probably wouldn't mind."

John dropped his head, shaking it in fake despair. "What kind of outfit did I sign up with?"

* * *

Van Sant navigated through the woods, leaving his watch camp deserted. Disgusted that his plan had so far failed, he weighed his options. He was tired of the journey, yet his resolve drove him forward.

He reached the trail and stopped. *North or south?*. Returning solved nothing—all his time and effort were wasted if he gave up now. Going north didn't appeal either, now that he was likely days behind his quarry.

The possibility was real that Palmer received the deceitful telegram, turned around, and passed in the night.

He cursed himself again for the shortcomings of his plan. He needed to regroup, collect his thoughts, and come up with a new strategy. *I need a hot meal and a decent night's sleep.*

Knowing the Tazlina Roadhouse was only a couple miles away, he pointed the horse south. The trail was easy and, after crossing the Tazlina, he arrived, passing only two wagons headed north.

The roadhouse was of simple log construction—nothing fancy, but it was new, having been open only a year. Compared to the tent, it was a palace—a thought that made Van Sant realize he may have been on the trail too long already. Compared to the accommodations he occupied in Seattle, this place was a shack. But it was a dry shack, with a wood stove, hot food, and a real bed.

"Headed south are you?" asked the short man with thick glasses as he brought Van Sant a cup of coffee, spilling some as he sat it on the table.

"Not sure," said Van Sant, realizing immediately how strange that sounded.

The man scratched his balding head and gave him a quizzical look.

"I mean, I'm looking for my partners and I'm not sure which way they've headed."

"Ah," said the man.

"Maybe you've seen them—name's John Palmer and he's traveling with a younger fellow named Thornton."

The man thought for a moment, again scratching his head. "Nope, doesn't ring a bell."

"Are you sure?"

"Most people headed either direction stop in here for

a bite or a drink, but I don't always catch their names."

Van Sant smiled and feigned civility. "Thanks anyway."

The man shuffled off to the cook stove in the other room. "I'll fetch your breakfast."

Blast it. Now what to do, thought Van Sant.

The man brought the food, and Van Sant ate slowly, all the while looking out the window with the passing of every horse and wagon.

Analyzing the plan, he realized Palmer would most likely send a message to Valdez to find out more about Emily's so-called condition. The reply would, of course, reveal the deception. He was almost certain now that Palmer had continued on. Worse than that, he likely aroused their suspicions with the odd message that proved false.

Stupid.

As he finished his meal, a plan emerged. Palmer by now certainly knew his fortune had disappeared and if he inquired of the bank, would know who had withdrawn it. The direct approach was called for—the next telegram would certainly make Palmer come to him.

* * *

"Where you want this sent to, mister?" said the telegraph operator at Tazlina.

Van Sant glared at him. "I believe I already told you. Do you have a hearing problem?"

"Just wanted to make sure. Most people don't send a message to every station up the line."

"I'm not most people. Just send it."

The operator added the message to the bottom of the queue. "Will do—we got a few ahead of you."

"Send it first."

"Sorry can't do that."

Van Sant started to pull his overcoat back to reveal the Colt strapped to his side, but reason got the better of him.

"Just send it as soon as possible then."

The operator nodded as Van Sant turned and left without a word.

He mounted up and pointed the horse back toward the roadhouse. Not looking forward to the next fifty miles, he decided to spend another night or two at the roadhouse, fine tuning his plan and recuperating from the vigil at the watch camp. There was no hurry—with the telegram sent, success was now assured.

Chistochina, he thought. *Fifty miles and a few days time I'll finish this.*

* * *

August 18, 1903

Thomas stood on the bank of the Tanana River, happy there was a bridge in place. The thought of crossing without it was something he couldn't imagine. He returned to the wagon and with one bound, leaped into the seat. The mid-morning sun felt good as he leaned back and took another drag on his cigarette.

I wish John would hurry up, he thought, wondering what was taking so long. He had left him at the telegraph office and scouted ahead the short distance to the crossing.

Thomas was pleased with their progress in the last day or so. The trail from Mentasta Pass proved to be in excellent shape, gently sloping as they followed the river first east, then northward. After camping at Mineral Lake, they made another thirty miles the day before and were now facing a change in the trail.

Thomas pulled out the map and studied the route, certain John would have questions when he returned. In just a few miles the trail traversed much higher terrain than they'd experienced in the last several days. Thomas estimated the trail gained almost two thousand feet in elevation from the flat ground at Tanana Crossing. This wasn't good—the fact that it was up and down from here on out meant progress would be slower.

John's not going to be happy.

Thomas wasn't too happy either, especially when he added up the time required to return to Valdez before freeze-up. It meant very little time on the claim.

Thomas finished his cigarette just as John rode up. "Get the telegram sent okay?"

"No. The line's been down since the day before yesterday. Nothing's getting through for several days they said."

"What happened?"

"It appears some of the poles were leaning after the winter storms and the wind came blasting through one of the valleys and blew them down."

"How long before they fix it?"

"Nobody seems to know. May be more problems they haven't found yet. News is only coming in bit by bit from travelers. Seems the problem is somewhere between here and Tazlina."

"I'm sure Stella and Emily are expecting word from us by now."

"I wrote the message and gave it to the telegraph operator. It will go out once the line is repaired and the backlog clears."

"Did you tell them we were almost there?"

"I said your optimistic estimate was three more days or so."

"I hope I haven't been too optimistic—been looking at the map while waiting for you."

"Oh?"

Thomas explained the trail ahead and the ups and downs they faced. "I still think we can make it to the claim in three days."

John frowned. "We're going to be nearly out of time before we arrive."

"I know, but we knew it was close when we planned this trip. Maybe we should have waited until spring, but we have to make the best of it now."

"Well let's get moving then, or I might just decide to turn around."

Thomas was worried for an instant—until he looked at John and saw him smiling. They were now only ninety miles from the claim and Thomas was growing more restless with every mile.

"You lead for a while," said Thomas.

John pointed his horse toward the bridge over the Tanana River, raised his arm, and motioned forward. "Follow on."

* * *

Van Sant pushed slowly forward, hoping the pace would put him at the next roadhouse before nightfall. It was less than twenty miles to Gakona, from there another thirty or so to Chistochina. He resolved to not spend another night in a tent, camping among the bugs and bears. The crude existence along the trail wore on him.

I'm ready for San Francisco.

He put it out of his head. Focus was required for the business at hand. As he rehearsed the plan in his mind, there was no hesitation. Palmer must die, and Thornton with him. There could be no witnesses. Further, the daughter was also a threat—but there were complications.

Perhaps an explainable accident would set all well with San Francisco.

Then there was the woman at the boarding house. A problem or not—he wasn't sure.

Yes, she may have to go as well.

It was a messy business, yet necessary. He was not afraid to do what fate demanded. No fear of reprisal, no hesitation in violence. He was much more dangerous than anyone who met him would ever imagine.

As the horse plodded along, he made plans for his new and completely free life that was so close to realization.

* * *

August 20, 1903

"What do you mean the telegraph is down?" demanded Van Sant, slamming his fist on the counter. After arriving in Chistochina the night before to find the roadhouse closed for repairs, spending the night in a tent, and having nothing to eat, his temper was short.

"It means what it means," said the operator. "The lines are down and we're not getting anything from south of here."

"When?"

"When will it be fixed or when did it happen?"

"Don't even begin to play with me," said Van Sant, the contempt in his voice growing.

"No need to get your feathers riled. It's been down now for let's see..."

Van Sant grew impatient as the man counted on his fingers, peering up at the ceiling as if it held the answer.

"Four days," said the operator. "Went down in the evening on the sixteenth."

"I'm Preston Van Sant," he said, staring directly into the man's eyes. "I sent a telegram from Tazlina that day to all stations between there and Eagle. Was it received?

"Who was it to?"

"John Palmer."

"Oh, I know him," said the operator. "Him and that

young fella Thomas was here a while back. I helped them with some odd telegram from Valdez. You a friend of theirs?"

Van Sant saw an opportunity. "Yes, in fact I'm looking for them. When were they here?"

"Almost a week ago now, I think."

Blast it, he thought, realizing his strategy had put him much farther behind them than he hoped.

"Did my telegram make it here?"

The operator again looked up at the ceiling, rubbing his chin.

Van Sant slammed his fist on the counter, startling the man back to attention. "Don't you keep any kind of records?"

"Uh...Oh...yeah. Let me look it up and see."

The operator pulled out a stack of papers and started shuffling through them, dropping half of them on the floor. "Probably easier to check my log book, if it's up to date," he said with a sheepish look. He flipped through the tattered pages of the book, running his finger slowly down each line. "Hmm, I don't see it. My last on the sixteenth wasn't from Tazlina and I see nothing from you. I would've remembered your name anyway—got a mind like a steel trap, I do."

Van Sant thought of another word to describe the operator's so-called mind, but kept it to himself. With nearly a week lead and the failure of his message to get through, his plan was unraveling. *Time to change tactics.*

"I'm sorry I was short with you—I spent a long uncomfortable night in the tent and am not looking forward to another since I may have to be here a while."

The operator rubbed his chin and chuckled. "Thinking of moving here?"

Van Sant restrained himself, smiled, and said, "No, I was hoping to join up with my friends here."

"I think you're way off the mark there, friend. They was pressing on to get to their claim out of Chicken. Don't think they're headed this direction."

This is getting me nowhere, thought Van Sant. "I guess you're right—I'll have to make other plans. Is there a place around here I can stay?"

"Not with the roadhouse closed. You can get meals over at Mrs. White's place, but she don't take boarders."

Van Sant reached into his vest pocket and pulled out his wallet. "I could pay her well."

"Don't think she would be interested."

Van Sant pulled out a wad of bills and thumbed through the pile of fifties and hundreds. "Are you sure?"

The operator stared at the stack of money, eyes wide.

Van Sant extended two, one hundred dollar bills toward the man. "I'd be happy to pay you to convince her,"

He snatched the money from Van Sant, quickly stuffing it into his pants pocket. "I guess I could try. Nowhere to spend it around here, but it'll come in handy some day. Let's go talk to Mrs. White."

* * *

In the fading light, Thomas took in the view from atop the ridge, looking south into the Mosquito Fork drainage. It was a grueling journey after crossing the Tanana, going up and down the mountains and hills. Even so, the trail was better than expected and they made good time. Now only a few short miles from their destination, the desire to push on was strong.

"I think we need to make camp," said John. "There's only a little daylight left, the horses are tired, and I need some food."

Thomas knew he was right. No sense in going forward tired and in the dark and doing something stupid like driving off the ridge top.

"No, we have to go forward," said Thomas, trying to hide the grin that was slowly forming.

"Are you serious? It's dangerous and you—"

Thomas burst into laughter. "I'm kidding. Let's make camp."

"Glad you said that. I was thinking about mutiny."

"We'll get an early start tomorrow, get into Chicken, and find somebody that can direct us to the claim."

John dismounted, tied the nag off to the wagon, then grabbed the axe. "Sounds good. You set up camp while I scrounge for some wood."

* * *

"Well, I'm not really set up to take on a boarder," said Mrs. White.

"He's willing to pay you well," said the operator. "I seen his stack of money."

She hesitated. "Do you think he is okay?"

"I think so. He's friends with Palmer and Thornton. You remember them right."

"Oh yes, pleasant fellows they were."

"So what do you think?"

"Go fetch him and bring him in."

The man went out and returned almost instantly, Van Sant following close behind. He elbowed past the man and extended his hand to her. "I'm Preston Van Sant, pleased to meet you," he said, gently shaking her hand.

"Pleased to meet you. You can call me Matilda. I

understand you need a place to stay for a few days. What are you proposing?"

"I'm in a bit of a bind and sorely tired of staying in a tent and doing my own cooking. I'll gladly pay you fifty dollars a night, and throw in some extra for my meals."

She took a step back. "Mister, I've never been offered that much money for something so simple. I was expecting you'd offer me five dollars."

"No, I'm in a pinch and happy to pay you."

"I'm not sure I can take that much from you. Doesn't seem fair."

Van Sant grew weary of the conversation. *Who refuses money when shoved in their face? Perhaps a bit of charm....*

"My dear lady, please let me do this for you. I can see you are a most deserving soul."

She paused, then said, "If you insist. Get your things and I'll show you to the spare room. Are you hungry?"

"I haven't eaten since yesterday, and that was some dried jerky and pemmican."

"Get settled and I'll fix you some breakfast."

"Thank you, ma'am."

"Call me Matilda."

"Thank you, Matilda."

Unpacking what he needed from the horses, he analyzed the situation. He could go forward—Palmer certainly wasn't on his way to meet him. Or he could wait until the telegraph was repaired and hope to make contact.

By now they could have arrived at the claim.

This would take some thought. A day of rest, a bit of food—the plan would become clear.

* * *

Part III

The Mine

August 21, 1903

"Today's the day," shouted Thomas, causing John to lurch awake.

"What time is it?" said John, prying his eyes open to see that Thomas was not in the tent.

"It's 4 o'clock by my watch."

John groaned. "How can you even see it? The sun's not even up yet."

"Light enough to read my watch, light enough to get going."

John roused from the sleeping bag, pulled on his clothes, and crawled out of the tent into the cool August air. "I'm glad you weren't like this the whole trip. Can we at least have a proper breakfast first? We're less than twenty miles from Chicken—don't want to get there before the town's awake."

"You're right. At least we'll have most of a day to get settled on the claim. I can hardly wait."

"This is our thirteenth day on the trail. How long before we have to head back?"

Thomas smiled. "You're thinking about heading back before we ever get there?"

"Just thinking ahead. Trying to determine how much time we have on the claim."

"It all depends on when it snows. I think we can probably get in at least thirty days, maybe forty before it gets too cold and the snow too deep to return."

"That would put us at the end of September. At least the bugs won't be as bad by then."

"Ah, they haven't been all that bad. You only had to wear your head net once or twice."

"Still, I can do without them."

"See if you can get that fire going, and I'll start packing what we don't need for breakfast."

John pulled on his coat, then laughed. "Okay, but I wonder if Emily knows what a hard taskmaster you are."

* * *

The five hours it took to travel the ridge and reach the descent into the town of Chicken seemed like an eternity to Thomas. He was both excited and wary, uncertain of what truly faced them when they arrived. *Will we have trouble finding the claim? Will the claim be worth it?* The thoughts weighed upon him as the town came into view.

"I think we've arrived," said John.

"Amen," said Thomas. "Where to first?"

"Let's check in at the post office. They ought to know everything that goes on around here. After that, we'll send a telegram off to Emily and Stella."

"Good idea. The map of the claim is pretty crude. Don't want to get shot as claim jumpers our first day here."

There were a few people out and about on the main street of Chicken, a narrow dirt path, lined with small log structures and a few wood frame buildings. They stopped in front of a building that looked as though it might be a meeting hall or roadhouse. A man was seated on the steps, drinking coffee.

"Excuse me, sir. Can you direct us to the post office?" said Thomas.

The man looked up at Thomas seated on the wagon and said nothing. He stood, walked around the back of the wagon, lifted the canvas, and looked under. He grunted, then sized up John.

Thomas frowned. *Not a very nice welcome to the town*, he thought.

"Cheechakos, eh?" said the man.

Thomas, still frowning started to respond, "Look mister, I—"

"We've just arrived from Valdez," said John, stepping in as the diplomat. "We're not exactly new to the country, just looking for a little friendly assistance."

"Well, come on then," said the man.

John and Thomas looked at each other, puzzled.

"Get down off your rig and let's go inside. There's fresh coffee on."

John smiled and dismounted, winking at Thomas. With the horses secure, they followed the man inside.

The dimly lit room was larger than Thomas expected, and though dark, was clean and orderly.

"Have a chair," said the man, pointing to a table and chairs in the middle of the room. "I'll be back in a moment." He disappeared into an adjacent room that Thomas surmised must be the kitchen.

He returned with three cups of steaming coffee. "Sorry, no cream up here."

"No problem. We've been on the trail for almost two weeks so this is welcome," said John, trying to build a bit of rapport with the man.

"I'm Frank," he said, in a deep voice that seemed out of place for a man of his stature.

John took the lead. "I'm John and this is my future son-in-law Thomas."

Frank nodded. "Where you headed?"

"To the claim we bought on Angel Creek from a couple of fellows. We thought the post office would be a good place to get some information."

"I been here for a long time. Post office is new this summer and they brought a postmaster in from down south. Don't know nothing about things around here."

"I guess we came to the right place then," said John.

"So let me guess, you bought that claim from a fella named Olson and his partner Clyde."

"You know them?" said Thomas.

"Know 'em? I helped run them out of town."

Thomas looked at John, obviously worried. *Please don't tell me we've been had.*

"What did they do?" asked John.

Frank's look turned serious. "They stole gold."

Thomas sighed, but didn't say anything. They waited for the rest of the story.

Frank sipped on his coffee and looked out the window. "Gonna be a nice day."

Thomas couldn't stand it. "Tell us what happened."

Frank smiled. "Eager, aren't ya."

"I admit we are a bit concerned about what we've bought into," said John.

"It was a simple matter," said Frank. "They was going around at night and digging around in the first couple riffles of folk's sluice boxes. Getting the heavy gold, then claiming it was theirs when they went to sell."

"How did they get caught?" asked Thomas.

"Well," said Frank, "Everybody knew those two weren't running any pay up on their claim and with people missing gold..."

"They could tell?" said Thomas.

"Yeah, those two simps didn't even cover up what they done. You can tell when all the gravel and gold has been scraped out of your riffles."

"Unbelievable," said John. "It's lucky their fate wasn't much worse."

"It was close. Simpson up on Stonehouse Creek came hunting them, rifle in hand, but we convinced him it wasn't worth it. We searched 'em best we could and sent them packing."

Thomas sighed. "So the claim is no good."

Frank sat his cup on the table. "Didn't say that."

"Why didn't they work it then?"

"Two reasons—lazy and stupid. They had no idea what they were doing—had no business in this country."

"They showed us a bag of nice nuggets that supposedly were from the claim."

"Probably mine and several others. They must've hidden them well before we searched."

"Well, this is certainly a disappointment," said John.

"Where do we go from here?" said Thomas, nearly certain the whole venture was a bust.

"To your claim", said Frank, "Finish your coffee and I'll take you up there."

"We need to send a telegram to Valdez before we head up," said John.

"No can do," said Frank. "Lines are down, but the rumor is it'll be fixed in a day or so. Now drink up so we can get going, I can't fiddle around with you fellows all day, you know."

* * *

"Your claim is just over the crest, in the drainage below," said Frank as they neared the top of the low hill.

Thomas was excited, yet apprehensive after learning they bought a claim from liars and thieves. *I hope this wasn't a mistake.*

The trail didn't go straight over the hill, but traversed around on the contour. As they rounded the hill, the valley came into view. The stands of birch and aspen obscured the creek below, adding to the anticipation. The leaves were already hinting at yellow, signaling that winter was planning its arrival.

"Fall comes early here," said Thomas.

"Early and fast," said Frank. "In another month everything will be yellow and red."

They descended into the valley, John and Thomas both anxious for the first look at their purchase. Finally the trees yielded and they rode out into the clear, the claim in full view. All their imaginations and expectations were dashed.

Frank grinned and pointed. "There she is—your new home."

The narrow creek flowed down through a deep cutbank, probably fifteen to twenty feet high Thomas estimated. The water was only a foot or two deep and if you got a good run at it, you could probably jump across it.

"Where are the sluice boxes?" said Thomas.

"There aren't any," said Frank. "See that small pile of gravel over there?"

They nodded.

"That's the winter dump—the only pay those simps ever stockpiled."

"Stockpiled?" said John.

"Yes, for sluicing in the summer."

John looked at Thomas, puzzled. He shrugged and turned back to Frank.

"I'm afraid I don't understand."

"Oh. I guess they didn't tell you—you bought a drift mine."

"Drift mine?"

Thomas knew what this meant, but waited for Frank to explain.

Frank pointed at the cut-bank. "Sure. All the ground here is frozen and covered by muck."

"Muck?" said John.

"Yup. See that dark black soil above the creek? That stuff is frozen and when it thaws, it sloughs into the creek. It's sticky stuff that makes quite a mess if you try to walk through it."

"How are we supposed to mine it when it's frozen?"

"Follow me," said Frank.

They rode along the creek, deep in the cut on the small trail that had been terraced just above the water level, reaching the small pile of gravel Frank pointed out earlier.

"Your shaft is up that path on the bench. Let's take a look," Frank said as he dismounted.

"That's a pretty steep path to...," John started to say, only to see Frank bound up and onto the bench like a mountain goat.

They looked at each other, then followed. Above the creek the bench was flat, probably one hundred yards wide before the next bench above it. In the middle was some sort of frame built of logs. They hurried to catch up to Frank who was already standing there.

Thomas realized what the frame was—a windlass for hoisting from the shaft. It was in disrepair, looking as though no one had used it in a long while.

"Well, here's the shaft," said Frank, looking down into an open hole about eight feet deep.

"It's caved in," said Thomas.

"More like sloughed in. That's what happens when you don't cover it properly and insulate it during the summer. This frozen muck doesn't stand when it thaws."

"Wait a minute," said John. "I don't understand. I thought we would be moving gravel through sluice boxes."

"Not on this claim," said Frank. The only thawed ground is right under that creek bed. Not enough room in that narrow cut to mine, besides, there's not much pay there."

"So how does this work?"

"You fellows really aren't ready for this, are you."

Thomas knew he was right. Moving gravel through a sluice box was one thing, but this was a completely different proposition.

Frank began to explain the process of drift mining, gauging their response as he spoke. "It's pretty simple. You sink a shaft through the frozen ground, using a wood fire to thaw it a bit at a time, then shoveling and hoisting out. When you get through the muck and into the gravel, you start following the pay streak and stockpiling the gravel."

"Why do we have to stockpile it? Can't we just sluice it as we go?"

Frank laughed. "No, you'll drift in the *winter*, sluice in the summer."

Thomas knew this was the case, but expected to be sluicing thawed gravel, not working underground.

"Well this is a fine mess," said John.

"Pretty typical for a lot of creeks around here," said Frank. "Not enough water for hydraulicking."

"Hydraulicking?" said John.

"Using big, high-pressure nozzles to thaw and wash away the muck, then direct the pay towards your boxes. You can see from the size of the creek and how short it is, no way you can get the head to do that."

John was overwhelmed by all the mining terms. *I thought the trip was bad, this is looking worse by the minute.*

"Is the ground any good?" said Thomas.

"No telling. You can pan color down in the creek, but the jokers you bought the claim from never ran any of the gravel from the shaft."

"Well, this is certainly a mess," John said again. "I think we should take a day or two to rest up, put this pig in a poke up for sale, and head home."

Thomas shot him a glance. He didn't want to hear that—not just yet.

"You want my advice?" said Frank?

Thomas nodded, while John just stood there, staring at the muddy, caved hole in the ground.

"I'd take and sluice that small winter dump by the creek. I don't know if them fellas got to bedrock or not, but running that stockpile will give you an idea of what you might have. Then you can decide from there what to do."

"What do you think, John?" said Thomas.

John shuffled his feet, stared down the caved hole again, then taking his hat off, looked up at the bright blue sky. He sighed deeply. "I guess we might as well give it a go. We're here aren't we?"

Thomas slapped him on the back and grinned. "That's the spirit."

"You're going to need some lumber to put together a sluice box. How you fixed for supplies?" said Frank.

"We don't have any lumber, but we've got nails and tools," said Thomas.

"We've got a community-run sawmill down in the valley. You can get some rough-cut lumber there, if you've got money or goods to trade."

"I think we can manage that," said John.

"Looks like we'll be tenting it, even though we were told there was a cabin," said Thomas, looking around the claim.

Frank laughed. "No, you've got a cabin, or at least something like it. Follow me."

They walked along the bench toward a stand of trees and rounded a small curve in the trail to where the cabin stood. Thomas noticed to the left a wagon trail that wound it's way back to the creek downstream, following the bench. He wondered how he missed it when they came up the creek.

The cabin was small, built of logs and poorly constructed. The roof sagged a bit in the middle and the cap was missing off the stove pipe chimney, meaning rain had likely made its way down to whatever was on the other end. Thomas hoped it was a wood stove.

Approaching the cabin, they could see the door was latched, providing some protection from the elements and the wildlife.

Frank grinned and unlatched the door. "Go on in, she's all yours."

Thomas pulled the door open and stepped in. It was dimly lit by a single window and smelled bad—more like an outhouse than a living space. There was indeed a wood stove attached to the stove pipe, along with two bunks built into the far wall, one above the other. A homemade table graced the center of the small space, with two log stumps serving as chairs. A counter ran below the window and apparently served as the kitchen area.

John took one look over Thomas' shoulder and said, "Well, this is nice. What's the smell."

As their eyes adjusted to the light, it became clear that some small animal had made the cabin its home since the previous owners vacated. Whatever it was, it lacked a sense of proper cleanliness and sanitation, leaving a mess in nearly every place one could step.

"Better open it up and air it out," said Frank. "Even though it's sagged a bit, the roof looks in good shape. It ain't fancy but should keep you mostly dry and warm."

"Looks like we've got our work cut out for us," said John as they went back into the open air, with a remarkably fresh smell.

"I've got to get to work, already been away from my boys on the claim too long this morning. Gotta keep a close eye on 'em. I'll ride up and check on you in a day or two."

"Thanks for all your help," said Thomas. "Be sure and let us know about the telegraph when you come back."

"Good luck—you're gonna need it," said Frank as he bounded down the cut bank to his horse.

They looked at each other, then watched Frank ride out of sight.

Thomas turned back toward the cabin. "Well, John,

we knew it was going to be work."

"That's the understatement of the year."

* * *

Thomas pulled the wagon up the last of the hill and stopped next to the cabin. *At least the access is good,* he thought. It quickly became apparent the cabin wasn't big enough to store all the supplies and still have room to get in the door. There were no out buildings—no place for the horses to get out of the weather. He was conflicted. *Where do we even begin.*

John was already in the cabin, planning to stow his personal gear from the nag, but realizing the mess needed to be dealt with first.

Thomas jumped down from the wagon and looked in the door.

"Wish we had a broom," said John.

"Yeah, that would've been helpful."

Thomas removed the canvas covering their supplies and started digging around to find a shovel. The floor in the cabin was dirt, hard packed from use, but not a bit level.

"Here", said Thomas, handing John a square-ended shovel and taking one himself. "Maybe between the two of us we can scrape and scoop this mess up."

"We're going to need some water to clean the bunks and table."

"I'll fetch some after we get the floor cleaned up so we can quit tracking this mess everywhere."

Thanks to the size of the cabin, the work went quickly. Thomas fetched water from the creek and after a couple of hours, the cleanup was done. The place still reeked, but with only one door and no windows that opened, the air circulation was minimal. After a while they got used to the smell to the point it was unnoticeable—except after being out in the fresh air for a couple of minutes and coming back inside.

"It'll air out eventually," said Thomas.

"Hope so," said John.

By now, it was early afternoon and, after a quick lunch, they took a stroll around the property, trying to take inventory of what equipment was left by the con men.

"Remember what they said before we bought the claim?" said Thomas. "All the equipment needed to start moving gravel was here."

"I remember. They said everything was set up and ready to go."

"We were had."

"Yes, and their description of the cabin as 'real nice' is laughable."

After a walk around the bench and up and down the creek their inventory was complete—it was dismal. Some rusting tools—a pick, two shovels, some buckets, two complete with holes, and a large spool of rope, possibly usable. Along the creek bank, Thomas found a large metal chest containing a good set of hand tools, already beginning to rust. It looked as though the con men had bought used equipment and made a halfhearted attempt at mining. It was clear no one in the Fortymile would buy the claim for what he and John paid.

"We need to sit down and decide what to do," said John.

"Agreed. Let's see if that wood stove works and make some coffee. I saw some wood that might burn stacked against the back of the cabin."

* * *

With coffee boiling on the stove, they sat silently at the table, each reflecting on the situation. The original plan of rushing to the claim, mining a little gold, then returning before winter was in jeopardy. They had only a small stockpile of gravel, and while Frank called it "pay", there was no telling if it held any gold. The lack of thawed ground prevented further sluicing, and the only pay lay under perhaps tens of feet of frozen muck. With a little work, the cabin was livable, but there was no place to store supplies and process gold—if they ever found any.

Thomas tapped the coffee pot with a spoon to settle the grounds, then poured each of them a cup. Handing one to John, he joined him at the table.

"Well," said Thomas.

"That's a big well," said John. "More like a muddy hole in the ground."

Thomas sighed.

"The way I see it, we have a couple options," said John.

Thomas waited—he had his own course of action already set in mind, but it would remain his alone for now.

"First, we can take Frank's suggestion to build a sluice and run that stockpile to see if we can get any gold. Or, we can close up this place and try to sell it, most likely at a loss, then head home as soon as possible."

Thomas knew immediately which option John preferred—but leaving was not an option—at least not yet. Briefly his mind drifted back an eternity ago to Seattle, to old man Haskell and the huge nugget worn around his neck. No, the dream was still alive and he was here. *If not this claim, then somewhere,* he thought.

"What do you think?" said John.

Was it deceptive? thought Thomas. *Perhaps, but reasonable.* "I think we should build a decent sluice box and run that stockpile. If we find gold, then it can be a selling point for the claim." *There, the deception, the half-truth.*

"Well, that kind of makes sense. Given my financial situation, it would be nice to recoup as much of the cost as possible."

"I don't think it will take long to get set up to run the gravel."

John finished his coffee and poured another cup. "Okay, I'm in."

Thomas poured a cup as well, then sat the pot on the wood stove to warm. "Let's try and get things sorted out here, supplies unloaded and stowed so we can haul some lumber tomorrow."

They spent the rest of the day unloading the wagon and stacking what they could in the cabin, the rest outside. Thomas cut some poles and built a crib next to the wall to support everything, then he and John secured the canvas over the goods. Keeping the animals out of their food stuffs was the biggest problem. Fortunately most was in hard containers. Bears, of course, were another matter—they could get into most anything, but so far they had seen no sign.

By nightfall they had been on the go for eighteen hours. Sleep came easy, despite the uncertainty ahead of them.

* * *

August 22, 1903

After a quick breakfast, Thomas and John headed back to Chicken in search of some lumber. Neither had ever built a sluice box, but were confident it wasn't difficult.

"How much lumber do you need?" asked the operator of the sawmill.

"Just the standard," said Thomas. They hadn't really thought about dimensions or what they needed, assuming they were all the same.

The operator laughed out loud, eliciting a frown from Thomas.

"No such thing as standard, boy."

Thomas realized they were going to need some help. "We want to run a small stockpile of pay so what would you recommend?"

"What creek you on?"

"Angel Creek," said John.

The operator pulled off his gloves and grinned. "Nothing angelic about that one, is there."

Thomas grew impatient with the ridicule, thought about a reply, but realized this was the only game in town, short of whipsawing their own lumber.

"Not much water in that one. You won't need a long box to catch the gold—I figure twelve feet or so ought to do it. You need material for riffles too?"

"We didn't bring anything suitable," said John.

"Okay, let's get you fixed up. Need nails?"

"No, we're set on that front."

"Follow me."

Thomas waited at the wagon while John and the man headed to the stack of lumber. *Maybe I should make sure he's not giving us poor quality goods,* thought Thomas.

The man poked through the stack, shuffling the lumber as he looked for straight pieces. After several minutes, he had a neat pile set aside. "Come get it, ain't going to load it for you."

Thomas joined John and they carried the rough-cut lumber to the wagon a section at a time. It was surprisingly heavy. With enough for the sluice, the man waved them over again.

"Here's material for your riffles," he said, pointing at a stack of square stock, roughly two by two inches and in eight foot lengths.

"How much do we need?" said Thomas, expecting another ribbing.

"Uh, let's see." The man started pulling the wood out of the stack eight at a time. "This ought to be enough. I threw in some extra so you can use it for bracing the box if you need to."

Thomas looked at the riffle material, wondering if square two-by-twos would actually work. He knew there were all kinds of riffles, but he had never seen any in action to know what worked and what didn't. "Are these riffles going to—"

"You're going to want to shave the downstream side of those at an angle so you get a nice little area for the gold to drop out. You got something to do that with?"

"We have a block plane and a draw blade," said Thomas,

recalling the contents of the tool box by the creek.

"That'll work. I'd use the plane so you get a nice consistent angle."

"How much angle?" asked John.

The operator picked up one of the two-by-twos and drew a line across the end with his finger. "Oh, just a bit, like this."

"Thanks, said John.

"Come in and we'll settle up", said the man, pointing to the small wood frame office.

Thomas was about to ask how the riffles are supposed to be assembled and attached to the box, but was afraid of the retort he would likely receive. *We'll figure it out,* he thought as he secured the load to the wagon, leaving John to the financial matters.

John returned and joined Thomas on the wagon.

"Got any money left?"

John smiled. "Some. It wasn't as bad as I expected."

"I'm not sure how all this goes together."

"Great, I was depending on you to figure it out."

Thomas released the brake on the wagon and nudged the horse ahead. "Pretty simple, I guess. Just make a long skinny box and put riffles in the bottom."

John laughed. "No problem."

* * *

By mid-afternoon John and Thomas had the sluice box frame assembled next to the creek, just downstream from the winter dump of gravel. The task of shaping the riffles was next—simple compared to how they were going to attach them to the box.

Thomas used the block plane to angle the two-by-twos. As he finished each one, John cut them to match the width of the box. They weren't sure how far apart to place them, so they cut plenty, just to be sure.

John cut the last one to length and added it to the stack. "We can just nail them in."

"Okay. I guess that will work."

They flipped the box on its side and began attaching the riffles. John held each in place while Thomas nailed from the backside.

Nearly half of the riffles were in place when Thomas looked up. "Here comes someone. I think it might be Frank."

John looked downstream and, as the horse drew closer, saw indeed it was.

Frank dismounted, walked up, and took a long look at the sluice box. "How goes it?"

"Doing great," said Thomas. "Almost got our box built."

Frank bent over and looked at the riffles, then walked around the other side to where Thomas had been nailing. He raised his eyebrows and adjusted his hat. "That's a mighty fine piece of work."

"Thanks," said Thomas. "I grew up on the farm so I'm pretty handy with tools."

"I see. How do you plan to remove the riffles when it's time for a cleanup?"

Thomas dropped his hands to his side and looked at John. John shrugged.

"They're supposed to come out, aren't they."

A big grin spread across Frank's face. "Well, they don't have to, but it'll sure make cleanup a whole lot easier—and faster."

"Now what?" said Thomas.

"Look, this is what you need to do. Take a couple

of long two-by-twos and then nail your riffles to them so it ends up looking like a ladder. Make sure you get the width right so it will fit in the box."

"Okay. Then nail the ladder in?" said John.

"No." Frank went on to explain how to attach angled blocks to the side of the box and create a wedge to drive between the block and the ladder to secure the riffles.

John looked at Thomas. "Why didn't we think of that?"

"I guess because we don't know what we're doing."

Frank chuckled. "Your box needs some modification too."

"More?" said Thomas.

"What will happen when you set this wooden box in the creek?"

"Uh...it will float away, won't it."

"Yup. Look, just take some of your bracing and nail it to the bottom so that it sticks out beyond the box a foot or so. Then cut a triangle from your wide stock and nail it to the side of the box for reinforcement. This gives the box some feet to support it and you can pile big rocks on to hold it down."

"That makes sense. How many feet do we need?"

"I'd put one near the head and the end, then one in the middle. That ought to do the trick."

"Thanks a lot, Frank," said John. "Anything else we should do?"

"You might want to put a gate at the head—just a board you can slide in to shut off the water for cleanup."

"Good idea," said Thomas. "I think we have enough scrap around to finish all of it."

With a single motion, Frank flew up into the saddle. "I'm off, boys. Good luck. I'll check in with you in a few days. You should be ready to start shoveling tomorrow."

"Wait, Frank," said John. "Any word on the repairs to the telegraph line?"

"Word from down the trail is it should be fixed sometime tomorrow. Probably going to be a big backlog of messages, I expect."

"I guess we'll drop into town and check tomorrow or the next day," said John.

They both shouted thanks again as Frank rode off.

"Well, we looked pretty stupid," said John.

Thomas started prying riffles out of the box with the claw hammer. "Yeah, but just think how stupid we'd look if he hadn't come along."

"True—very true."

In three hours the box was finished and Thomas was eager to set it in the creek and start shoveling. His partner, however, was not quite as enthusiastic.

"I'm tired and hungry," said John. "Let's start fresh tomorrow—besides, it's going to take a while to get this thing properly set and secured in the creek. We don't want to wake up tomorrow to find it halfway to Chicken."

"But if...," Thomas began to protest, then thought better of it, realizing that he was hungry and tired as well. In their frenzy to build the box, neither had eaten since breakfast.

"You're right again, John. Let's call it a day."

After stowing the tools and making sure the box was high and dry in case the creek came up overnight, they trudged up the hill to the cabin. Being tired, neither was interested in cooking.

John gnawed on some dried moose meat from their stores. It was salty and tough, nearly pulling your teeth out when trying to get a bite. "We need to see about getting some fresh meat."

"I've been told there's a big caribou herd that roams around here. Maybe we'll get lucky and one will walk up and knock on the door."

"Well, let's leave the door open and maybe it'll come in and field dress itself as well."

Thomas gave up and pitched his chunk of moose meat into the bucket on the counter. "Might be fish in the creek, or maybe in the bigger streams in the valley. We should ask around and find out."

"Fresh fish would be fine too."

Thomas' thoughts drifted back to the gravel pile. "Wonder how long it will take us to run all that stockpile."

"I guess it depends on how fast you shovel and how far we have to carry it."

It was then they both realized the distance between the pile of pay gravel and the creek. Carrying buckets was going to wear them out in a hurry.

Thomas looked at John. "We need a wheelbarrow."

"There must be one around here somewhere. Surely those ninnies didn't carry all that by hand from the shaft to the creek."

"Agreed. Could be hiding in the brush perhaps," said Thomas. "I'll take a look while you clear the table."

"I'll come with you."

Thomas set his cup and the counter and grinned. "No, you rest up. I need you at full strength tomorrow."

"Okay, if you insist."

Thomas pulled on his coat and grabbed his hat from the hook on the door. "I won't be gone long."

* * *

Thomas began his search on the bench near the slumped

shaft, then moved further from the creek through the low brush. He couldn't imagine someone tossing a wheelbarrow so far from the workings, but given the nature of the former owners, anything was possible.

Seeing no sign in the brush, he returned to the shaft, his curiosity derailing him from the task at hand—at least for a moment.

The shaft measured roughly six feet on a side, wide enough for one man to work in and still be able to maneuver. The dark slimy muck sloughed in as it thawed, slowly reclaiming the hole.

This is ruined, he thought as he took one last look—then saw it. A wooden handle protruding from the muck at the bottom of the hole. It was hardly noticeable, with just an inch or two still visible. *I wonder...*

He looked around for something long enough to reach the bottom of the hole. None of the collapsed frame members were long enough to do the job. He headed for the trees at the edge of the bench and in short order found a scrawny dead spruce still standing. Grabbing it as high up as he could reach, he pulled hard, only to have the tree fight back.

Changing tactics, he jumped as high as he could and grabbed the tree, then began swinging his legs back and forth until the tree bent, then cracked, crashing to the ground on top of him. Unfazed, he easily stripped the dried branches from it, then headed back to the shaft.

Poking around the exposed handle, he worked to push the muck away. The tree was plenty long, but brittle at the top and immediately broke two feet from the end when he shoved too hard. Now it was too short, a problem solved by laying on his stomach at the edge of the hole.

After several minutes of poking and pushing muck

around, he confirmed it was indeed a handle. *But to what?*

He continued to work at the muck, clearing the area, all the while fighting as it flowed back in. Two feet or so from the handle he struck something. Working quickly to stay ahead of the flow, he uncovered the end of another handle. Now he was sure it was a wheelbarrow, shoved into the shaft in frustration by the con men.

For an instant he thought about climbing down to fetch it, but realized that would be a big mistake. He returned to the cabin.

"Found a wheelbarrow. At least I think I did."

"Where?" said John, still finishing up an evening cup of coffee, complete with swirling grounds.

"I think it's under the muck in the shaft," said Thomas, explaining his discovery.

"Can we get it out?"

"I think so. Are you up for a try yet today? If we can get it out we'll be set for tomorrow."

John gulped the last of his coffee, then spit the grounds back into the cup. "Let's do it."

* * *

"You ready?" said Thomas.

"If you think this is going to work, yes, go ahead," said John.

John stood holding the reins of the Appaloosa, about twenty feet from the shaft. Thomas, at the edge of the hole, rope around his waist, stood ready to descend. "Back her up."

John backed the horse slowly and Thomas began his descent into the mucky shaft. As soon as he went off the edge and his feet touched the side, it began to slough off, sliding down and covering what little was exposed of the assumed wheelbarrow.

"Keep her coming," yelled Thomas, "until I holler whoa."

The horse continued backing and Thomas reached the bottom, only to find himself suddenly knee deep in the muck.

"Whoa!"

The sides of the shaft continued on a slow creep, threatening to make Thomas a permanent resident. Working quickly, he dug around with his hands, finding one of the handles elbow deep. He pressed further, finally feeling the cold metal frame of the wheelbarrow.

He grabbed on, then shouted, "I think I got it. Go slow."

John led the horse slowly as Thomas attempted to hold on, only to lose his grip or lose his arm.

"Whoa!"

John halted the horse. "What's wrong?"

"It's stuck and I can't hold on to it."

"You're going to have to tie on to it."

"I don't have enough slack, back up a bit."

John backed the horse and Thomas loosened the rope around his waist, slowly working the knot around until he had an extra two feet or so behind him.

"Let me down a little more—about three feet."

John backed the horse until Thomas was able to thrust his hand into the muck, and work the rope around the frame. He pulled it up and tied a double overhand knot.

"Okay, go real slow."

The horse began to move and the rope tightened, digging deep into the ground at the edge of the hole. Thomas tried to walk his feet up the sides, but his legs sunk in. He resigned himself to being pulled out of the hole like a fish on a line.

Just when it looked like the rope would break and he would be buried, the wheelbarrow emerged, hanging below his feet as he was dragged up and out.

"Whoa," said John as Thomas emerged.

Thomas lay on the ground, covered in dark muck.

John looked at him, bathed in mud, and laughed. "You stink."

Thomas stood and pointed at the wheelbarrow, laying upside down and dripping with mud. "That's the thanks I get for saving your back."

"Sorry. Let's get the two of you cleaned up."

Thomas untied the wheelbarrow and flipped it over, and, after freeing himself from the rope, examined it closely.

"Looks in pretty good shape," said John, "once the mud is off it." "Let's take it to the creek and wash it off before it dries."

"Okay, but I wonder...," said Thomas.

"Wonder what?"

"What else is at the bottom of that hole."

John watched the muck ooze in to fill the void left by the wheelbarrow. "Odds are we may never know."

* * *

August 23, 1903

John awoke early, only to find Thomas already up and gone. The stove was cold with no sign of fresh coffee to be found. Finding wood next to the stove, he built a fire, made some coffee, then went to look for Thomas.

Walking to the edge of the bench above the creek, he found Thomas, leaning on a shovel next to the sluice box. He already had the wheelbarrow full of gravel, ready to be dumped in the box even though it still sat on dry ground.

"Ho there!" shouted John. "Coffee—and breakfast."

Thomas waved, leaned the shovel against the wheelbarrow, and headed toward the cabin.

John handed him a cup of coffee as he entered. "Eager this morning, are we?"

"A bit."

"Drink your coffee and let's eat, otherwise you'll fade out before we get started."

Thomas gulped his coffee, poured a second cup, and tapped his foot all the while John was rustling up something to eat.

"You know, I hope you're not disappointed if that pile of dirt has no gold," said John.

"Of course I will be. This claim represents a lot of money down the drain if it's worthless—most of it other people's money."

"You know Stella and I threw in with no strings attached."

"I know, but it's not like any of us have money to throw around, especially you."

John smiled. "Thanks for the reminder, but don't worry about me. I'm a survivor. Come on, finish up and let's run some gravel."

* * *

"I've already cleared the big rocks from the channel and leveled it so we can set the box," said Thomas, standing next to the sluice.

"It can't be level, can it?" asked John.

"No, we'll need to have some slope to it—not sure how much."

John picked up the tail end of the box. "Let's set it and figure it out. I'll get this end."

Thomas grabbed the other end and they set the box in the water. Immediately it began to float and twist in the current. They pulled it back into position and Thomas sat on his end.

"I'll hold it down on this end. Put some of those bigger rocks on the feet to hold it down, then we'll do the same on your end."

With rocks stacked on the feet, the box remained stationary. To Thomas, the slope of the box looked adequate. He pushed the wheelbarrow and dumped the full load of gravel into the head of the box. Nothing happened, apart from water backing up behind the pile of gravel. The current wasn't enough to move the material.

"Not going to get rich that way," said John. "Now what?"

"I guess we need more water. We'll have to make a wing dam."

They spent the next hour collecting the largest rocks they could find and placing them at an angle from the box towards the opposite bank of the creek. This improved the flow, but it still wasn't enough—too much water was flowing through the makeshift dam.

More shoveling in the creek improved things, filling the gaps with smaller rocks. At last material started to swirl down the box, though dumping an entire wheelbarrow on top the first three riffles proved not to be the best practice.

"I think we have a problem," said John.

"Right," said Thomas. "Dumping that much at once on the riffles just clogs them up."

"I think we need make a modification to the riffles."

Thomas leaned on the shovel and sighed. *Another delay.* "What's that," he asked.

"Let's pull the riffles and remove the first few. That way we'll have a smooth area in the box at the head to feed the material. Sorta let it get a running start at things."

Thomas nodded. "Putting riffles the whole length of the box sounded like a good idea. You sure you haven't done this before?"

"Nope. Come on, this won't take long. Let's get this gravel out of the box as best we can, then knock off a few riffles."

It took them but a few minutes to remove the riffles and make the modification. Thomas scanned the box looking for nuggets from the first load of gravel, but found none. They were able to recover most of the first load of gravel, hoping not much was lost.

"Okay," said Thomas, pushing a fresh load up to the box. "I'm going to feed it slowly this time till we make sure it's working right."

"Good plan," said John. "Dump away."

Thomas tipped the wheelbarrow up and rocked it side to side, letting the gravel pour out slowly. John stood opposite, washing and tossing aside the big rocks too heavy to travel the sluice. After dumping just a few buckets worth of pay, the box was loaded with gravel its entire length.

"We need more slope," said Thomas. "Or more water."

"Don't think we're going to get more water. Let's see if we can lower the tail end."

Working with shovels, they attempted to clear the stream gravel from beneath the lower end of the box. This proved to be more difficult than expected. In order to lower the tail, they had to try and scrape gravel from under nearly the whole length of the box. Raising the head would be easier, but that would reduce the flow and water would run under the box. In the end they pulled the whole thing out and reworked the gravel bed, making sure there was enough slope.

"We can always raise the tail end if it's too steep," said Thomas.

"Yes, that will be easier than going the other route."

Thomas did another test dump and this time the sluice worked much better. It looked like the riffles were working and the flow was enough that the whole box didn't clog.

"Now we're in business," said Thomas.

John took off his hat and wiped the sweat from his forehead. "Finally—now the work really begins."

* * *

After an afternoon of shoveling, the stockpile was slightly smaller, but Thomas could tell it was going to be several days to run it all. The sluice was working pretty well, as long as it was fed at a reasonable rate. The gravel had some good size boulders, but none that John couldn't handle. Often they were caked with a sticky gray clay. It slowed them down a bit to wash each boulder, but Thomas knew the clay could contain gold—at least that's what he heard somewhere.

"Shall we call it a day?" said John after several hours. "I'm getting a bit tired."

Thomas was eager to continue, but no need to try and do it all in one day. "Sure. Let's knock off for the day." He flipped the wheelbarrow upside down against the pile and plunged the shovel into the ground—then the temptation overtook him.

"Now what are you doing?"

Thomas was pawing through the gravel behind the first few riffles and seemed not to hear the question.

"Thomas?"

"What? Oh, I'm looking to see if we got anything. Maybe we should pull the riffles and cleanup."

John knew that meant shutting off the flow to the box and trying to flush all the collected gravel down into a bucket, without losing any of it. They might even have to pull the box out of the water to get it done—he wasn't sure. "That's going to be a lot of work, Thomas. And it'll just slow us down."

"I know, but the anticipation is killing me."

"How about we run for another day or so and then cleanup? That will give us a good idea, and I'm not too keen about having to set the box again."

Thomas reluctantly agreed. He knew John was right, but still he just had to see some gold—one way or the other.

"Come on, let's get some dinner," said John.

Thomas cleared the grit from the gate at the head of the box and slid the board into place. Rolling a couple of large rocks in front of it to displace the flow of the creek, he checked his handiwork. *Should do it.*

"That'll keep it good until morning," said John as they headed up the hill to the cabin.

* * *

John leaned back on the lower bunk, his feet propped up on the crude stump that served as a stool, sipping his evening coffee. *Tomorrow I need to get into town and send word to Emily and Stella,* he thought, hoping the line was repaired. The women would be wondering what happened to them and he was just as concerned to hear of their welfare. About to drift off, his thoughts were interrupted by scraping, banging, and crashing against the outside wall.

"What's going on out there?" shouted John, jumping up while wondering if they had an unwelcome four-footed visitor.

"Just me," said Thomas. "I'm looking for something."

John exited the cabin to find Thomas digging under the tarp covering their supplies. "What in the world are you looking for?"

"A gold pan. Can't figure where they went to."

"Why do you need it tonight? I'll help you look for them tomorrow."

"I'm going to go down and pan some of the gravel."

"Now?"

"Just as soon as I find a pan."

"Thomas, you surely have gold fever. I guess this old man just doesn't have the drive you do."

"You're not that old," said Thomas, emerging from under the tarp, gold pan in hand. "Found it."

"Going to be dark in a couple of hours."

"I won't be long. Want to join me?"

John didn't have to think twice about it. "No, I'm going to relax in the warm cabin rather than stand in the cold creek."

"Suit yourself. I won't be long."

John returned to the cabin, all the while admiring the ambitious nature of his future son-in-law. He was bound to find success, if not in gold, then certainly in some other endeavor. When Emily first brought him home, he was concerned the young man wouldn't be able to provide, even though his character was immediately admirable.

John fetched the small book and began to write. He kept a journal of their adventure thus far, though many entries while on the trail were brief. Today's accomplishments were certainly worth expounding upon. He was nearly finished writing when he heard hollering from the direction of the creek. From inside the cabin, he couldn't make out words. *I hope it's not a bear,* he thought, grabbing the carbine and heading out the door.

He ran to the edge of the bench, afraid of what he might see when the creek came into view. It wasn't a bear. There was Thomas, prancing around, gold pan in hand and a huge grin on his face.

"Gold," he shouted, waving John down to see.

John half ran, half slid down the trail to the creek to get a look. Breathing hard, he walked the last few steps and peered into the pan.

"Where?" said John, seeing nothing but little rocks and some black sand in the little bit of water left in the pan.

"Watch." Thomas tilted the pan down and shook it gently to work all the material together, then tipped it gently up and began swirling water. The rocks and sand began to move away, revealing the cause of all the excitement.

In the fading light of the day, John saw the first gold from their claim. It wasn't a lot, mostly small specks the size of a grain or two of salt. Thomas continued swirling the pan until all was revealed.

"Well, it's a start," said John.

"Oh," said Thomas, "and there's this..."

He reached into his mouth, between his lower lip and gums where one would normally stash chewing tobacco and pulled it out, placing it in his open palm. "A nugget."

John's eyes widened at the sight of it. It wasn't huge, about the size of a popcorn kernel, but somewhat flat. John picked it up and dropped it into his hand. It was big enough to feel the weight as it landed. "Now that is *real* encouraging. How many pans have you done?"

"This is my first one. I wonder why we can't see any in the box."

"Don't know. Maybe scraping around in there makes it hard to see—or that pan could just be the luck of the draw."

Thomas continued swirling the pan, as if it would make more gold appear. "Time will tell. We can run even more gravel tomorrow."

John handed the nugget back to Thomas. "Maybe in the afternoon."

Thomas cocked his head and looked at John. "Why?"

"Because tomorrow morning I'm going into town and send a telegram, one way or the other."

* * *

August 24, 1903

After an early breakfast, John left Thomas to the claim, figuring he would have half the pile run through the box before lunch rolled around. Of course, that wasn't possible, but given the young man's enthusiasm he would certainly make a good dent in it.

Arriving in Chicken, John went directly to the telegraph office, only to find the door open and no one around. This didn't bode well—perhaps the line was still not repaired. He quickly changed his mind, as it appeared there was a fresh stack of messages in the "To Deliver" bin on the counter. He was tempted to leaf through them, but thought better of it.

"Anyone around?" he shouted.

Hearing no response, he turned to leave just as a man came busting in the back door, pulling on his suspenders and stumbling his way to the counter.

"Sorry, had some business to attend to out back."

John smiled. "I can understand that."

"What can I do for you?"

"Well, I'm wondering if the line is back up. I need to send a message, as well as check to see if anything has come in for me."

"Line's back up as of late yesterday and we've been clearing quite a backlog of messages. What's your name and I'll check."

"I'm John Palmer," he said, extending his hand to the man.

"Name's Wayne. Pleased to meet you," he said, shuffling through the stack of messages. "You're new in town. Plan to stay long?"

"We bought the claim up on Angel Creek and we're just checking things out for a month or so."

"Oh. You bought *that* claim."

"Yeah, I know, but we're hoping to make the best of it. Looks like there's a little gold there."

"For your sake, I hope so. Those two yahoos never worked hard enough to find out," said Wayne as he continued shuffling. "Ah, here's one," he said, handing the message to John.

It was from Emily and Stella.

```
JOHN PALMER / THOMAS THORNTON
TANANA CROSSING / CHICKEN, ALASKA

ALL WELL HERE. HOPE YOU ARRIVE
ON CLAIM SOON.

LOVE,

EMILY AND STELLA
VALDEZ, ALASKA
```

"I need to send a return to them so they know we made it here safely." John.

Wayne handed him a blank form. "Sure, just write 'er down and I'll get it out for you."

John kept the message short, not wanting to reveal the sad state of the claim and the possibility they were cheated. He finished writing and handed the message back over the counter.

Wayne took the message, added it to the outgoing stack, then continued organizing the newly arrived telegrams. "Oh, here's another for you."

John assumed it was also from Stella and Emily, probably worried at receiving no word. He was wrong.

JOHN PALMER
ALL STATIONS TANANA CROSSING TO CHICKEN

I HAVE YOUR MONEY. SORRY FOR THE MISUNDERSTANDING. MEET ME IN CHISTOCHINA IN SEVEN DAYS.

/S/ P. VAN SANT
TAZLINA, ALASKA

John read it again to be sure he wasn't mistaken. *Preston is in Alaska?* "When was this sent?"

Wayne took the message back and looked at it.

"It was originally supposed to go out on the sixteenth, but it just came in yesterday, what with the line being down an all."

Eight days ago, thought John. This was a problem—why did Van Sant feel compelled to travel all this way when he could set things right with a simple telegram?

"Something wrong?" asked Wayne. "You look a bit flustered."

"No, just a little mix up it seems."

He didn't know what to do. By this time Van Sant was in Chistochina, or maybe he had moved on.

"How far to Chistochina from here?"

"Whew," said Wayne. "You're talkin' um...probably almost two hundred miles."

"That's nearly halfway to Valdez."

"Sounds about right. Need to send another telegram?"

"No thanks. I need to do some checking on things

first. Just send that one and I'll probably be back to see you tomorrow."

"No problem," said Wayne, "Have a good day."

* * *

The ride back to the claim gave John an opportunity to contemplate the strange turn of events. Perhaps Van Sant had gotten wind of the police investigation in Seattle and was on the run. Or, maybe he truly wanted to make things right. *Perhaps I misjudged him,* he thought. After all, they had been friends for as long as he cared to remember.

The money was important, but traveling south halfway back to Valdez didn't appeal to him at that very moment. The rigors of the trail were still fresh in his mind from the journey north. *Might as well toss all this on Thomas and see what he thinks.*

It was late morning by the time John made it back to the cabin. Thomas, of course, was nowhere in sight, likely down at the creek pushing gravel through the box as fast as he dared. He staked the horse out so she could graze, then wandered down the trail toward the creek, still deep in thought.

"How's it going," shouted John as he approached.

Thomas was in the middle of dumping a load into the box. He looked over his shoulder. "Doing fine."

John could see that a fair amount of gravel had been moved in his absence. At this rate it would only take them a week to process it all—if there were two of them working.

"How are things in Valdez?" said Thomas. "Did you get word?"

"Yes, got a telegram from them and all is well. I sent

a short message off to them. I'm sure they're anxious to hear from us."

"I'm sure they are."

"And then there's this," said John, handing the other telegram to Thomas.

"Well this is a strange turn of events," said Thomas, handing it back. "What do you make of it?"

"I'm not sure," said John. "I'm just not sure."

The more he thought about it, the more it seemed likely Van Sant was the author of the previous telegram regarding Emily's mysterious trouble. The strange telegram coupled with Van Sant's latest was more than suspicious.

"I can't think of anyone else who would have sent it."

"What's that? said Thomas.

John realized he was thinking out loud. "Sorry, just trying to figure out who would have sent the telegram about Emily being in dire trouble."

"You think it was Van Sant?"

"It seems likely. I can't imagine who else would attempt to derail our trip, but I don't know what he's up to. If he truly wanted to reconcile, why not deposit the money somewhere and send a telegram with some plausible excuse for the mix up, rather than come up here and follow us."

"What are you going to do?" said Thomas.

"I'm going to sleep on it, then send a telegram first to Stella telling her to be on the lookout for him. Then I have to figure out what to send to Chistochina. I'm certainly not going to head that way based on what I know now."

Thomas started shoveling again. "Sounds reasonable. Let's run some more gravel—it'll take your mind off things."

"Or give me time to think about it even more."

* * *

"Nothing?" said Van Sant as he stood in the Chistochina telegraph office, his clenched fists resting on the counter.

"Sorry, mister," said the telegraph operator. "Haven't seen anything for you yet."

He swore under his breath. *What now?* He was used to being in control of every situation—this was something else.

"You can have this blasted country." He left the office, walking toward the bluff that overlooked the vast Copper River. *Nearly three weeks in this God forsaken land and still no closer to finishing the matter.*

Again he faced a decision—go forward and try to find Palmer or stay and wait for him to show up. In frustration, he swore again—not knowing whether to stay or leave was gnawing at him. Sending another telegram to Chicken may be the best plan, but what should he say? At this point he wasn't sure he could lure Palmer his direction and it would take at least six days to reach him, possibly more. He returned to the telegraph office.

Seeing Van Sant enter, the operator began nervously shuffling papers on the counter. "Yes?"

"I need to send a telegram to Chicken."

The operator handed him a pad and pencil. "No problem, write your message and we'll get it going."

Van Sant took the pencil to write, then paused, suddenly at a loss for words. He considered himself clever, smarter than everyone he met, and certainly superior. This essence is what drove him toward revenge, yet now he faced a blank page, not knowing what to do. He didn't like the sensation. Uncertainty would lead to mistakes—he pushed the feeling down and wrote.

```
JOHN PALMER
CHICKEN, ALASKA

NEED TO MEET HALFWAY. ADVISE
WHERE AND WHEN. IF NOT, ALL YOURS
IS LOST.

/S/ P. VAN SANT
CHISTOCHINA, ALASKA
```

He handed it to the operator. "Send it."

"Curious message, mister."

A scowl crawled across Van Sant's face. Glaring, he said, "Is it your job to comment or send it?"

"I'm sending it, I'm sending it. Calm down."

If there was one thing Van Sant detested was rebuke from a lesser. His first impulse was to pull the Colt and give the man a whipping across the face. Knowing such an act wouldn't get the telegram sent, he resisted. At the moment, this man was his only access to Palmer. He took no action, but vowed not to forget this moment.

"Fine," he said, hiding his contempt. "I suggest you keep the contents of my messages to yourself. Sharing them would not be healthy."

The operator nodded as Van Sant turned and left. As he proceeded to send the telegram, his concern deepened. *I think I might send my own message to Chicken.*

* * *

"Looking good," said Thomas as he sized up their progress.

By mid-afternoon they had run nearly a quarter of the stockpile. At this rate, they would be done in less than a week. There was debate about cleanup—Thomas ready to cleanup at the end of every day. John proposed a more conservative approach, recognizing the amount of work required to cleanup and get everything back in place to continue sluicing.

"I know you're anxious, but how about we wait and cleanup after we've got about half the pile gone?" said John.

Thomas leaned on the shovel, looking at the amount of gravel remaining. "I guess I can wait that long, but it's going to cost you."

"How's that?"

"I get half the gold."

John laughed. "You mean half after we pay off our debts."

"You had to go and remind me, didn't you."

"Sorry, reality hurts sometimes."

"Let's get back to work," said Thomas, digging the shovel deep into the pile, only to strike a huge rock just under the surface. "This would go faster if there weren't so many big rocks."

"Slow and steady," said John. "Any faster and you'll wear your partner out for good."

Thomas realized he was perhaps pushing a bit too hard. The lust for gold drove him, but he also felt the press of the season. Each day it was a little cooler, the leaves a little more yellow, and the nights longer. Only three days on the claim and he couldn't help thinking about the return journey that faced them in just a few weeks time. *Perhaps there was another way.*

"You'll be on your own for a while again tomorrow,"

said John. "I've got to go back to town and send a telegram or two—once I figure out what to say."

"Are you considering leaving and meeting him on the trail?"

"Perhaps."

"I'm not sure that's a good idea. We've spent a lot of time to get here. Can't Van Sant just meet you here?"

"Well, it is my money. He sort of holds all the cards, and if I hope to get it back, I may have to play the game his way."

Thomas dumped a shovel load into the wheelbarrow. "I don't like it—not one bit."

* * *

August 25, 1903

Thomas gulped the last of his morning coffee and looked across the table at John. "What happens if you ignore Van Sant's telegram?"

"I don't know what he would do, but I risk losing the opportunity to recover the money if I ignore him."

"I'll go with you."

"No, that's not fair to you, especially since we have so little time here."

"I don't think it's wise for you to meet him alone. I don't trust him."

"I don't either. I think the odds are pretty good that he sent the fake telegram about Emily. If that's the case, he's up to something."

"Do you think he intends to return all the money, or work out some deal?"

"Judging from the telegram, he wants to bargain with me—or perhaps worse."

"What do you mean?"

"Perhaps he views me as a loose end."

Thomas' expression changed, worry spreading across his face. "That means Emily could be in danger as well."

"I'm afraid so."

"I thought this man was your friend."

"He was, but something has changed."

"I say we make him come here—offer him an enticement he can't refuse."

"Meet him on our turf—I'm not sure he'll go for it."

"You could lie to him—tell him you'll give him a stake in the claim if he comes."

"I'm afraid he may see right through that."

"Not if you pitch it the right way."

"It's worth a try," said John.

After breakfast, Thomas headed for his shovel, while John rode off to send a telegram, the contents of which still uncertain. The trip from the claim to Chicken gave him time to think.

It was certainly out of character for the man he thought he knew so well. He struggled to understand what had changed him so. *Was it simply greed?*

Whatever the reason, John now realized he entrusted too much to Van Sant. Complete access to his financial, business, and personal affairs allowed this to happen. He wondered what else Van Sant may have done.

John wasn't sure the lie would succeed in drawing him north, but he had to try. *The further Van Sant was from Valdez, the better.*

* * *

Wayne was leaning back in his chair, staring at the ceiling when John entered the telegraph office. He sat upright and grabbed a stack of papers, then looked his way. "Welcome back."

"Thanks. I've got a couple to send this morning."

"Here you go," said Wayne, handing John the message pad.

The first telegram was easy—he needed to warn Emily to be on the lookout for Van Sant and to steer clear of him if at all possible. It wasn't likely he would return to Valdez, but John wanted to warn her anyway. He framed the wording carefully, not wanting to raise too much alarm. That done, the next was more difficult—he stared at the blank pad.

"Problem?"

"No," said John, dodging the issue. "Just want to make sure I word this correctly."

"Take your time."

John began to write, stopped, then continued. *Yes, this just might work.* John handed the pad back over the counter. "Here you go. This one goes to Chistochina."

"Got it."

"How soon will they go out?"

"Right away," said Wayne as he sat down at the telegraph key and began tapping away.

* * *

As Van Sant walked to the telegraph office, he plotted his next move, should he not hear from Palmer. He expected an answer by now, angered that this game continued to drag on. Five days in Chistochina was too long—five days of inaction. Something better happen soon—this wasn't how he operated.

As he entered the office, the telegraph operator winced, dreading another interaction with the man. Before he could speak, Van Sant beat him to it.

"Anything?"

"Yes, sir. Just came in a short while ago."

"Well, where is it."

"Oh, here, let me get it for you." He fumbled nervously through the short stack of messages, wishing he had set it aside when it first came in. "Ah, here."

Van Sant grabbed it unceremoniously and read.

```
PRESTON VAN SANT
CHISTOCHINA

UNABLE TO TRAVEL NOW. RICH GOLD
STRIKE BEYOND BELIEF. WILLING TO
PARTNER IF YOU COME TO ANGEL
CREEK.

JOHN PALMER
CHICKEN
```

This was unexpected, yet it made him suspicious. Perhaps he truly wanted to reconcile. A smile spread across his face. *Palmer always was naive, too trusting.*

It didn't really matter if Palmer was sincere or not. Here was another opportunity—an opportunity to walk away even richer, no strings attached. It meant even longer before he could return to civilization, but once done, they would be set for life.

"How far to Chicken?"

"Huh?" said the operator, still sitting at the key.

Van Sant didn't like to repeat himself, especially during an interrogation. "How long to Chicken?"

"Oh, uh, I don't know—probably six days, five if you push hard."

Without further word, he left the office for his lodging, all the while kicking himself for delaying so long. *I should have pressed on.*

Though it meant more time on the trail, once he had concluded his business there were other ways south. He vowed not to cover this ground again. From Chicken it was only ninety miles or so to the town of Eagle on the banks of the Yukon River. He could catch a sternwheeler to Whitehorse, then the White Pass and Yukon railroad to Skagway, where passage on a steamer south could be had. This was much better than the return journey he dreaded with each step north. It was all coming together, the money, the gold, a comfortable journey south, and, of course, there was her.

Packing up, he abandoned the spare horse, turned the other toward Chicken, and whipped her hard.

* * *

"Get it sent?" yelled Thomas as he dumped the load of gravel into the sluice.

John waited until he got to the creek to answer. "It's done. I lied about a big gold strike and offered to make him a partner."

Thomas whistled and smiled. "Maybe it'll come true."

"I don't make it a habit of lying, but in this case..."

"You had to. Now what?"

"We wait I guess. I'll probably make a quick trip to town each morning to see if we get a response."

"I'm going to have to change our split if you keep dodging work," said Thomas, trying to keep a straight face.

"I'm sorry about that, but it looks like you're making good progress on your own."

"No worries. I think we're going to be ready for a cleanup soon." He handed a shovel to John. "Move some dirt, it'll take your mind off things."

* * *

August 27, 1903

Two days and still no word from Van Sant. This left them wondering if the deception worked. John felt the daily trips to check were a waste of time, but an unfortunate necessity. The work on the claim was a welcome diversion, yet with each passing day they became more alert, not knowing if and when Van Sant would make an appearance.

After four days of running gravel, the pile had shrunk to half its size and Thomas was eager to cleanup. John felt that the gold, if there was any, was safer in the box should Van Sant appear, but knew he couldn't fight the enthusiasm of his young partner.

"Okay, you've convinced me—let's do it," said John. "What's the first step?"

Thomas stared at the box for a moment. The idea was simple—get the gravel out of the box and pan it down to get the gold. After all the hard work running the gravel, he was concerned about washing the gold downstream. Clearly the first step was to shut off the water.

"Can you go upstream and turn off the creek?" said Thomas.

John laughed. "Sure, no problem. How about you just put the gate in the head of the box."

"That works too. Then what?"

John moved toward the head of the box, then turned and grinned. "Get the gold."

Thomas realized that an elevated sluice box would have made cleanup much easier, but in their hurry to get started, that idea never formed. Even though they could shut off the water, there was still the issue of pulling the riffles and flushing the box without all the material going out the end of the box.

Thomas shoved the gate into the slots at the head of the box, causing the water to boil up and nearly overflow into the sluice.

"We have to open up the wing dam, otherwise we're going to flood everything out," he shouted.

John nearly dove into the creek and began rolling away the bigger boulders in the dam to cut down the flow. With a four-foot section of the dam opened, the flow subsided to a manageable level.

"Now what?" said John.

"Can you fetch that big wash tub from behind the cabin while I start digging a hole at the foot of the box?"

"Ah, got it," said John, realizing the plan.

Thomas took a shovel and moved to the downstream end of the box. Digging away in the water, he worked at creating a hole big enough for the wash tub. To catch all the material in the box, the tub would have to fit under the lip of the sluice.

John returned with the tub and watched Thomas labor away in the water. Digging gravel in the water was quite inefficient. Thomas would get a good load on the shovel, but as he brought it up to toss it aside, the water washed half or more back into the hole.

"Looks like fun," said John. "I think we're going to have to do some renovation on our setup if we plan to do more of this."

Thomas grunted and continued working, finding that scraping the gravel away and downstream worked far better than trying to shovel it out. "Let's try it," he said, after another ten minutes of effort.

John handed him the tub and he put all his weight on it to sink it in the hole, then shoved it forward until the edge was under the lip of the box. As soon as he let go, the tub drifted up and out of position.

He sunk the tub again and held it underwater. "Get me a big rock."

John splashed into the creek and dislodged a boulder weighing nearly twenty pounds, then set it carefully into the tub while Thomas held it in position.

The tub remained in place, the rim just sticking above the water by an inch or so.

"That'll do," said Thomas. "Let's pull the riffles."

Thomas went along each side of the box, knocking out the wedges that held down the riffles. With that done, they each grabbed a side and pulled. Nothing happened.

"They're stuck—what's going on?" said John.

It only took a moment for them to realize the problem. Very small rocks had worked their way into the tiny gap between the riffles and side wall of the box, preventing their removal.

"We're going to need a pry bar," said Thomas. He headed up the hill to the cabin while John continued to struggle with the riffles, but made no progress.

Thomas returned with a pry bar, a small block of wood, and a hoe. Working his way along with the pry bar and block, he loosened the riffles, careful not to put too much pressure on any one section. "We're going to need a bit of flow to wash the gravel off the riffles before we flush everything into the tub."

John moved to the head of the box and slowly lifted the gate until a couple of inches of water filled the box.

"That's enough." Thomas worked the riffles up and down, rinsing them clean of gravel.

"See any gold?"

"Not yet—too much material still in the box."

Thomas was tempted to start pawing through the gravel looking for nuggets, but decided to get on with the job at hand.

"I think the riffles are clean," he said, carefully turning them over and looking for any remaining material. He sat them on the creek bank and fetched the hoe. From the lower end of the sluice, he worked at scraping material into the tub, careful not to wash any down the creek. "Give me a little more water."

Little by little, John opened the gate until there was enough water to begin moving the material down the box. Thomas continued working his way up the box with the hoe.

"Look!" shouted John, pointing at the area near where the first riffle had been. "Nuggets!"

Thomas nearly fell in the creek trying to get a look. John was already bent over, picking gold from the box.

"How big?" said Thomas, his eyes wide.

John held out his hand to reveal three nuggets, nearly the size of a pumpkin seed and just as flat. Thomas took one and held it in his hand, mesmerized by the golden sheen.

"I can't believe it. We actually found something."

"Yes," said John, "but where did it come from?"

He was right. There was obviously a pay streak up on the bench where the shaft was sunk, but with it caved and unusable, they had no idea which direction the previous owners had drifted, if at all.

"Well, we'll just have to figure it out," said Thomas. "Let's get the rest of the material in the tub. I can't wait to see what we have." He handed the nugget back to John. "Pocket those and make sure you don't lose them."

Together they worked the rest of the material down the box and into the tub. Thomas took a gold pan and splashed the sides of the box to get every last little piece of material from the sluice. Altogether, it looked like five gallons or more to pan down. Using his pan, Thomas bailed as much water out of the tub as he could. John removed the big rock and made sure it was clean before he tossed it into the creek.

"Let's see if we can get this ashore without spilling anything," said Thomas.

They each grabbed a handle and struggled to lift their treasure out of the creek and up onto the bank. It was heavy, but not more than they could handle.

"Whew," said Thomas, sitting down next to the tub and wiping the sweat from his forehead.

"How do you want to do this?" said John.

Rubbing his head, Thomas stared at the gravel in the tub. "Seems like that's a lot to pan."

"I agree, but it couldn't be any more work than shoveling half that pile through the box."

"True. How about you work on washing off some of the larger rocks and tossing them while I run up to the cabin and fetch something."

"What are..." John began, but Thomas was already out of earshot.

John sat down and started pawing through the tub of gravel, taking the larger rocks and, after making sure they were washed well, tossing them back into the creek.

This will take forever, he thought as he rubbed the sticky clay from yet another rock.

"This will help," said Thomas, shouting over the noise of the creek as he returned.

John looked up to see him carrying yet another tub and what looked like a large screen.

"What's your plan for those?"

Thomas dropped the tub next to him. "We'll screen the material down, toss the oversize, and have less to pan."

John looked at the screen. "What about losing the nuggets?"

"It's a half-inch screen. We should be able see any nuggets that big."

Placing the screen over the second tub, Thomas began to shovel from the other tub onto the screen while John shook it back and forth.

"That's working well," said John. He tossed another screen full of oversize, being careful to paw through it first in case a big nugget was hiding.

"Yep. Should get us down to a more reasonable amount to pan."

They worked at it without pause, taking turns shoveling and screening. Much to their dismay, no large nuggets appeared on the surface of the screen, despite their extreme diligence.

Tossing the last screen full of washed rocks, Thomas took off his hat, wiped his forehead with his handkerchief, and sat down. He pulled out his tobacco pouch and began rolling a cigarette. "Time for a smoke break."

"I'll go for that, but I think we missed lunch—again."

Thomas realized he was hungry, but not hungry enough

to let the washtub of screened gravel sit. "I'm going to finish this smoke and get to panning. I can eat later."

"You are sure anxious," said John, not admitting that he was excited to see what their labor had brought.

Thomas flicked the remainder of his cigarette into the creek. "Hand me those two gold pans."

"Two?"

"Yep, I need one for a safety pan."

"Ah."

Thomas filled his pan with concentrate from the tub, submerged it in the creek, and worked it back and forth vigorously to settle the gold. Holding it over the empty pan, he began to work the excess material off, repeatedly swirling the pan to make sure no gold was lost. It took a good ten minutes to work the material down to a mason jar's worth.

"See anything yet?" said John.

"Just about to look." Thomas swirled the pan and tipped it upward to gently move the black sands away. "Got some."

John rushed over to look, only to see a few meager flakes in the bottom of the pan. "That's it? Pretty small and not much of it."

"Put some water in that jar and hand it to me." Thomas stared into the pan, using his finger to isolated the flakes from the black sand.

"Yes, sir!" said John, hurriedly grabbing the jar and dipping it in the creek.

"Sorry, I should have said 'please'."

John smiled and handed him the jar. "No worries. I know you're just too focused on that yellow stuff."

Thomas touched his finger to each flake, then dipped it in the water, dropping the gold to the bottom of the jar.

"That's going to be slow going," said John.

"You're right. I think we need to change tactics."

"I'm concerned with how little you got in that first pan," said John.

"Well, we did shake the tub up pretty good. Most of the gold should be at the bottom."

"True. So how do we speed this process up?"

"Let's pan it down as best we can, then put the concentrate in jars. We can work at getting the fine gold out later."

"Sounds reasonable, but I'd rather be picking nuggets."

"I'm just going to check this safety pan to see if I missed anything."

Thomas quickly panned the contents of the safety pan, only to find a couple of very small pieces of gold remaining. *Not bad, but I need to improve my technique a bit,* he thought.

"How's it look?"

"Not too bad. I missed a couple of fines."

John laughed. "I guess that won't break the bank."

"Grab a couple of pans and let's get to it," said Thomas.

Working together, they slowly made their way through the tub of gravel, collecting the concentrates, but not able to resist swirling the pan now and then to see if anything glimmered. Stepping up the pace, they were down to the last few shovel-fulls of gravel.

"This should be the good stuff," said Thomas.

"Hope so. We're not getting rich so far."

"True, but at least we're getting some gold, even though it's kinda small."

Thomas filled John's pan, then tipped the tub up and scraped the remainder of the gravel into his. Using his hand, he repeatedly splashed water from the creek up into the tub to wash every last bit of gravel into his pan.

They now worked more slowly, hoping to find real money in the last two pans. Thomas worked the material down, flicking the larger pebbles out of the pan until only a few cupfuls remained. *The moment of truth,* he thought.

He slowly tipped the pan up as he swirled it, bit by bit moving the black sand aside. One last swirl revealed a long, thick line of gold, most of it flat and smaller than a pea, but with several nicer chunks. He smiled broadly and showed the pan to John. "I did pretty good."

"Looks good! How much you think that is?"

"Not sure, but I'd say with this and the rest of it we're talking several ounces. How about you?"

John turned back to his pan. "I'm not quite done."

Thomas looked at the pan and realized it was still two-thirds full. "Want me to finish that for you?"

"No, I can get it."

"Okay, I'll start putting the sluice back together. We still have a lot of that pile to go."

Thomas replaced the riffles in the sluice, driving the wedges in to hold them securely, all the while keeping an eye on John. He opened the head gate to allow the water to flow through the sluice, then began to repair the wing dam to get the flow in the box moving. He looked at John who was now picking through the gravel in his pan rather than actually panning. He stopped for a moment and watched.

Thomas could see John move the material in the pan around with his index finger, pick something up, smile, and put it in his pocket. Unaware he was being watched, this continued for several minutes until Thomas decided it was time to step in.

Thomas stepped out of the creek and looked over John's shoulder. "Finding anything?"

Startled, John jumped, nearly dumping the pan. "You scared me," he said, then smiled and reached into his pocket. "Look at these." John held out half a dozen nuggets, some larger than those picked out of the sluice box. He dumped the nuggets into Thomas' outstretched hand. "I wanted to surprise you."

"Amazing," said Thomas, staring at the gold sparkling in the sunlight. He handed the nuggets back to John. "Here, take these. I'm going to finish your pan."

John took the nuggets, smiled, and didn't resist. "Bet the bottom of that pan is going to be good."

Thomas worked the material down quickly but carefully, anxious to see the result. Within minutes he reduced the contents of the pan down to where the gold was visible—and there was a lot of it.

"Look at this—more than I had in mine!"

John looked at the thick band of gold in the pan and whistled. "We have to get all this cleaned up and weigh it."

"I think we're going to have quite a lot," said Thomas, adding the concentrate to the jar. "I'll pan this all down, then we can dry it on the stove in the cabin to finish separating it."

"Sounds good," said John, reaching into his pocket. "Here, take a couple of these for good luck."

Thomas held out his hand and two nuggets landed with a thud. He marveled at the weight and the beauty of each. Even though they were smaller than the nugget old man Haskell wore in Seattle, they were better—they were his.

* * *

August 29, 1903

Thomas emptied another wheelbarrow of gravel into the sluice. "Maybe he's not coming."

Another two days, and still Van Sant had not made an appearance, nor was there any word from him at the telegraph office.

"Maybe," said John. "I'm tempted to stop going down to check for a telegram every day. Seems pointless—since he never answered my last, I don't expect anything more from him now."

"At this point we have no idea what he's doing. I guess we just need to be vigilant until we can determine his intentions."

John looked at the carbine strategically leaned up against a large boulder bordering the creek. *I hope it doesn't come to that.*

* * *

He pushed the horse hard, harder than reason dictated, but it made no difference. The end was in sight—one final deed and the hardship would cease—the rest would flow easily. *One more miserable night in a tent in the middle of nowhere,* he thought, jabbing his heels hard into the horse's ribs.

He shivered, still trying to shake off the cold that

invaded his entire body overnight. The end of August brought the changing of the season, and cold temperatures in the mountains. He looked northward, hoping the snow that draped the higher peaks would refrain from descending until his business was done.

Van Sant wasn't sure exactly where he was, but he knew he was getting close. Roadhouses were few and far between on this stretch of the trail, but it didn't matter. He couldn't afford the luxury of timing his travel to coincide with a good night's rest in a real bed.

The trail had been following the contours of the hills high above a fairly large river. Rounding a corner, Van Sant saw a bridge in the distance, several hundred feet below his elevation. He pushed the horse again with a swift kick, but she balked as she slipped on the rocky trail. He backed off—no point in risking a fall now.

"Mosquito Fork," he said, reading the crude sign that marked the bridge. He dismounted, tied the horse off to the sign post, then pulled the map from his pack. Using the crude scale on the map, he confirmed what his gut told him—forty miles to Chicken.

He looked out his pocket watch—11 a.m. *Too far to make it today,* he thought. But he would be there tomorrow—not in time to conclude his business, but at least he would be off the trail. *I can wait one more day—this will be done right,* he thought, smiling to himself as he folded the map and pressed on.

* * *

John put another log in the wood stove and closed the door. "Almost finished?"

Thomas ran the small magnet over the gold concentrate that was spread out on a newspaper on the table.

"Not quite, but I don't think you need to stoke the fire anymore—I'm done cooking the gold."

"I know, but it's going to be a cold one tonight and I want to be warm when I retire."

The temperatures at night were now dipping into the low thirties, and there was a light frost each morning. This filled John with a sense of urgency and anticipation, trying to determine when they should head south before winter really hit.

"We have another month before it snows, I'll bet," said Thomas.

"I don't want to find out," said John. "I want to be firmly planted in Valdez before that happens. You can already see it dusting Taylor Mountain."

Thomas continued to work on separating the gold from the remaining black sand and grit. Using the wood stove and a gold pan, they cooked the material to dry it completely, then spread it out on newspaper on the table. The process consisted of picking out the bigger chunks, then using the magnet to pull out the black sand. Lastly, the remaining gold was separated from the grit by blowing gently across the paper, leaving the fine gold.

"Two nights in a row working on this—gotta be a better way," said Thomas, even though he was happy to see the mason jar filling slowly with bright, shiny gold.

John hefted the jar carefully so as not to shatter it on the dirt floor of the cabin. "How much do we have?"

"We'll know soon, but with the nuggets added in I think we're pushing twelve ounces."

John frowned.

"What's wrong?"

"Twelve ounces? That's roughly two hundred and forty dollars at current prices."

"That's good."

"I was hoping for more."

"We haven't really processed that much material. I think we're doing good, especially when we get set up to move a lot more gravel per day."

"I guess so," said John.

"You were expecting to come up and pick nuggets off the ground, eh?"

John laughed. "In my dreams, I guess."

"Look, another day or two and we'll have that stock-pile licked, then we can cleanup the sluice and go from there."

"Right," said John, grabbing another log and heading for the stove.

"Hold up. You're going to drive me outta here tonight if you keep stoking that thing."

John hesitated, then opened the stove and quickly shoved the log in. He turned toward Thomas, a big smile on his face. "Just one more."

* * *

August 30, 1903

It rained overnight, morning breaking with a damp chill hanging over the late August landscape. The willows were already turning yellow and the pucker brush in the high country was a deeper red each day.

Van Sant cursed as he recklessly stuffed his wet gear in the pack and loaded up the horse. *Miserable. I won't need this slop tonight*, he thought, hoping to be lodged firmly in the roadhouse at Chicken. He finished his coffee, kicked dirt on the campfire and mounted up. As he slapped the reins and nudged the horse, it began to snow.

He pulled his coat tight around his neck as he rode, shivering slightly in the morning air. The threat of an early winter was constant in his mind, driving him forward with a sense of urgency. He pushed the horse harder, all the while rehearsing the plan that would be set in motion tomorrow.

* * *

"Cold last night, wasn't it," said John.

Thomas kicked the door shut with one foot, a big load of frost-covered firewood in his arms. He dropped the wood next to the stove. "A bit chilly. There's a pretty heavy frost out there."

"I'm thinking we may have to leave sooner than we

planned. I don't want to be caught here when freeze up hits."

Thomas knew their time was limited. As the temperatures dropped, so would the flow in the creek, eventually bringing an end to any further sluicing. He hoped to process more gravel than just the stockpile, but it all depended on the weather.

"About that..." said Thomas.

"Yes?"

"I think I'm going to stay," said Thomas, dropping the news unexpectedly.

John set down his coffee cup and looked at him, eyebrows raised. "What do you mean stay? Over the winter?"

"Yes."

"That's all you have to say? How will you get by? We sold half our supplies, there isn't enough firewood cut for the winter, and this cabin has enough holes in the walls to freeze you solid if the wind starts blowing."

"There's a bit of work to do to get ready, I'll admit that."

"I'll say. And it's not a bit, it's a bucketful of work. And what about Emily?"

Thomas stared at the dirt floor for a moment. "Well, she may not like it, but I think it's the chance I've been waiting for—to be able to support her once we do get married."

"I don't think it's wise. Too much can go wrong up here by yourself."

"I won't be the first man to spend the winter alone in Alaska," said Thomas, immediately realizing he sounded a bit surly.

"I can't stay," said John. "There's too many loose

ends I need to take care of, and I certainly don't want to leave Emily alone all winter."

"I didn't figure you would stay."

"Promise me you'll reconsider."

"I'll think about it, but my mind is pretty well made up."

John poured the last of the coffee into his tin cup, then sat down on the bunk.

"I'm going to get to work," said Thomas, grabbing his hat and heading out the door.

John sat staring into his coffee. He should have seen this coming, given his future son-in-law's ambition and tenacity. Not only did it mean Thomas would spend the winter alone, he was now faced with a solo journey south—something that didn't appeal at all.

Conflicted, he had a decision to make—when to leave. If Thomas was going to stay he could certainly use the help to get ready for the first snowfall. On the other hand, there was a nearly two week journey ahead of him in ever decreasing temperatures. Though he fought it, resentment built as his cup emptied. *Thomas is thinking only of himself,* he thought.

* * *

By the time John made his way to the creek, Thomas had already made several trips with the wheelbarrow from the winter dump to the sluice and was in the middle of dumping a load into the box. John silently took up a position at the stockpile, pulling the shovel from the gravel where Thomas left it. Thomas returned with the empty wheelbarrow.

"Look," said John. "I understand your desire to stay, but certainly you can see my position, can't you?"

Thomas took the other shovel and dug into the pile, dumping the gravel into the wheelbarrow, John looking at him all the while.

"Well?" said John.

Thomas took off his hat, slapped it against his leg to clear the dust, then stared at the ground for a moment. Finally he looked up.

"I know you're against my staying. I know Emily won't like it—"

"But?"

"But this is why I came to Alaska. We're just getting started here and leaving just doesn't sit well with me. I have to stay."

"And do what? You plan to sit up here in the dark in that musty cabin all winter?"

"No, I plan to mine."

"How?"

"I'm going to drift mine and stockpile pay over the winter."

John looked at him through a squint. "You can't drift mine by yourself."

"I think I can."

"How do you hoist out of the shaft? You going to go up with each bucket of dirt, dump it, and then go back down? You'll make little progress that way."

Thomas sighed. They disagreed in the past, but only in a minor way. This was the first time he and John were truly at odds, but he was stubborn enough not to give in.

"If you're going to stay, you have a lot of work to do in the next month. I think we need to pay Frank a visit."

"Why?"

"Let's get his take on your plan," said John, hoping Frank would make it clear a one-man drift operation was not only inefficient, but downright dangerous. *Then Thomas will return with me for the winter.*

"Good idea," said Thomas. "I need his advice on how to get started anyway. Let's ride over there after supper."

* * *

"It's a tough proposition," said Frank, handing each of them a cup of hot coffee.

"In what way?" said Thomas.

"Well, drift mining is nothing but hard work, and going it solo is darn near impossible."

Thomas sat down his coffee and rubbed his forehead. Already the conversation was headed in a direction he didn't like. "But it's been done before, right?"

"Probably, but I can't remember anyone around here doing it. Is your ground good enough to even consider it?"

"The stockpile has been promising," said Thomas, "but we—"

"I guess that clinches it," said John. "Looks like you'll be heading south with me."

Thomas shot him a glance.

"You could hire someone to help you," said Frank unexpectedly.

"Who?" said Thomas.

"Well, there's a bunch of folks in Chicken that winter over after the mining season. I'm pretty sure you can scare up someone to help."

"We don't have much in the way of cash to pay wages," said John, hoping to quash the idea.

"Most guys around here will work for a percentage of the take after it's processed," said Frank.

"What percentage?" said Thomas.

"Well, that depends on how rich your ground is I guess. I'd suggest some sort of guaranteed amount plus five or ten percent of the take."

"Is that pretty standard?"

"Don't know about standard, but if you can't pay an hourly wage, it's about all you're going to get someone around here to accept."

"Sounds workable to me," said Thomas, looking at John.

"You know my objections."

"Look fellas," said Frank. "You bought a drift mine. Most drift miners dig in the winter and sluice in the summer. If that's not in your game, you best get out now."

"Most?" said Thomas.

"Well, some operations are drifting and sluicing in the summer. That way they don't have to thaw gravel in the summer to sluice the winter dump. Been thinking about going that route myself, but haven't yet. Be nice to spend the winter south for once."

"Maybe we should sell," said John.

"And do what?" said Thomas.

Frank intervened again. "With the gold you got out of the stockpile you can probably convince a buyer, but I'm betting you'll not recover your cost. What did you pay?"

"We paid—" began Thomas.

"Let's just say we're into it for several thousand when you consider our supply costs," said John, not being in the habit of providing specifics of his financial dealings.

"Going to be tough to get that for it, especially this time of year. There's a lot of other ground for sale around here—ground with proven reserves. Yours is still an unknown," said Frank.

"We need to follow this through," said Thomas.

John stared into his empty coffee cup. They went into debt to Stella for nearly the whole amount. It was a risk, but at the moment, there seemed little else to do but hang on to the claim. With little money of his own remaining, he felt cornered—unless he could recover his fortune from Van Sant.

"Okay," said John, "but you're going to write a letter to Emily explaining why I show up in Valdez without you."

"Done," said Thomas without reservation.

"Now," said Frank, "what's your plan?"

Thomas looked puzzled. "What do you mean?"

"How are you going to get started drifting?"

"Well, I guess we need to repair that shaft first."

"That'll be tough going this time of year, but you might be able to timber it as you go until you get the thawed muck out of the way and get into frozen ground."

"Sounds messy," said John.

"Well, it's best to be doing this work in frozen ground rather than thawed," said Frank, "but if you can get it cleaned up now, you'll be ahead of the game. Just remember, if you don't insulate it you'll continue to have problems."

"It's getting cooler now," said Thomas.

"Yep, that'll help. Your other option is to sink a new shaft, but you know the old one found pay."

Thomas didn't want to start over. Getting the old shaft fixed up would allow them to start stockpiling pay much sooner, assuming they could fix it without difficulty. "I think we'll give the old shaft a go and see if we can't open her up."

"You're going to need some timber. Ever timbered a mine before?"

Thomas laughed, then realized it wasn't really a funny question. "No."

"Come around tomorrow and I'll give you a peek at how we're set up."

"Sounds good. I guess we better head back to the claim—kept you long enough for one night."

"Here's the names of a couple of experienced fellas that will likely be happy to work through the winter," said Frank, handing Thomas a scrap of paper.

"Thanks for your help, Frank," said Thomas as they got up to leave, "and the coffee."

The twilight ride back to the claim was mostly silent, Thomas excited at the winter that lay before him, John dreading the trip south and the explanations that must follow.

* * *

August 31, 1903

Thomas woke early, his mind racing with all the things to accomplish before freeze-up. First order of business was to hire a worker—everything hinged on that. Stumbling around to stoke the fire and get coffee going, he woke John.

"What's all the racket?"

"Sorry, couldn't sleep any longer. Just trying to get some coffee on."

"A little early to be out shoveling. Still dark, isn't it?"

"Still dark, but I'm heading to Chicken this morning to see if I can hire someone.

John sat up in his bunk and rubbed his eyes. "They're probably all still working since the season isn't over. What makes you think you'll find them in town?"

"Good point. I guess I'll head over to Frank's first to see if he can tell me where to find them."

"Good plan, except I don't think their boss will be happy with you trying to hire them away while it's still sluicing season."

"You're probably right. Wouldn't hurt to make some inquiries though, would it?"

"I guess not—if you have to," said John.

Secretly he hoped Thomas would fail in finding labor and be forced to abandon his foolish plan of fixing the shaft and mining through the winter. In his mind, the best they could hope for was to put the claim up for sale next summer and try to recover some of their cost.

"I'll just see if I can set things up for when the season is over," said Thomas.

"What will you do in the meantime?"

"Depends on how long you're staying."

John mulled it over, not wanting to commit to anything and still hoping to bring Thomas back to Valdez with him. Barring that, he resigned himself to leave as early as possible—yet there was guilt in abandoning Thomas unprepared for winter. "Don't know yet. Are you sure I can't get you to come back with me?"

"Nope. I'm staying." Donning his hat and coat, he walked out the door, leaving John staring at his empty cup.

* * *

Van Sant yawned as he lifted his second cup of coffee. He arrived late in Chicken the night before and had a restful night, despite what he considered the primitive conditions of the roadhouse. With his goal in sight, his attitude changed—he was in no hurry to rush in headlong. He had to proceed carefully, without arousing suspicion. Inquiries must be made, some reconnaissance accomplished before completing the task.

If it took a few days it didn't matter now. There was still time to make it to the Yukon River and catch a sternwheeler south before freeze up. First order of business was to get directions to Angel Creek. His hand could be forced, however, if he encountered Palmer in Chicken—something that would make things all the more difficult and attract unwanted attention.

No, he would lay low, be discreet, move carefully.

* * *

"Come to see how it's done?" said Frank as Thomas rode up.

Frank was standing near the creek, watching his crew as they sluiced the remainder of last winters drifting. Thomas was impressed—the operation was well thought out, with an elevated sluice box and a permanent dam to control water flow.

Thomas dismounted and shook Frank's extended hand. "Looks like you have a good operation going. Much easier to clean up than our little setup."

Frank smiled. "You'll want something similar if you're going to get serious about your operation."

"I can see that." Thomas examined the sluice box and dam, noting how everything was situated to make processing stockpiled gravel more efficient. "Can I see the shaft?"

"I'll show you the windlass and the covered shaft, but we won't be opening it up today—don't want to risk any thawing."

They walked a short way from the creek, climbing the bench to where the shaft was located. The windlass was set over the shaft and was powered by a small steam boiler nearby. The shaft opening was boarded over and covered with what appeared to be several layers of dirt and moss.

"Here she is," said Frank. "Not much to look at this time of year."

Thomas looked over the setup and realized his was going to be much more primitive. "I don't have a boiler."

"You can operate the windlass by hand, or use a horse to raise and lower your bucket."

The bucket itself was quite large, obviously meant

to haul a good load of gravel with each trip. Thomas thought the setup was ingenious, with a cable that ran to the dump area and a self-dumping mechanism for the bucket, all powered by steam.

"I'm not sure we can afford to get set up like you are," said Thomas, worrying that his plan may be in jeopardy.

"Well, you can start small, with a hand-operated windlass and dumping into a chute and wheelbarrow. Be a lot more work, but at least it would get you going and you'd be able to prove up your ground—see if it's worth going bigger."

"I see. Looks like I'm going to have to elevate that old windlass to do that."

Frank smiled. "Yup. You've got a lot of work ahead of you."

Thomas held back a sigh. He just wanted to get into the gold, but there was a huge amount of work ahead before that would happen, especially if John deserted him early—and he still had no idea of how to actually mine once the shaft was repaired.

"So I just get the shaft opened up then start hauling gravel up from underground?"

Frank laughed. "If only it were that simple."

Frank went on to explain that once the shaft was down to bedrock, a drift running parallel to the creek needed to be constructed, both upstream and down. With that complete, perpendicular side drifts were run at regular intervals. Beginning at the end of the main drift, the gravel was extracted in a retreating manner, allowing the workings to cave as progress was made towards the shaft.

"Whew," said Thomas. "That's way more than I anticipated."

"My guess is you'll be lucky to get your main drift

down and perhaps one or two side drifts this winter. The good news is, all that will be gravel you can sluice. Hopefully those crooks you bought the claim from sunk the shaft near the middle of the pay streak, otherwise you'll have to adjust your plan."

"How can I tell?"

Frank tipped up his hat and laughed. "Well, you probably won't know until it's all mined, but it's important to keep sampling your gravel as you drift to make sure you aren't hauling worthless material top-side."

"Makes sense," said Thomas, more overwhelmed than he was a minute ago.

"Take it slow. If I were you, I'd use the windlass you have for now, and timber the shaft as you clear the muck. You can get by using spruce poles for most of the cribbing."

"Last time I was in that shaft I nearly sunk up to my shoulders and had to be pulled out."

"Well, you know better now. Get a ladder and anchor it at the top so you don't have to sink out of sight."

"Good idea," said Thomas, wondering why he didn't think of it himself.

"When do you think you'll start?"

"I'm ready to get things started today, if I can get John on-board."

"Sounded like he was ready to head south."

"Yes, he's worried about leaving me here because of the effect it will have on his daughter, especially if things take a turn for the worse."

Frank nodded. "Ah. I think you have another good month before things start to freeze solid—but you never know how the weather will go around here."

"Not sure John will want to stay that long."

Frank didn't say anything as he turned and headed in the direction of the sluice box.

"Oh, I wanted to ask you how to find those fellows you suggested yesterday."

"I'm pretty sure they're both still working. I suggest you wait a couple weeks before approaching them—wouldn't want their boss to come after you with his scatter gun."

Thomas laughed, realizing that Frank was joking—at least partially.

"Okay, I'll check with you in a couple of weeks. Right now I've got a ton of work to do."

Frank watched Thomas mount up and head off. Turning to bark orders at his crew, he thought, *That boy is gonna get an education this winter.*

* * *

After driving the horse hard back to the claim, Thomas could barely contain himself as he told John everything he learned. John didn't understand half of what Thomas was saying, particularly the part about parallel drifts, perpendicular drifts, and caving ground.

"Sounds pretty complicated—and labor intensive," said John.

"It is, but Frank will help us out. I'm anxious to get started."

"What about our stockpile and the gold we have in the sluice? There's still a few days work to finish that up."

Thomas thought for a moment, torn between getting the rest of the gold in the pile of gravel and getting started on the shaft. "You mean the winter dump," he said finally.

"What?"

"The stockpile—it's called a winter dump."

"Oh, more mining terms. I stand corrected."

"I'm inclined to get started on clearing the shaft since the winter work depends on that. According to Frank we still have a good month before things freeze up tight."

John sighed. *Decision time was near.* "One thing we've forgotten in the last couple of days."

"What's that?"

"Van Sant."

The threat still loomed large, and Thomas was slack in keeping an eye out, even leaving the carbine at the cabin during his morning trip. For that matter, they didn't even know if he was coming or if it was all a bluff. "We need to be more careful. Better keep your rifle handy from now on."

"For how long?" said John. "I wish I knew what he was up to."

"Well it's been days since the last telegram and no confirmation he even received yours. He could be close for all we know."

"I know, that's what worries me."

"I'm planning to take the wagon down to Chicken and get a few things we'll need to start on the shaft. I'll stop in at the telegraph office and see if they have anything for us."

"I'll go with you."

"I really think it's better if you stay here. Van Sant doesn't know what I look like and, since we don't know his intentions or whereabouts, you'd be better off here than meeting him on the road somewhere."

"Good point," said John. "I'll go run some more gravel, but keep the ole' Winchester nearby."

* * *

Van Sant found the proprietor of the roadhouse quite helpful, providing him with directions to Angel Creek. The ruse of being a "partner" from the south was fully swallowed. *Mindless fools*, he thought as he rode along, his hat pulled low and his collar high.

The trail to Angel Creek wound along the Mosquito Fork valley, then up a ridge line to a fork. So far he met no one along the way, but was watchful nonetheless. Once at the fork he was to bear right, following another ridge for a short distance to where the trail forked again, one branch descending into the creek and the other continuing along the ridge.

After winding to the creek bottom, the trail meandered up to the claim site. He planned to approach it a bit differently, not wanting to be seen on the stretch along the creek, should Palmer or his partner happen to be on the trail.

It took him nearly thirty minutes to reach the fork, passing only one grizzled old fellow headed downhill on foot. In another ten minutes he was at the second fork, where he paused to survey the trail leading down to the creek. Seeing no one, he continued.

Van Sant crossed the creek and, rather than following the trail upstream, detoured into the brush and black spruce, navigating the series of benches paralleling the creek. *This should be high enough*, he thought, reaching the third bench above the creek, which was now nearly four hundred yards below. He dismounted and, pulling out his binoculars, scanned from the trail below him as far upstream as he could see. *Nothing.*

The proprietor of the roadhouse told him there was a cabin and the owners were actively sluicing gravel. The word sluicing meant little to him, mining being an occupation for the lower class. So far, there was no evidence of activity along the creek. Mounting up, he pushed further upstream along the high bench, stopping occasionally to glass the area below. Finally he was in sight of the head of the valley, the brush thinning as he continued on. He was now a good five hundred yards above the creek, with a clear view of most of the drainage. Then he saw it—*movement.*

Training the binoculars on the trail far below, it came into view. It was a man driving a wagon down the trail, apparently headed toward town. Van Sant struggled to focus on the person, but all he could be sure of was a man with a hat, driving an empty wagon.

His first impulse was to fall in behind and slowly advance, then finish his task. Restraint took hold. *It might not even be him.* Realizing he didn't know what Thornton looked like, he couldn't risk revealing himself and word getting back to Palmer. Surprise was essential. He made note of the wagon so as to recognize it again, then continued scanning the drainage.

Though the brush and trees had thinned, he still found it difficult to get a good look at everything. Moving around allowed him to gain a better view, finally realizing the dark object below was the roof of a cabin. *Ah, there they are.*

It only took another minute for him to locate an individual near the creek. At this distance there was no way to tell who it was, but it was clear the person was shoveling into a wheelbarrow and wheeling towards the creek.

Van Sant watched for more than an hour, hoping to determine who he was watching, but it was pointless—he was too far away. Briefly he considered moving in closer, but realized he would be in plain view as he came down the benches to the creek. Approaching along the trail would also leave him open to discovery much sooner than desired. Looking to the head of the valley, another plan began to materialize.

Pushing his horse up the final bench and finally to the ridge line that separated Angel Creek from its neighbor, he dropped just below the backside and traveled to the head of the valley. The creek made a turn to the west just before the head of the valley. Dropping back over the ridge into the Angel Creek drainage, he was now out of view of both the cabin and the man working near the creek.

This will do nicely.

* * *

Thomas returned from Chicken by noon, loaded with lumber and other supplies needed to begin rehabilitation work on the shaft. While most of the cribbing could be done with spruce poles, the shaft cover and upper timbering required rough-cut lumber. Heavy rope was needed for the windlass as well, the weather making the original useless and unsafe. Although the operator of the mill was more than happy to take gold in payment, Thomas found it difficult to part with even a small amount of his treasure—something he did out of necessity.

He drove the wagon to the shaft and began unloading as John walked up from the creek.

"Got everything?" asked John.

"Yes. I'm going to get started building the ladder and repairing the windlass after I grab some lunch."

"Any telegrams?"

"I stopped and asked but there was nothing for either

of us. I sent off a quick one to Emily and Stella just to let them know we were fine."

John rubbed his chin. "I don't know what to make of this whole thing with Van Sant."

"I also asked around to see if there had been anyone new in town asking about us, but drew a blank."

"Maybe he's not coming. He certainly had time to get here by now."

"Could be, but I don't think we should let our guard down—not for a while anyway."

John grabbed another board from the wagon and tossed it on the stack next to the shaft. "Agreed—we need to be careful."

* * *

"Two of them," said Van Sant to himself, watching the men unload the wagon far below. He had made his way around the head of the valley and was now on the ridge on the other side of the creek, tucked in to a small stand of brush.

Still, he could not tell which was Palmer. *No matter, today is not the day*, he thought as he mounted up and crossed over the ridge out of view of the men below.

His scouting mission complete, Van Sant made his way along the backside of the ridge in the general direction of the trail he came in on. Before long he reached the fork he used to descend into Angel Creek.

This is perfect.

His plan of action was now complete. Rather than descending into the creek at the fork, he would head up along the ridge to the head of the valley, then descend. Assuming they were watching for him, they would expect his route to be along the trail from downstream, not above. Hidden from view, he could leave the horse at the head of the valley and discreetly make his way down the creek, choosing cover carefully until he reached them.

Content in his plan, he nudged the horse onward, knowing he wouldn't meet either of them on the return.

He made his way slowly—there was plenty of time.

Another night at the roadhouse it is, and then...

* * *

Thomas was pleased with the progress on the shaft. Together, he and John built a ladder long enough to reach the muck pile at the bottom, with plenty extra sticking above the collar. They shored up the windlass supports and replaced the fraying rope with new, attaching the bucket which was still in serviceable condition. By mid-afternoon they were ready to get down to business.

"How do you want to go about this?" said John.

Thomas thought for a moment. "I'll go down, you lower the bucket and I'll start filling it," he said as he grabbed a shovel and put it in the bucket.

"Okay, just don't step off the ladder or you'll end up over your head."

Thomas stepped onto the ladder and started down. "Right."

Immediately it became clear they had a problem. As he descended, thawing muck from the upper part of the shaft sloughed in, threatening to fill it even more. Thomas climbed back out and stared down the hole.

"Well, that's not going to work," said John.

"We need to get the cribbing in as we go, otherwise it's just going to keep caving on us," said Thomas.

With that, they regrouped and spent the next several hours building a platform around the shaft opening to support the cribbing from the top down. Fortunately Thomas had brought back enough lumber, although some of it was originally meant for an insulating cover. By dinner time, several feet of cribbing was complete, but was still well short of the bottom of the shaft.

"Looks like we won't be doing any digging tomorrow," said John.

"Maybe. I'm thinking of working some more after dinner."

"Don't know about you, but I'm getting tired," said John as they headed for the cabin.

* * *

The light began to fade as Thomas resumed work on the shaft. Working alone, progress was slow. Eventually the darkness crept in and he was forced to stop. *Should have brought a lantern,* he thought as he climbed the ladder and headed toward the cabin.

"Done for the night?" said John.

Thomas closed the door behind him. "Nope, just need a lantern."

"How long you going to work?" said John, feeling a bit guilty for not helping.

"Till I run out of lumber, which won't be too much longer."

Thomas grabbed the spare lantern from the shelf and fueled it, then started for the door.

"I'll give you a hand. I think I'm getting my second wind after having something to eat."

"Thanks, probably won't be out there very long."

John grabbed his coat and followed out the door. The night air was cold, and likely to get colder under the cloudless sky. The chill only served to remind John about the journey that lay before him.

"If you can run the windlass for me I won't have to climb out to fetch more lumber," said Thomas as they arrived at the shaft.

"No problem," said John, looking down the shaft. "Looks like you've made good progress on your own."

Thomas tied the lantern to a spare bit of rope and descended into the shaft which was now properly timbered to a depth of nearly six feet. He hung the lantern to a rung just above him and called to John.

Thomas pressed himself against the ladder. "Send the bucket down, just don't hit me in the head with it."

The bucket came down and Thomas got to work. After several round trips and more hammering, the timbering was extended another foot or so, bringing it near the top of the muck in the shaft.

"I need some more lumber," said Thomas.

"Here you go." John lowered the bucket with the last of the lumber he'd already loaded in anticipation. "That's the last of it."

Thomas tipped the bucket a bit so he could see what was left to work with. "Doesn't look like enough to finish up. Let's call it a night," he said, climbing out of the hole.

Thomas stepped off the ladder and tried to knock some of the muck off his clothes. "I'll head back to the mill in the morning to get the rest of the lumber. Should be able to finish the timbering and actually move some of that muck out of the hole tomorrow."

John nodded. "Sounds good. I'll run more gravel through the sluice while you're gone. Don't know if you noticed, but that pile is getting pretty small."

"Good. After we get some of the muck moved, maybe

we can finish it off and do a final cleanup."

"Right. Now let's get some sleep—you wore me out today."

Thomas grinned and said, "Old man," carefully avoiding the backhand that came swinging by his ear.

* * *

September 1, 1903

The frost still glistened on the pucker brush as Van Sant reached the fork. He left just before first light, wanting to be off the trail before any chance of an encounter. Following his previous route, he left the trail and followed the backside of the ridge above Angel Creek, moving carefully towards the head of the valley.

It was cold. He pulled his collar tight about his neck, wishing he was somewhere else—but only for a moment. His task was too important—too critical for his future.

By the time the sun made it above the hills, he was dropping down into the creek bottom at the head of the valley, out of sight of Palmer's claim. He considered riding down along the creek, but the risk of being seen was too great. He tied off the horse near the creek, leaving enough rope so she could graze and drink. He cared little for the horse, but he would need her later.

Van Sant removed the rifle from the scabbard and took the small backpack, checking to make sure his binoculars were inside. There were two options for moving downstream to a good vantage point. One was to walk along the creek, the other to move along the lowest bench. He considered the creek, but quickly realized he would need to walk in the water a fair bit of the way, as the bank was too steep and mucky. The bench was the better option, as long as he made careful use of cover.

It was slow going, mainly because he had to be wary of being seen. An hour passed and he was still up around the bend, out of sight of his goal. He quickened the pace, making his way through the maze of brush and fallen black spruce.

It happened quickly—stumbling over a root, he fell headlong into tundra, jamming the barrel of his rifle deep into the moss and dirt. He stood up quickly, brushing himself off and cursing the root as if it could care. Realizing the noise the fall and his subsequent tirade made, he quickly ducked down, even though the claim was still well in the distance. *Can't risk it,* he thought.

He moved slower now. There was time.

* * *

Thomas stood over the shaft, coffee in hand, surveying the work from the day before. He was anxious to get down to it and start clearing the muck, but that would have to wait—more lumber was needed first.

He walked slowly back to the cabin, despite the pressure of all that needed done before John left—before winter settled in.

John met him at the cabin door. "Going to be a great day. Looks like plenty of sunshine to drive this frost away."

"You're in a good mood this morning. Guess that late night work did you some good."

"It did good alright. My back feels like a horse used me for a mattress last night."

"You just need to get out there and start shoveling gravel. That'll loosen you up," said Thomas, grinning as he sat his cup down on the table and poured another.

"I figured you'd be anxious to head in for more lumber."

"I am, but I have to give the guy at the mill a chance to have his breakfast. I'm leaving soon."

"We should be able to make good progress today," said John.

"Hope so. I'm anxious to see where the shaft bottoms out. I hope it's not too deep to bedrock."

"Me too."

"Judging from the size of our stockpile, I don't think the workings are very extensive."

"I suspect you're right." John finished up his coffee and grabbed his coat from the hook on the back of the door. "Guess I'll head down to the sluice and get busy."

"Good. I expect you to have it all run by the time I get back," said Thomas, chuckling as he followed him out the door.

* * *

Van Sant crouched in the brush, carefully surveying the creek below. Having rounded the bend in the creek, the claim was now in view. Through binoculars he could see a sluice box and further up the bench, a small pile of gravel. *This is it.*

There was no sign of movement—he scanned further up the bench towards a stand of trees, hoping to catch a glimpse. Slowly the cabin appeared among the trees. He steadied himself against a small tree, struggling to get a clear view.

For five minutes he saw nothing. Lowering the binoculars, he rubbed his eyes, then continued glassing. Finally he spotted it—movement near the cabin. He was able to make out two people moving about. One of them disappeared for a moment, then returned leading a horse. He couldn't tell who was who at that distance, but it appeared the person with the horse was hitching it to a wagon.

He watched intently, trying to determine the best course of action. It wasn't long before the wagon pulled out, leaving a lone individual. Van Sant watched as the other person made his way from the cabin to the gravel pile and began shoveling. *Was it Palmer?*

The wheelbarrow full, the man pushed it down to the creek and dumped it into the sluice box. He stood, removed his hat, turned his face to the morning sun, eyes closed, and wiped his brow. Van Sant had a clear view—it was Palmer.

Immediately he began running over his options. The man on the wagon must be Thornton, unless it was someone else and Thornton was still in the cabin. He waited a while longer and no one else emerged. Palmer continued to work alone.

Perfect, thought Van Sant. With Palmer alone his job was all the easier. No threat of witnesses, no complication of having to deal with both of them. He could take care of business and be gone before Thornton arrived, assuming he was gone to town and would be a while. *Time to move quickly.*

Moving directly toward Palmer was not an option—he would be seen before he got within five hundred yards. He quickly decided to move back up the creek until he was out of sight, then cross and climb the bench. Crossing the shallow creek was easy—climbing the bank of thawing, sloughing muck was not. He struggled, taking two steps forward and sliding one back.

Out of breath and covered in mud from the knees down, Van Sant finally made it out of the creek and up on the bench. He paused for a moment, hoping his position hadn't been revealed. Confident he was still in the clear, he moved further away from the creek toward the base of the second bench. From there he could work his way toward Palmer without being seen.

He inched closer, ever so slowly. Palmer was plainly visible now without the need for binoculars. He raised the rifle and aligned the sights on Palmer's chest. Exhaling, he slowly, steadily applied pressure to the trigger—then stopped. *This is too easy.* No, he would have his say—he didn't come all this way to end it silently. He would make sure Palmer knew who was taking his life, his money, and why.

* * *

John pushed the wheelbarrow to the sluice, tipped it up, and began shaking it back and forth to dump the gravel. A couple of larger rocks hung up in the riffles at the head of the box. Bending over he tossed them out, then fanned the remaining material with his hand to get it moving down the box. Satisfied, he stood and turned—and saw him.

"Hello, John," said Van Sant, rifle cradled in his arms and a twisted smile on his face.

John was silent, sizing up the situation and glancing beyond Preston to the carbine left standing next to the gravel pile.

"Quite a little operation you have here. Seems a bit different than your telegram implied."

"It has promise," said John bluntly. "Why are you here?" he said, delaying the real question that burned in his mind.

"Quite simple, John. I've come to kill you."

Though he suspected Preston was up to no good all along, the revelation from his longtime friend was shocking. He was no longer looking at a man he knew, but a stranger.

"I don't understand. We've been friends forever. Why?"

"That's your problem, John. You just don't get it. You don't see. You never have."

"You're right. I don't understand."

"Where's your partner?"

"He's up at the cabin," said John, lying in hopes of putting Preston off.

"You're a terrible liar, John. I saw him leave with the wagon. Where did he go and when will he be back?"

"He just went down the creek a bit to fetch some timber. He'll be back any moment."

"Again, John, you're a terrible liar. I know you too well. I can tell by your face you're lying."

John started to move towards the gravel pile. Van Sant leveled the rifle at him, stopping him in his tracks.

"You're not going anywhere, John. Not until you've heard me out. Then you'll be going on a one way trip."

John stood his ground. "What do you want? You already have my money."

"Well, it's pretty simple, John. "You're right, I have the money, and what I want is you to go away, permanently."

"I've never done anything to you."

"True, but you've never done anything *for* me either."

"How can you say that? I've employed you and entrusted my finances to you."

Van Sant sneered. "For a pittance."

"You never complained."

"You had all the advantages, all the choice business opportunities while I, your trusted friend, was shut out—forced to work for clients that couldn't pay near what I was worth as a lawyer. You could have cut me in, but you didn't."

"I thought you were doing well," said John, taken aback by the allegation.

"See, you're blind. You lived in a near mansion while I lived in a small flat in Denny Hill."

"I'm sorry you feel that way, but I paid you well."

Van Sant let out a laugh that quickly turned into a sneer. "Well enough in your eyes. I wanted more and I took it. I've been embezzling from you for years but you were too stupid to know."

It now became completely clear to John. Apart from the jealousy and rage, Van Sant was a thief and wasn't about to be caught.

"So I'm a loose end," said John.

"That's all you are to me, nothing more. When you came to Alaska I saw my chance—my chance to have it all."

Suddenly John realized the implication. "Did you set the fire—kill my wife?" he blurted out.

Van Sant laughed aloud. "Your wife? That's hilarious, John."

"What do you mean? Answer me. Did you set the fire?"

"None of that matters now, John," said Van Sant as he raised the rifle. "Your life is over, and what's yours is now mine."

"You're planning to shoot me in cold blood—with that rifle?"

"You're not as stupid as you look. You always did have a flare for the obvious."

"You'll regret it if you pull the trigger."

"Doubt it," said Van Sant. "I've pulled the trigger before."

It wasn't much of a hope, but it was all he had. "Pull the trigger and you're dead—the barrel is full of dirt," said John, contemplating rushing him, but unsure of the outcome.

Van Sant looked shaken for a mere second, remembering the fall and the barrel plunging into the ground. *Too late to clear it,* he thought.

John rushed forward, made it halfway to Van Sant before he dropped the rifle and pulled his .45 from under his coat and aimed it at John's chest.

Before he could slide to a stop, the shot rang out and John rolled to the ground, then back on his feet.

Van Sant was lying on the ground, blood streaming from a hole below his right collar bone. The .45 lay on the ground beside him and fear gripped his face. John moved quickly and kicked the revolver away. Confused, John looked up and it became clear. Thomas was running down the hill towards him, carbine in hand.

"I don't know what you're doing here, but I'm glad you are," said John.

"You all right? said Thomas, his voice quivering. "I forgot the gold pouch so I could pay for the lumber. Left the horse just behind the cabin and went to fetch it when I saw what was going on. I grabbed my carbine and snuck in closer. Didn't want to shoot him in the back but it looked like he was about to fire."

Van Sant groaned, tried to sit up, then fell back to the ground. He was losing blood quickly and began to cough, pink foam spilling from his lips.

"It's fatal," said Thomas, still shaking.

John was torn between trying to save his former friend

and getting the truth. He knelt down beside him and applied pressure to the wound, causing him to wince. Van Sant reached up with his left hand and pulled John close, whispering to him quietly.

"She is mine...waiting...for me," said Van Sant hoarsely, barely audible. "She hated you—you were too stupid to question her attitude, you never..."

John was in shock, unable to fully grasp or accept what he was hearing.

"And the house? The fire?"

"To...cover...up," said Van Sant, his voice even lower. His lungs rattled now with each breath as his grip on John's collar tightened. "You win again, but not...everything," he said, gasping as his arm dropped to his side. He coughed once more, blood spewing from his mouth.

"The money—where is the money?" John shouted at him, but there was no answer, only a cold lifeless stare. John stood, color draining from his face as he looked at Thomas.

"What did he say?"

John couldn't bring himself to vocalize the unbelievable truth. *Could it be that his wife was alive?Lydia—alive?*

* * *

September 2, 1903

Thomas sat in the dimly lit cabin, finishing off his second cup of morning coffee. "Shall we get back at it today?"

"I guess we should," said John. "I need to get my mind off things, but first there is something I must do."

The confrontation with Van Sant the day before ended all work on the claim. John and Thomas wavered on how to handle the situation, but in the end, they loaded his body in the wagon and took it to Chicken. There was no law enforcement in town, but, based on the account of what happened, the residents agreed the act was justified. Briefly there was talk of contacting the military post in Eagle, but ultimately Van Sant was buried in the town cemetery, a simple wooden cross marking his grave.

"What do you need to do?" said Thomas

"I'm going back to town and send a telegram off to my investigator. I need some answers."

On the way to bury Van Sant the day before, John told Thomas of the confession and the possible implications. Thomas found it inconceivable, but his main concern was Emily.

"I should have done it yesterday," said John, "but I was too out of sorts."

"No worries. I'll just run gravel until you get back. One thing bothers me though."

"Only one?"

"True. I never killed a man before. Not something I want to repeat," he said, the image of that moment once again flashing through his mind.

"Terrible, but unavoidable. You saved my life. What else is bothering you?"

"Well, how did Van Sant get down to the claim? He must have a horse, and if so, where is it?"

"Obviously he left it somewhere. He was on foot when he arrived."

"Did you see which direction he came from?"

"No, I was busy dumping a load into the sluice."

"Well, he clearly didn't come up the trail to the cabin or I would have seen him. He must have come from upstream."

"I'll bet you're right."

"While you're off sending your telegram, I'll take the old nag upstream and see if I spot anything. Wouldn't want the poor thing tied off out there somewhere."

John nodded in agreement, grabbed his coat and hat, and headed out. Thomas finished the last gulp of coffee and did the same, heading for the nag to get her saddled up.

"I'll be back as soon as possible," said John as he mounted up. "I don't expect an answer right away so I'm not going to hang around."

"Okay, I'm going to make a quick trip up the creek and then sluice some gravel. When you get back we'll get to work on the shaft."

Thomas mounted up and rode along the first bench, picking his way through the scrub brush and black spruce. He wasn't sure where to look, but felt he had to give it a try rather than leave the animal out there somewhere.

Within twenty minutes he reached the bend in the creek that would take him out of view of their claim. He paused and looked, then seeing nothing, continued on.

A sudden snapping of timber on the bench above brought him to full attention. He stopped the horse, pulled the carbine from its scabbard, and prepared himself. The dark form emerged from the brush above and came barreling down the slope toward him.

Thomas laughed. It was a horse, obviously stressed and trailing its lead. He called to it, talking gently as he dismounted. It walked slowly toward his horse and Thomas was able to grab the lead, all the while soothing it with his voice. *No doubt about it, this has to be Van Sant's horse,* he thought. Tired of being tethered overnight at the head of the creek, the horse had apparently tugged long enough to loosen the knot and set itself free.

Thomas mounted up, lead in hand, and took the horse back to the cabin. He removed the saddle, brushed her down, then staked her out with the old nag to graze. *I guess we just acquired a horse,* he thought. Given the money Van Sant stole from John it was only right—little did Thomas know the origin of the horse.

Satisfied the horses were cared for, he headed for the creek to sluice, hoping to finish off the stockpile soon and cleanup one last time. He was spread pretty thin—sluicing, working on the shaft, fixing up the cabin for winter, and cutting firewood. He dared not think of it all at once, lest he be totally overwhelmed.

* * *

John handed the completed telegram to Wayne.

"I'll get this right out for you."

"Thanks," said John as he turned to leave.

"Heard about that business up on the claim."

John opened the door and paused. "Yeah, it was unfortunate. Thanks again. I'll check back for an answer in a day or so."

"Good enough," said Wayne.

John stepped out on the street and hesitated, then headed in the direction of the roadhouse. As he walked, he hoped his decision not to tell Emily anything was correct—at least for the time being. *I need to handle it in person.*

Reaching the roadhouse, he inquired about Van Sant's stay, hoping to learn something that might help the investigator. The proprietor had little information, indicating only that Van Sant left early the day before, taking all his belongings—obviously not planning on sticking around.

The backpack he was carrying when Thomas shot him didn't contain anything helpful with regard to Lydia or the money. If he was headed out of the country afterward, perhaps his horse was carrying something useful—if Thomas could find it.

* * *

"I see you found the horse," said John, yelling at Thomas from the cabin.

Thomas raised his hand and motioned that he was coming up.

"She actually found me," said Thomas when he reached the cabin.

"Oh, loose was she?"

"Yes, she'd gotten loose and was running scared when I found her not too far up the creek."

"Van Sant didn't leave anything at the roadhouse—he wasn't coming back. Was there anything on the horse that might help us?"

"You know, I didn't even look. Let's find out."

Thomas pulled the saddle and bags down from the rack under the lean-to and they began looking through Van Sant's belongings. Odd there wasn't much for a man that was traveling across country in Alaska—no camping gear, just some extra clothes, tobacco, a small flask of what Thomas assumed was whiskey, and a wallet.

"Didn't Van Sant have a wallet on him?" said Thomas.

"Yes."

"I wonder why he has a second," said Thomas, looking through the wallet and finding a picture of a man, woman, and a small child. Next to the picture he came upon a ticket stub for a steamer. "Wonder who Charlie Wilson is?"

John immediately made the connection. "Probably the same guy that owned this saddle," he said, patting the letters "C.W." engraved on the side.

"Hmm," said Thomas. "Now that you mention it, Van Sant's rifle had the same engraved in the stock. It looks as though you weren't the only victim of his thievery."

Little did they know the crime went far beyond theft, to two bodies, stripped of all personal belongings, hidden in the brush along the trail far from the mining claim.

"There's nothing that provides any answers," said John, slamming the saddle back on the rack.

"I know it's frustrating. Maybe the investigator can dig up something."

"I hope so, but at this point we don't even know where to begin."

"Did you send a telegram to Emily and let her know

the situation?"

"No, I decided to wait until I return. This needs to be handled in person."

That word—return. Thomas wondered if now John would want to leave even sooner. He really needed his help to get things ready for winter. Doubt began to creep in. *If I can't get prepared for winter, I may have to abandon my plan.*

"Come on," said Thomas. "Let's get our hands dirty and get our mind off things."

Thomas fetched the horse and hitched up the wagon that held the lumber needed for timbering the shaft. Jumping up into the seat, he drove the wagon the short distance across the bench.

"Guess that trip to town with Preston wasn't a total waste," said John as he began unloading the lumber.

"That's pretty callous," said Thomas.

John yanked another board from the wagon and tossed it on the stack next to the windlass. "I know, but I've got a lot to be bitter about."

"I wish it didn't end the way it did. Shooting someone isn't an experience I want to repeat," said Thomas, the guilt creeping over him once more.

Thomas wasn't a killer and shooting Van Sant was troubling, even though John's life was at stake. He tried to put it out of his mind—no one blamed him, yet the taking of a human life, no matter the situation, wasn't trivial, nor easily forgotten.

"I'll take the wagon back to the cabin and put the horse away," said Thomas, after they finished cutting the lumber to length. "I don't think we'll need it the rest of the day."

John nodded and began loading lumber into the bucket,

along with the rest of the tools Thomas would need at the bottom of the shaft.

"Ready?" said Thomas as he returned.

"Ready if you are."

Thomas nodded and descended the ladder, then signaled for John to lower the bucket. It was a bit dangerous to be in the hole underneath the bucket. If John lost control of the windlass and it unwound on its own, the bucket would come crashing down on him. The bucket was no small thing—Thomas judged it was as big around as a regular washtub, but at least twice as deep. He wondered if John would be able to winch a bucket full of wet muck out of the hole by himself. Then there was the matter of dumping it, but first the timbering had to be completed.

The bucket lowered, Thomas proceeded to timber the rest of the shaft down to the top of the muck pile. The thawed muck continually wanted to flow into the hole, so much so that there was now space between the timbers and the walls of the shaft. *We'll have to do something about that, or the whole thing will be unstable,* thought Thomas. It took many round trips with the bucket to finish the job, but it went faster than expected.

He climbed out the hole and signaled for John to raise the bucket. "We have to backfill around the outer walls or this is going to be unstable as we go down."

"What do you suggest?"

"I think we should run the rest of the stockpile through the sluice and capture the tailings as they come off the end, plus we can use some of those big rocks we tossed aside."

"Sounds like a plan—kill two birds with one stone so to speak."

Thomas laughed. "It means taking longer to start

clearing the shaft, but you're right—at least we'll have most, if not all, the stockpile run and we can do a final cleanup."

John smiled. "Right, then I'll have gold to take back with me."

Thomas didn't much care for that plan, but ignored the comment. "I think we should cover the shaft to maybe keep things from thawing during the day."

"Right," said John, "but we don't have a cover."

"I know, but I've got enough lumber here to make one. Shouldn't take too long."

By mid-afternoon, the shaft cover was in place and, after a very short lunch break, they were busy running gravel through the sluice. With the metal washtub in place at the tail of the sluice, the material was collected as Thomas dumped each load from the wheelbarrow. Each time it was full, John dragged the tub ashore and the two of them dumped it in the wheelbarrow to be wheeled up and dumped next to the shaft. It was slow going.

"We could just dig some of the thawed gravel along the creek and use it for backfill," said John.

"True," said Thomas, "but there's probably some gold in that gravel and we'd want to run it anyway. This is slower, but remember, we're making progress on both chores."

"I guess you're right." John took the wheelbarrow from Thomas and pushed it up the trail carved in the side-hill of the bench. "This would be easier going if we put some lumber down to roll over."

"Good idea. We may have enough to spare to cover the path up the bench."

"Hope so. If not, we can always buy more since we're rich—or going to be."

By the time the sun started to dip below the hills and the temperature began its slow slide into night, they had processed a fair bit of the gravel and a nice little pile sat next to the shaft. Calling it a day, they trudged back to the cabin to rustle up something to eat.

"Should be able to finish this off tomorrow and maybe even backfill. Then we can start clearing the shaft," said Thomas.

"Don't forget the cleanup," said John. That's going to take several hours."

"Well, we don't have to set the sluice back up so that will save some time. And we could just keep the concentrate in the tub and pan it later."

"Yeah," said John, "like you could resist."

* * *

September 20, 1903

Winter was coming, that was clear. With each day the temperatures got a little cooler, the chill in the air never quite diminishing during the day. Already the snow coated the mountains to the south. John was anxious to leave, feeling he'd already stayed longer than he should. Leaving now would mean he might make it to Valdez before the end of the month, depending on snow in the high country.

He felt guilty leaving Thomas, but then again it was his decision to stay. They had made good progress, completing sluicing of the winter dump. The final cleanup was good, yielding a few small nuggets, with the total take a little more than ten ounces, worth just over two hundred dollars. Not a lot of money, but then again there was no way of knowing if the winter dump included gravel from near bedrock.

Though work on the shaft progressed nicely, they still weren't down to bedrock. The muck was cleared, the shaft timbered, and gravel was exposed at the bottom. They were able to remove a few yards before encountering frozen ground. This slowed progress as they now had to thaw the gravels using a wood fire, making only a few feet on a good day. Even though things were moving slower, Thomas was happy to be in virgin ground. It was clear that the con men hadn't reached bedrock, yet the gravels from the winter dump produced a fair amount of gold. Thomas was sure a fortune lay just a few feet deeper, and the slow pace was exasperating at times.

Thomas knew John would want to leave soon, but never brought it up. Perhaps by not verbalizing it, he would stay longer. Little by little, mostly in the evening, the cabin was patched up and fresh moss chinking was shoved in all the open spaces. There was still a lot of work to do, mainly in putting up a store of firewood. Thomas could buy wood in Chicken, but he preferred to spend money on the things he now needed for underground mining, beginning with carbide lamps and additional hand tools.

The weekly telegrams to and from Valdez omitted any mention of the split that was about to take place—John returning and Thomas staying. Emily was anxious to know their return date, yet John was able to put her off, being somewhat vague in the telegrams. He would have to face things soon enough, to reveal to her both the events regarding Van Sant and the fact that her fiance was not returning.

It was time to make a decision, and John was ready. "I'm leaving in two days," he said abruptly during their pre-dawn breakfast.

Thomas set his coffee cup down and didn't say anything for a moment. He'd been waiting for John to announce, noticing that he seemed to be more distracted with each passing day.

"I figured it would be soon."

"I'm sorry I can't stay longer. I know this puts a halt to your underground work until you can hire someone."

"Don't worry about it. I'll ride out today and see if I can hire someone. Most of the folks will be done sluicing in another week. I know some have ceased already."

"Well, I'll help as much as I can in the next couple of days."

"Appreciate that. If you're up to it, I think we'll focus on cutting firewood. We'll just cut it long and I'll buck it up later. That way we can get a good start on the winter supply."

"What about food?" said John. "We left half in Valdez, then sold the other half along the way. That's three months worth and we've been here one already."

"I think I'll be fine. I'll supplement with some fresh meat. The caribou should be moving through anytime and I can always hunt down a moose once it's cold enough to keep without spoiling."

"Well, I'd hate to see you starve up here in the cold and dark."

Thomas laughed. "Me too. Worst comes to worst I can probably do some trading for staples. Gotta have my coffee—that's the only thing I'm worried about."

Thomas worried that John may not be up to the solo trip south, given the weather and not having spent a winter in Alaska. "You up to this trip?"

John stared at Thomas for an instant, then broke into laughter. "Sure, I had such a great time coming up, what's not to look forward to?"

"Seriously, it might be a lot rougher than our trip up."

"Don't worry about me, I've got it all figured out."

"Oh?"

"There's a government pack train returning to Valdez from Eagle. They'll be passing through here in two days time and I've already been in contact via telegram to see if I can travel with them."

"And?"

"They said no problem, as long as I pay my own way

and provide my own gear."

"Well, that's a relief. You'll be in good company and have help available in case your horse gives out."

"Speaking of horses I was hoping—"

"I want you to take the Appaloosa. She's in way better shape than the other two and better suited to travel this time of year."

"Thanks," said John. "I didn't really want to ask, but was hoping you'd offer."

"No problem. I still have to get some sort of shelter built for the horses, otherwise I'll have to see if someone in Chicken can board them over the winter."

"You need to have some sort of transportation."

"Well a lot of folks run dogs in the winter, but I'm not ready to get into mushing. I prefer a horse."

Yet another thing needing done before winter—shelter for the horses. John wondered how in the world Thomas would be ready in time.

"I don't see how you can get everything ready for winter," he said finally. "There's still time for us to close things up here and both leave for Valdez."

Though he didn't vocalize it, as the days grew shorter, Thomas often thought maybe returning would be best. He was conflicted—stay and get things established or return nearly as poor as when he left. He knew Emily wouldn't be happy when John returned alone.

"I can see you're thinking about it," said John.

"I've thought about it every day for a while, but I'm staying. If things go bad, I'll figure out a way to get back, maybe do the same thing you're doing."

John could see, despite some lingering doubt, Thomas had made up his mind. There was no point in pursuing it further.

Thomas grabbed his coat and hat off the back of the door. "Come on, let's go cut some trees."

"Right behind you," said John.

* * *

Part IV

Beginnings

September 22, 1903

The day had come—the day of John's departure. The last two days were productive. Together they made a good start on the firewood supply, stowed the sluice box for the winter, and laid out the beginnings of a lean-to for the horses. The long hours brought John to the point of near-exhaustion, an unfortunate condition on the eve of a three hundred and fifty mile trip.

Thomas attempted to slow the pace of work, but soon realized John was working hard out of a sense of obligation and perhaps a little guilt for leaving. Thomas didn't blame him, after all he was the one that changed the plan. Despite his urging, John insisted on working from daylight to dark.

His quest to hire someone proved unsuccessful. Of the two men Frank suggested, one was already working and the other was headed to Seattle for the winter. With John's departure imminent, he delayed another trip to see Frank for more options. He was confident someone would be willing to hire on—if not, it was going to be a long winter, working solo underground.

They were up before daylight, as was their norm for a working day, though this was not an ordinary day. Breakfast was a quiet affair, neither wanting to bring up what the day held. It was Thomas who, finishing his coffee, broke the silence.

"What time do you meet up with your traveling companions?"

"They overnighted in Chicken and will be leaving at nine this morning. I best be getting around soon and head down at first light. I don't want to miss them."

Thomas looked at his pocket watch. "Getting light out now. I'll help you get things loaded up. Are you sure you don't want to take a tent and some of our camping gear?"

"No, they said I could travel light and share their accommodations, such as they are. Most of the time we'll be overnighting at the roadhouses along the way."

"Well, that's far better than tenting."

"Agreed," said John, "but I'm still not looking forward to the trip."

"When will you make Valdez?"

"Not sure. I expect it to be at least ten days, maybe as long as two weeks."

"Are you going to tell Emily you're on the way?"

"No, not yet. I think I'll send a telegram once I get closer—maybe from Copper Center or Tonsina."

"I should have been in touch with her more over the last month," said Thomas.

"Me too, but I think they understand that we're off from town a bit."

"I hope she understands," said Thomas, handing John an envelope.

"What's this?"

"A letter to Emily I'd like you to deliver. I wrote it before Van Sant showed up. Wanted to have it ready in case you decided to up and desert me early," he said with a wink.

John, stuffed the envelope in the inside breast pocket

of his coat and patted his chest. "I'll keep it safe right here."

"You can give it to her right away. It doesn't reveal anything that she should hear from you."

John gathered up his hat and coat. "I'll make sure she gets it. Best be getting the horse saddled up. I don't mind getting there a bit early."

Thomas grabbed up John's carbine and tossed it to him. "Better take it with you—never know when you might need it."

"Right. Hopefully I won't meet a bear on the way to town."

"Not likely. We haven't seen one since we've been here."

"I saw some tracks on the trail to town a while back."

Thomas smiled. "Tracks won't hurt you."

"Smart as ever," said John as he headed out the door, the rifle and pack in hand.

"Hold on, I'll give you a hand," said Thomas, quickly grabbing his coat and slipping past John.

* * *

Thomas stood by the cabin in the crisp morning air, watching as John rode down the trail and disappeared below the hill. He remained, looking for a long while, a strange feeling welling up inside. They had exchanged goodbyes, shook hands long and hard, and wished each other luck.

With John on his way, Thomas immediately began to question his decision.

He was alone—not that it bothered him much, but he felt a sense of obligation to John—to ensure he made it home for Emily's sake. Yet John was in good company, with experienced men. No, John would be fine. The only question was—would he?

* * *

October 1, 1903

Day ten since John left. Thomas kept busy, completing the crude lean-to for the horses and sawing firewood. He was anxious to get back to mining, yet still had no luck in finding help. Frank assured him someone wintering over in Chicken would be looking for work, but thus far, Thomas hadn't found them.

The temperatures were colder now, already dipping close to zero several nights. The shortened days were still pleasant, filled with sunshine. Thomas kept a close eye on the creek, which already had a fringe of ice several inches thick. He hadn't thought about a winter water supply. If the creek froze solid he would be hauling water from Chicken Creek or Mosquito Fork.

It didn't take long for Thomas to realize there was a lot to learn on the frontier, far away from any semblance of civilization. He wondered how many things he either forgot or wasn't even aware of in the first place. If things got really bad he could always head into town and hope to board with someone until spring. *Not ready to give up yet,* he thought.

Thomas contemplated riding into town to see if there was word from John, but decided to wait another day or two, rather than waste time going to town for a message that might not be there. He decided to do something different today—mining.

He set about carrying tools and lumber to the collar. Though it was still cold, he worked up a sweat after several trips. The first thing to do was extend the ladder. Without someone topside, Thomas went down using the ladder and when it was time to hoist gravel from the shaft, climbed back out to operate the windlass. Though it sounded easy, he realized that, in practice, it would make for a long day and sore muscles.

The shaft remained covered since John left, idled by a lack of help. Thomas struggled to remove the cover, finally able to tug it aside and reveal the workings. He loosened the ladder, pulled it out, and began work on extending it. Half-way through he realized his mistake. *That was stupid.*

Rather than build a long ladder, it would be much simpler to nail cleats to the timbers that lined the shaft. This would eliminate the need for constantly adjusting a ladder, not to mention it wouldn't be in the way of the bucket. He set about making cleats from some scrap lumber.

Iron rungs would be better, thought Thomas as he put the ladder back down the shaft to begin the installation of the simple cleats, which turned out to be narrow enough to make it difficult to get a toe-hold. He started over, rebuilding the cleats so that each consisted of two blocks and a board for a rung.

Much better, he thought as he finished installing the last cleat at the bottom of the timbering. He could use a shortened ladder now in the bottom of the hole as he dug down, then install more cleats as he timbered the newly excavated area.

Thomas wondered how much deeper it was to bedrock. He really had no idea, but was aware that in some places it could be one hundred feet or more. He'd run out of money for timber before he got that deep and have to switch to spruce poles for cribbing. Many of the mines did just that, but his hope was to timber the shaft with sawed lumber at least to bedrock, then switch over to spruce for any additional support needed in the drifts.

He scratched about for a bit with the pick, but the gravel was frozen too hard to make any real progress. *Time to build a fire,* he thought as he climbed to the surface and set off to fetch some firewood. It wasn't an ideal situation—much of the wood he and John cut was green and wouldn't burn well at the bottom of a frozen hole. As he spent nearly a half hour digging through the wood pile, he realized they should have separated the green from the dry as it was stacked.

With the wheelbarrow loaded to the hilt with wood, a bit of dry kindling, and a can of kerosene, he pushed it to the collar of the shaft, then loaded everything into the bucket. Lowering it was easy—much easier than hoisting a bucket of gravel from the bottom.

Starting a fire at the bottom of the shaft was hazardous. The shaft was barely six feet square, leaving little room to maneuver. Hanging on to the ladder, Thomas unloaded the wood, first throwing the larger pieces, then finally dumping the rest from the bucket. Descending with the kerosene, he placed the kindling, then arranged the wood into a teepee shape. It took a good fire to thaw just a few feet of gravel, but he had to be careful—too big and it might ignite the cribbing of the shaft, sending the whole thing up in smoke and likely sending him south for the winter.

Satisfied the wood was arranged properly, he doused it with a good amount of kerosene, then ascended several feet up the ladder. Pulling a match from his breast pocket, he struck it on the dry cribbing, then tossed it on the wood pile.

Nothing happened.

He was certain there was enough kerosene to get it going, so he tried again, with no success—the match going out before reaching the wood. Moving down the ladder several rungs, he struck another match and tossed it. With a loud, booming sound the pile ignited, flames jumping up and nearly catching his pants on fire. He scrambled up the ladder while the flames licked at him, smoke filling the shaft as he ascended.

That was close, thought Thomas as he crawled out of the shaft, making a mental note not to do it that way again. Looking back down the shaft he could see the fire was burning, the dry kindling doing its job as the rest of the wood began to burn.

With smoke now rising from the shaft like a chimney, he brought the bucket to the surface, then gathered up his tools and loaded the wheelbarrow. The shaft had to remain partially open—covering it completely would deprive the fire of oxygen, extinguishing it. He pulled the cover over the shaft, leaving just enough of an opening to allow the fire to burn.

He could do no more today—it would be hours before the ground thawed and the fire cooled. He wasn't sure if he would need to add more wood before nightfall, deciding against it to see how well it thawed by morning.

Pushing the wheelbarrow back to the cabin, he stowed things under cover of the woodshed, knowing that soon snow would cover the ground and anything left out would disappear until spring.

Though he was tired from the cycle of work each day, he pressed on, sawing the long firewood logs that he and John harvested into lengths that would fit the wood stove. With John gone it didn't take long for him to realize the amount of time and effort required to accomplish his winter goal. He needed help.

* * *

October 4, 1903

The pack train spent the night at Wortmans Roadhouse, despite many in the group wanting to push on the last sixteen miles to Valdez. John was anxious to reach Stella's house, but the idea of pushing on alone in the fading light through Keystone Canyon made him think better of it. He was worn out from the trip, the days of facing snow and ice in the high country, and at times bone-chilling temperatures brought him to exhaustion. Sitting at the table, morning cup of hot coffee cradled in his hands, he dreaded the thought of making that trip again in a few months time.

They waited until daylight before departing, not wanting to risk any accidents along the narrow trail above the canyon. Though it was nineteen miles to Valdez, Stella's was five miles fewer. John hoped that by midday he would be there, in what would turn out to be a surprise for Emily and Stella. He wired them from Copper Center, but was vague about his whereabouts, saying only that he would be home within ten days. Though part of his ploy was to surprise them, it also would keep them from worry should he encounter trouble or delay along the trail.

By 7:30 a.m. the leader of the supply train summoned everyone, telling them departure time was in thirty minutes. There was a subsequent flurry of activity as men finished off the last of their coffee and scrambled to pack belongings, saddle up horses, and hitch wagons. John didn't have much to do, his pack ready to go—all that remained was to saddle the Appaloosa and mount up. He took his time finishing the coffee, tipped the proprietor, and left to ready his horse.

The pack train departed promptly, each traveler anxious to put the journey behind them. Progress was good, the trail dry despite the threat of snow. As he rode along, John rehearsed in his mind the conversation he would have with Emily. Yet, no matter the approach he took, it still came out sounding wrong, or worse insensitive and hurtful. He resolved to keep his bitterness and anger at bay, to tell Emily as carefully as he could—yet he knew there would be hurt.

* * *

The trip from Wortmans was largely uneventful, except for one of the pack train horses throwing a shoe on the trail above Keystone Canyon. Now less than two miles from Stella's, John took leave of his traveling companions, wishing them well and thanking them for allowing him to travel along. He waited for thirty minutes or so, walking slowly, leading the horse while having a smoke. He needed some final time to think about the reunion with Emily.

Her first reaction, of course, would be concern, perhaps fear, that Thomas wasn't with him. John decided to deal with this issue first, leaving the Van Sant incident and subsequent revelation for later. *No point in dumping it all on her at once.*

Finishing his pipe, he mounted up and nudged the horse gently, delaying the inevitable by little more than a few minutes.

Forty minutes later he rounded the last bend that brought Stella's place into view. Smoke was streaming from the chimney and the thought of the warm house and one of Stella's home cooked meals was more inviting than he imagined. He stopped the horse and looked for a moment. Seeing no activity, he rode forward, closing the distance quickly yet quietly. He tied the horse off to the rail and walked carefully up the steps, seeing no one through the windows.

Composing himself, he knocked on the door. Softly at first, then louder.

"Coming," came the voice from inside the house, John immediately recognizing it as Stella's.

The door swung open and there she was, just as he remembered her. "Stella, I'm—"

"John!" she said, throwing her arms around him in a tight hug, then realizing, awkwardly stepping back, blushing a bit. "You're home."

John smiled long at her. "Good to see you. You're looking well."

Stella took him by the arm. "Come in, come in." She ushered him to the sitting room, then turned toward the stairs. "Emily, it's your father!"

John came in, the smell of fresh baked bread filling the air and the warmth of the fire bringing a sense of comfort over him—at least for a moment.

Emily came bounding down the stairs, nearly missing the last one and grabbed her father, giving him a giant hug that lasted for a long while. She was crying.

"I was so worried the entire time you were gone. I'm so glad you're home."

Releasing him, she turned towards the door. "Where's Thomas? Taking care of the horses?"

The moment had arrived and there was no escaping it.

"Sit down, Emily, we need to talk."

She immediately collapsed into the nearest chair, gasping, with tears streaming down her face. "He's dead. I knew it."

John realized he was handling this poorly—not only was Emily distraught, but Stella's face was one of grave concern.

"No! No, he's fine. Please don't cry and I'll explain."

"But where is he, Father? Why isn't he with you?"

John thought about relaying the story from the beginning, but could see Emily was too impatient for a drawn out explanation. *Best to tell her first, there's time for stories later.*

Emily sat quietly now, looking at him expectantly.

"Emily, he's staying on the claim over the winter."

"What? But why?" she said, briskly wiping the tears from her cheeks, a scowl spreading across her face.

John explained how they were able to recover some gold, but the claim was nothing like they were told.

"I still don't understand why he stayed. That wasn't the plan at all."

"I understand," said Stella. "This is his dream, why he came here."

"But what about me? He loves his gold more than me?"

"No," said Stella, "but this is the opportunity for Thomas to make his way in the world, to be able to provide for you in a proper manner."

"Stella's correct," said John.

"You should have made him come back," said Emily.

"Believe me, I tried long and hard to convince him to return, but he would have none of it."

Emily wasn't happy, nor did she think much of the whole affair. "I've been waiting and praying every day for you both to come home soon. This just isn't fair."

"He's his own man, Emily—strong-willed, yet I know he cares deeply for you. In the long run, he's doing this for you. Here, look..." John pulled out a pouch and emptied some of the gold into his hand. "We were able to get over twenty ounces in the short time we mined."

"That's impressive," said Stella.

"What did you mean the claim wasn't like those men told us?" said Emily.

John went on to explain the condition of the cabin, the lack of sluice boxes, and saved the worst for last—the fact that it was an underground mine.

"Underground! What do you mean?" said Emily.

"It turns out Clyde and Olson are crooks, run out of the Fortymile country by the rest of the miners. They were stealing from sluice boxes and did little work on the claim."

"I was worried about that from the get-go," said Stella, "but there was no way to know for sure."

"But what do you mean—underground?" Emily asked again.

"It's what they call a drift mine," said John. "The ground is frozen and there is little to no gravel to sluice along the creek. Clyde and Olson started a drift mine, sinking a shaft and hauling out the gravel, but they never processed it. That's what Thomas and I did a good part of the time."

"So why did he stay if the ground is frozen and there's nothing to mine?" said Emily.

John went on to explain the whole thing to her, the excavation of the shaft, thawing of the ground with wood fires, and stockpiling the gravel to process in the summer.

"I can't believe you left him alone," said Emily, her concern now turning to his welfare.

"He's going to hire someone to help," said John, knowing there was a very good reason for his return—one that would remain unspoken for yet a little while.

"Well, I'm going to join him," said Emily.

John laughed, bringing a deeper scowl to Emily's face.

Emily stomped her foot. "You think it's funny? I followed him here from Seattle and I won't be stopped now."

"Be reasonable, Emily. The trip this time of year is long, cold, and dangerous."

"You'll go with me."

"And what will we do when we get there? The cabin isn't suitable for three of us, we don't have enough supplies for all of us for the winter, and besides, it isn't proper."

Emily slumped again, realizing that this one was out of her control.

"We have more plans to make," said John. "There are things I need to do here with regard to finding our money."

"And if you can't find it, then what?" said Emily.

"We'll cross that bridge when we come to it."

"Emily, let's allow your father to settle in a bit," said Stella.

Emily relented, finally thinking of what her father must have endured during his journey home.

"Come, John," said Stella as she sat a large bowl of

stew on the table. "You look tired and hungry."

"I am famished, but let me take care of the horse first," he said. "Oh, and by the way, I've been looking forward to your cooking for nigh on two months."

Stella smiled.

* * *

After lunch, John took a brief rest, then saddled the horse again.

"Where are you off to?" said Emily.

"I've got to ride into town and check for a telegram."

"From who?"

"Just from the people who are looking for our money," he said, not revealing the exact truth.

So far there was no word from the investigator following Van Sant's death. In his last communication, John told him he was headed to Valdez and to contact him there as soon as he had something. As he approached the telegraph office, John hoped there would be word—something to provide answers.

"Greetings, Mr. Palmer," said the telegraph clerk as John entered. "Haven't seen you in quite a while."

"I just returned from the Fortymile and I'm hoping you have a telegram or two for me."

The clerk nodded and looked through the undelivered messages from the last several days and found nothing. "When would it have come in?"

"Could be anytime in the last couple of weeks."

The clerk looked through the stack a second time, again coming up empty. "Sorry, nothing."

John sighed heavily, debating whether he should send off a message requesting an update, then deciding against it. He turned to leave.

"Palmer?" shouted the telegraph operator. "Just coming in now," he said while copying furiously.

John turned back to the counter, hoping it was from the investigator. *Has to be,* he thought as he waited impatiently.

"Here," said the operator handing the message to the clerk. John reached for it, but the clerk pulled it back. "Gotta log it in first, sir."

Finally, he handed the message to John, who read it eagerly.

```
OCTOBER 4, 1903

JOHN PALMER
VALDEZ, ALASKA

VAN SANT SAILED TO VALDEZ WITH WIFE
MARY, ARRIVING AUG 7. NOTHING
FURTHER AT THIS TIME. STILL
CHECKING STEAMSHIP COMPANY
RECORDS.

/S/ CHARLES JACKSON
JACKSON INVESTIGATIONS
SEATTLE
```

John sighed, folded the message, and placed it in his pocket. Thanking the operator and clerk, he headed out the door.

No answers, he thought, frustrated with the situation. Now he knew *when* Van Sant arrived, but nothing further. *But who is Mary? Had Van Sant married in his absence?* It seemed unlikely since, for as long as John could remember, Van Sant was a confirmed bachelor. He wondered if it was possible that this Mary was still in Valdez, even after nearly two months. It was worth checking.

"Nope, don't see no Vansan here," said the hotel clerk

as he checked the register.

"No, it's Van Sant. Two words—Van Sant."

"Oh, sorry. What day did you say he would have been here?"

"August seventh," said John, his voice tightening.

"Let me see," said the clerk, flipping the pages. "Ah, the seventh."

"Well?"

"Nope."

"May I look?"

"Uh, sure," said the clerk as he turned the register so John could read it.

He was right—there was no Van Sant registered that day. John wasn't surprised—though he used his real name to book passage north, once here he probably wouldn't risk using his own name. John scanned the names, looking for a possible alias that would fit—a man and wife.

"What about this man and his wife? Do you remember them?" said John, jabbing his finger at the entry in the register.

"John Preston?" said the clerk. "Uh...he checked in with his wife...uh, let's see...Mary." The clerk looked up from the register, rubbed his chin, and stared at the ceiling. "Preston...Preston..."

Growing impatient, John slammed his fist on the counter, causing the clerk to jump back and nearly tumble over the chair behind him.

"Sorry! I'm trying to remember."

"This is critically important. Do you remember him? Do you remember his wife?"

"Oh, now I remember. This must be the man that was asking about you. Funny I didn't remember that at first."

Real funny, thought John.

"I told him you were living at Stella's boarding house and gave him directions."

John was astonished at the man's lack of recall. "And the woman?"

"Real quiet she was. Don't think I heard her say a word the whole time they was here—at least when he was with her."

"When did they leave?"

The clerk slowly flipped through the register, looking for the names.

"Here it is. He left on the tenth of August, but she stayed a while longer." He flipped through more pages until he found it. "She checked out on the nineteenth. Said she was sailing south."

"What did she look like? Can you describe her?"

"Can't really say—dark hair, average height. Nothing remarkable about her, but she was probably about your age, maybe a little younger."

John was about to press for more, but realized the clerk wasn't the most reliable source of information. *Still no answers, but perhaps a clue,* he thought as he left the hotel and pushed the horse just a little harder toward Stella's.

* * *

John lodged the horse in the barn, then entered the house through the back door. Emily was waiting for him.

"Well, did you get the message you were expecting?"

"Not entirely. Come, sit and let's talk. Stella, please join us as well," he said, taking a chair at the dining room table.

Both had looks of anticipation, curious at what was to come next. For all they knew, there was little earth-shattering left to tell—just the details of the last two months. John wished he didn't have more to say, but he couldn't keep it hidden forever.

"Emily, this is difficult for me to say. I don't even know how to tell you."

"What is it, Father?" she said, her hands shaking.

He shot a glance at Stella, then proceeded.

"I found Preston, rather he found us—up on the claim in the Fortymile."

He looked at Emily, confusion spreading over her face.

"He stole our money and burned the house to the ground so he could cover his crime," said John, holding back the critical detail.

Emily gasped. "He killed mother?"

"No, dear, and here's the hard part. He and your mother were lovers, and she is still alive."

Emily's brow was wrinkled as she blinked repeatedly. "How do you know this?" she demanded.

"Preston came to the Fortymile to kill me, but Thomas saved my life. His dying declaration was a confession—that he stole all that was mine, the money and my wife, and burned the house to fake her death so they could run away together."

"He's lying—he's lying. Mother would never do such a thing."

"It explains a lot about how she behaved in the last year or so—at least toward me."

"I still don't believe it. If she's alive, where is she?"

"I don't know, but I have a man working on it."

"If it's true, we have to find her. We just have to."

Stella's face was drawn, color drained at the news. John wasn't sure why, but before he could say anything, she spoke.

"I believe Preston was here looking for you."

"When was that?"

"It was the afternoon on the day you left. He said he owed you money."

"That's an understatement."

"I didn't see him," said Emily.

"No, Emily, you were upstairs. When his questions turned to you I became suspicious and didn't tell him anything further. I offered to take the money, but he refused."

"I wish I had known this," said John.

"I'm sorry, I didn't have any idea this was the man who stole from you, but I think we're fortunate he didn't see Emily."

"Yes, you're right. That could have changed everything," he said, envisioning a kidnapping or worse.

"So what do we do now?" said Emily, hands still shaking.

"Not much we can do except wait and hope the investigator digs up something," said John, failing to reveal his suspicions about Van Sant's so-called wife.

* * *

The cold front moved in silently overnight, driving the temperature to near zero. Thomas felt the chill in the cabin—it kept him in his sleeping bag longer, till nearly nine. Reluctantly, he crawled out, swung the wood stove door open and tossed in a couple of logs, hoping the coals were enough to get it going.

He pulled on his clothes quickly, put his hand over the stove, and satisfied that it was going to take off, proceeded to dump coffee grounds into the near-frozen pot of water from the night before. He sat it on the stove to boil, then opened the door just a crack and peeked outside.

It was the thing he had been dreading—snow, and lots of it. *At least the wind isn't blowing,* he thought as he closed the door and contemplated breakfast. He shivered and checked the stove again—it was finally hot enough to where he couldn't touch it, but the cabin was still cold, at least from the waist down. By the time it was warm enough to thaw your feet, it was blistering hot if you stood up. *Need a way to circulate the heat,* he thought, knowing that wasn't in the cards.

By the time his second cup of coffee was history, it was plenty warm in the cabin. As he ate his breakfast of powdered eggs and bacon, he considered hibernating for the day, but pushed the thought aside. The fire he set yesterday was possibly snuffed by the snowfall and had to be dealt with. Hopefully the gravel was thawed at least some, otherwise it was a wasted effort. The shaft was twenty-two feet deep and still not to bedrock, but Thomas was certain it couldn't be much deeper, although he had nothing but hope to base it on.

Bundling up, he left the warmth of the cabin and trudged through the snow to the shaft. There was no plume of smoke rising from the hole, confirming his suspicions—the fire was out. With a little luck, at least some of the gravel was thawed. Thomas removed the cover, lowered the bucket, then descended. A small bit of warmth rose from the remains of the fire, despite the fact the snow had done its best to extinguish it.

He raked through the coals until the gravel was exposed, then swung the pick hard, expecting to be jolted with the shock of striking frozen ground. To his surprise, the pick sunk to the hilt. He worked at breaking up the gravel, scratching a full twelve inches before hitting frozen ground. He swung the pick hard again, and it didn't sound right. It wasn't frozen—it was bedrock.

* * *

October 6, 1903

Waiting was difficult. Only a day passed since last visiting the telegraph office, but John couldn't resist another trip to Valdez. Having no idea when the investigator would turn up something, he felt compelled to check each day.

Riding into town gave him time to reflect on not only the events at the claim, but also his relationship with Lydia. It made sense now, the bitterness and abrupt manner that developed over the last year. Though presenting a soft-spoken and mild temperament in public, at home she was often demanding, overbearing, and controlling. It struck him as strange, given the quality of life she enjoyed—money, a nice home, and pretty much anything she desired.

Perhaps if and when he found her, there would be an explanation. For now, both he and Emily were left to wonder. Of course, there was always a chance that Van Sant had lied—only time would tell.

He was jarred from his reflection by the sound of a wagon coming up the trail. He maneuvered the Appaloosa to the right to make room, then recognized the driver—it was Jack.

Jack pulled alongside and halted the wagon. "Greetings, John. Back from the Fortymile I see."

"Hello, Jack. Yes, been back a couple of days now, but I'm heading in to check for a telegram. What brings you out?"

"Delivering some supplies for Stella," said Jack as he reached into his breast pocket and pulled out an envelope. "And delivering a couple of telegrams for you."

John reached out and snapped up the envelope. "I didn't know you delivered."

"Well, you know I've been bringing messages to and from Stella's like you asked. I didn't know you were back, but figured you might be when I picked up that message addressed to you."

"Thank you very much. I just hope it's good news."

"Oh?"

"Long story. I've been waiting for news from Seattle with regard to some business issues."

"Understand."

John turned his horse around. "You've saved me quite a ride, only made it a mile or so this morning."

Riding along together, the conversation turned to the journey to the Fortymile, the condition of the claim, and the work that he and Thomas accomplished. Jack was very interested in all of it, having a mild interest of his own in the yellow metal. Though he could barely restrain himself, John resisted the urge to open the envelope.

Arriving at Stella's, John helped unload the supplies; staples including flour, bacon, and dried fruits. John heard the stories of the scurvy epidemic that afflicted early miners in the region. Having brought nothing in the way of foods rich in vitamin C, by the first winter many were ill and died—so many that the military launched a rescue mission to provide relief and medical care. The odd thing was, plenty of wild foods—blueberries, currants, and rose hips—were available had the miners known. The dried fruits had since become a necessity over the winter.

"Thanks, Jack," said Stella, handing him a cup of coffee. "Have a chair—you're not in any hurry, are you?"

"Always time for coffee," said Jack, taking the cup and a seat in the front room.

Stella brought a cup for John as well and he sat across from Jack. "I want to thank you for looking after things here while I was gone," said John, the telegrams burning a hole in his pocket.

"Yes, saved Emily and me lots of trips back and forth," said Stella.

"No worries, happy to help out," said Jack, as he gulped the last of his coffee. "Best be going now. Got anything that needs to go to town?"

"No, I think not," said Stella.

"I can take a return message for you, John."

"Message?" said Emily.

John looked quickly at the floor, then back at Emily. "No, that's fine. I haven't had time to read it yet."

"Is it about mother?" said Emily. "Please read it now."

"No, I'm sure it's just boring background stuff regarding the bank investigation," said John, dodging the issue. "No need to wait, Jack. Thanks, but I'll take care of it later."

"But, Father—"

"Emily, we'll discuss it later. Right now I have to get the saddle off the horse and get her some feed."

* * *

Alone in the barn, John finally opened the envelope and read the first message.

OCTOBER 6, 1903

JOHN PALMER
VALDEZ, ALASKA

FINALLY HIT BEDROCK. FIRST PANS YIELDED TWO NUGGETS, EACH OVER ONE OUNCE.

HAVE HELP NOW. STARTING TO DRIFT ON THE PAY STREAK.

WE MAY BE RICH. WISH YOU WERE HERE TO SEE IT.

/S/ THOMAS
CHICKEN, ALASKA

John smiled. *This was good—very good news,* he thought, wishing he could have been there to witness the discovery. Relieved that Thomas now had help and wouldn't be struggling alone, he read the remaining message.

OCTOBER 6, 1903

JOHN PALMER
VALDEZ, ALASKA

NO PROGRESS ON LOCATING YOUR FUNDS.

NOTHING FURTHER REGARDING VAN SANT'S WIFE MARY, HOWEVER MANIFEST CONFIRMS LYDIA PALMER SAILED FROM VALDEZ AUGUST 16 ON THE NORTH PACIFIC.

John stopped reading, his suspicions confirmed. She was alive and she was here. Odd she came incognito, then used her real name on the return trip. *A mistake perhaps, but where is she now?* he thought. He paused, took a deep breath, and continued to read.

```
SORRY TO REPORT NORTH PACIFIC STRUCK
A REEF OFF VANCOUVER ISLAND AUG 23.
ALL SOULS LOST. MY CONDOLENCES.

/S/ CHARLES JACKSON
JACKSON INVESTIGATIONS
SEATTLE
```

His hands dropped to his side, the crumpled message dropping to the barn floor. "Unbelievable," said John aloud, his thoughts turning to Emily and the emotional roller coaster they were on. Bitterness ruled—he felt only a twinge of sadness at the latest news, his concern now for how his daughter would take it. Could he put off telling her? *No, it was best to deal with it now.* The only question was, which to tell first—the good news about the claim, or the bad.

* * *

Emily sat in the front room, wringing her hands and looking at her father, waiting for him to speak. Stella sat next to her, concerned.

John started, stumbled over his words, then stopped.

"Just say it, Father," said Emily, sensing the news wasn't good. "It can't be any worse than what has already happened."

It was worse—being jerked back and forth, thinking Lydia was dead, then alive and unfaithful, now dead.

"I have some good news, and some bad. I'll start with the bad if you don't mind."

"If you must," said Emily, her handkerchief at the ready.

"I know the news has been difficult for you already and what I have to tell you isn't any easier."

"Your mother was in Valdez in August, arriving with Van Sant under an assumed name. She stayed a week and then sailed south. Unfortunately—"

"How do you know it was her if this person used a different name?" said Emily, her chin quivering.

"Fair question. As I said, she sailed south, this time using her real name. There is no question—the ship manifest confirmed it."

"Where is she now then?" said Emily, a glimmer of hope spreading across her face. "I want to find her and get the truth."

Here came the hard part—the part John dreaded telling his daughter a second time.

"Emily, she's gone."

"I know that, but where?"

"No, you don't understand. The ship she sailed on struck a reef north of Seattle and sank. There were no survivors."

At this news, Emily broke down, crying and unable to speak. Stella put her arm around her in a vain attempt to comfort her, all the while looking at John, expecting more.

"This time it is finished," said John. "There is no doubt."

"Will there be a memorial for her?" said Stella, her arm still around Emily while patting her hand with the other.

"We did that," said John abruptly, the sting of betrayal coloring his words.

John rose and put his had on Emily's shoulder, paused, then lifted her up by the hand and hugged her.

"I'm sorry. I know this is hard on you, but now it's over. We may never understand all that your mother felt and why she fell in with Van Sant, but now we need to look to the future."

"And what future is that?" said Emily, wiping tears from her cheeks as she stepped back. "My world is falling apart—mother, Thomas—it all seems so futile now."

"Not that you care at this moment, but there is no word on the money Van Sant stole, but the investigator is still looking. And don't forget, I have some good news."

"Thomas is coming home?" said Emily, staring straight ahead.

"Not quite that good, dear. But Thomas has struck gold in a big way. It looks like he may be a rich man soon."

Emily perked up a bit at the news, still wishing Thomas was returning, but if he was gone, deep down she wished him success.

"And he has some hired help now. I expect by spring we'll be sluicing lots of gravel and getting lots of gold. He's already found some good size nuggets just panning off bedrock."

"I don't understand all that," said Emily. "But I'm glad he's having success."

"I know you miss him," said Stella, "but his dream is finally coming true."

"When will I see him? Is he ever coming back?"

"It could be a while," said John, knowing she wouldn't like the sound of it. "I promised him I would return in the spring."

"Then we should make plans to go," said Emily.

"We have a lot of work to do to make the camp suitable for four of us."

"Four?" said Emily, her eyes narrowing.

"Stella, I have something to ask you," said John.

Stella stood apprehensively, looking a bit unnerved.

"Stella," John began, dipping to one knee, "will you marry me and come with us to the Fortymile?"

Stella dropped back down on the sofa. Emily looked on silently, biting her lip.

"Look, I know it seems sudden, but the wife I knew was gone long ago. Things are slow here with all the roadhouses up the trail. You've said yourself business was nothing like it used to be, and I think you know how I feel about you."

Stella averted her eyes, and turning her head, looked out the window to the flower covered hill behind the house. He shocked her, timing the proposal poorly and in front of Emily. A sinking feeling began to descend upon him as he waited, hoping he hadn't misjudged her feelings.

Stella turned from the window and looked up, a smile on her face. "Yes."

* * *

Part V

Appendix

Historical Facts and Fiction

- Chicken is a real town in Alaska, being the second incorporated in the state in 1902. Legend has it, the residents wanted to name it Ptarmigan after the white bird prevalent in the area, but no one could spell it—thus "Chicken."
- The gold price in 1903 was $20.67 per troy ounce.
- Angel Creek is a fictitious creek in the Fortymile country.
- The *North Pacific* was a real sidewheeler that brought miners to the gold fields turn of the century. It struck a rock in 1903 and sank. All aboard were rescued.
- Effective October 1, 1903, Congress enacted a hunting limit of two moose, harvested between September 1 and October 30, ending legal market hunting in Alaska.
- Much of the current highway system from Valdez to Chicken follows the original trail described in this story.

Glossary

This is a glossary of mining and other terms used in the book. For some terms there may be more than one definition, but the one provided here is in the historical context of the story.

bench: A terrace on the side of a stream

cheechako: A person newly arrived in Alaska

collar: The opening of a shaft

cribbing: Timbers constructed at right angles to each other to support a shaft

drift: A horizontal underground working in a mine.

placer: A gold deposit found in recent or ancient stream gravels

sluice box: A wooden box with riffles used to process gravel and capture gold.

sluicing: Running gravel through a sluice box to recover gold

shaft: A vertical mine working that provides underground access, usually timbered for support.

wing dam: An angled dam in a creek used to increase water flow.

winter dump: Material excavated from an underground drift mine during the winter and stockpiled for sluicing during the summer.

Made in the USA
Monee, IL
02 April 2023